MICHAEL VAUGHN

PREMONITION

TRUE
TERROR BEGINS

MICHAEL VAUGHN

BOOKS
BY
MICHAEL VAUGHN

(Romance)

Maid In Heaven

Sex In Malibu

(Drama)

Stroke Of Genius

Power Of The Order

(Mystery/Suspense)

Sam Pepperell Private Investigator Series

Faith And Legend

Who's Guilty

Call To Duty

Finders Keepers

It's Not What It Seems

Special Delivery

We All Need A Hero

(Paranormal Psycho Thriller)

The Hayden Keller Trilogy

Premonition

Resurrection

Walk Through Fire

For more about the author and upcoming books visit:

http://michaelvaughn.wix.com/books

Published in the United States by Powerhouse Press
Premonition / Michael Vaughn

First Edition: May 2013

ISBN-13: 978-0615812045
ISBN-10: 061581204X

1. Paranormal psychic powers-fiction 2. Murder investigation-fiction
3. Serial killer satanic ritual-fiction 4. Crime horror killings-fiction
5. Abduction violent deaths-fiction 6. Police good v/s evil-fiction

Manufactured in the United States of America

Table Of Contents

Chapter 1

The Slaughterhouse

Evening was fast approaching as the autumn air blew across the field outside a small town few had ever heard of, and it was there where evil took shape once again, preying on its next victim as it had done countless times before.

No one could have imagined what lurked within the field of wheat, except for one woman gifted beyond all others. She saw the bloody images in her mind, and she herself could feel the pain evil inflicted upon the innocent, but there was nothing she could do to stop it as Mrs. Ferris picked up the potholder resting on the counter beside the spice rack. She pulled a baked hen from her oven, placing it on top of the stove next to the field peas and stewed tomatoes. Everything smelled mouthwateringly delicious.

With little concern, she turned toward the sink to wash her hands, and over the noise of the running water she heard the screen door creak as it opened behind her. Without so much as looking over her shoulder, she said, "I told you supper wouldn't be ready until six o'clock." She naturally assumed it was her husband coming in from the barn ready to eat dinner. He was a big man with a hefty appetite. Woefully, however, she could not have been more wrong.

Her worst nightmares were revealed to her in an instant as she turned to tell him he was early, and in complete horror at the sight of what stood before her, she became paralyzed with fear as she stammered to ask, "who are you?" The segmented question had trouble making its way out of her mouth as she found herself face to face with the tall dark haired man standing in her kitchen.

He looked sinister in every sense of the word. His eyes were menacing, and they didn't move. They were focused intently on her. He had perfected the cold dark stare he possessed, which he gave to every one of his victims at some point prior to snatching their soul from their body.

She felt as if he was staring right through her, his face utterly grimacing, and it carried with it a hideous scar. The terror she felt increased as he snarled, revealing his teeth to her, and the look on his horrid face showed without question his demented intent to do her great harm.

Without so much as a word said, he tilted his head slightly as he reached for the butcher knife laying on the counter beside her freshly baked squash casserole. Emma tried to back away from him as she let out a scream, but there was nowhere she could run as he began to slash her face, arms, and chest with the razor sharp blade. He wielded the knife without mercy as she raised her hands trying to shield herself from his relentless attack. It was vengeful and barbaric. He continued slicing away, cutting on her as if she were a piece of meat hanging in a butcher shop, and he smiled the whole time.

Mrs. Ferris fell to her knees holding her chest with one hand as she whimpered and cried, attempting to crawl away from her assailant. He enjoyed watching her squirm across the floor like the lowest form of life on earth. Reaching down, he grabbed her by one of her ankles. That's when he pulled her back across the kitchen floor, leaving a blood trail which ran from the screen door to the kitchen sink.

She continued to look at the floor, too afraid to even turn her head in his direction to take another look at his face. She knew she was going to die. She could feel it in her wounds. Everything seemed so unimportant at that moment. She saw the blood which covered the floor, realizing it was hers put her in a state of shock where she could no longer think whatsoever.

At that very moment, she could hear him behind her as he sampled some of the food she had prepared. She found it increasingly hard to breathe as he calmly said, "not bad," before taking another bite of her squash casserole. Gripping the fork prison style in one hand, and the bloody butcher knife in the other, he stood over her listening to her sorrowful whimper, which was muffled by her hair, and the kitchen floor itself.

Slowly, he knelt down on one knee beside her. He leaned forward with his fist still clinching the bloody knife in his left hand. His other hand held the fork, which he deliberately touched to her back. Slowly, he raked it over her dress and skin, moving it closer and closer to her neck. Using the fork to pull her hair away from her ear, he placed his lips next to the side of her head. She could feel his breath against her cheek as her body started to grow colder. That's when he sadistically whispered into her ear, "my name is Hayden Keller, and don't worry. I know we are going to have a real good time together."

Hayden stood staring out the kitchen window as Mr. Ferris exited the barn to get something out of the back of his truck before going back inside. He just watched the old man as he devoured the food Emma had worked so hard to fix for her husband. She could see the heel of his bloody boot as he stood in front of the kitchen sink staring out at the barn, some of the food managing to find its way to the floor landed next to it.

Hayden looked across the counter, his hands slowly tightened their grip, clinching the knife and fork. Rage built deep in his eyes, listening to the pitiful sounds Emma was making from the floor. Still, gripping the knife tight in his left hand, he let go of the fork dropping it on the floor next to his feet. He then reached over pulling one of the legs off of the hen Mrs. Ferris had baked. Taking a huge bite out of it, he glanced down at the floor where she laid helpless. He took that opportunity to compliment her on her cooking by saying, "you have really outdone yourself this time. Your husband is a lucky man. I guess you know that though."

Hayden continued to stare out the kitchen window as he tossed the partially devoured drumstick on the counter before turning to make his way to the back door. He looked back at Mrs. Ferris as he opened the creaking screen door. Hearing that he said, "this place really needs some work, huh. Now don't you go running off without me, okay. I promise, I'll be back."

Lying there on the kitchen floor, bleeding profusely from numerous lacerations, Mrs. Ferris could have done without his promise to return. All she could do was roll her eyes in his direction to gain a final look at him. A sinister grin emerged on Hayden's scarred face, and Mrs. Ferris thought, *oh God*, but she physically could not speak those words out loud.

Chapter 2

Out In The Barn

Clouds were forming off in the distance as Hayden strolled on out to the barn to check on Mr. Ferris. He paid no attention to the approaching storm though, it mattered little to him. Hell, he was no farmer. He simply began whistling a sorrowful tune which had existed for ages. It was only drowned out somewhat, and made even more ominous by the faint sound of thunder occasionally accompanying it as the sky grew darker, and clouds moved closer.

Nearing the open door to the barn, he looked over at the bales of hay stacked just outside. His lip curled slightly, pulling to the left side of his face, as he reached over retrieving the bailing hook. He could hear Mr. Ferris inside hard at work as he hammered away at the hitch attached to his plowshare.

The ting, ting sound of metal striking metal resonated outside the barn. It was no wonder he couldn't hear Emma screaming for help in pure terror when she was able to do so. His hearing wasn't that good to start with, but his sense of smell was very acute. There wasn't a smell on that farm he wasn't thoroughly familiar with, until Hayden walked into the barn.

Mr. Ferris was losing light, and it was almost time for dinner. He paused briefly as he slowly turned his head to glance over his shoulder in the direction of the open barn door. Hayden had already taken cover inside an empty stall within the barn close to the door. He watched Mr. Ferris tinker with his farm equipment as he peered through a crack between the boards.

The horses began to neigh a little as they moved their heads up and down, side to side. They seemed nervous for some reason, and it didn't make sense. Never had they cared for bad weather, but the rain hadn't even started to fall, and lightening was nowhere nearby. Something had definitely rattled them though, and Mr. Ferris had no idea what it was. He looked over at the horses and then around the barn once more before he returned to his work, but something made the hairs on the back of the old man's neck stand up.

Hayden just carried that eerie sense of eminent danger with him in the form of a cold chill which ran through the veins of others, and Mr. Ferris could feel its clutch on him at that moment as he whaled on one the cotter pins, trying his best to dislodge it. Removing the pin, he no longer felt his mind was playing tricks on him, not with the way the horses reacted. He had smelt Hayden's presence and so had the animals, but he didn't show it.

Hayden continued to watch him patiently through a small crack which separated two of the boards in the empty stall where he stood. The horses were still acting strange. Suddenly, Mr. Ferris stopped as if he were tired of working altogether, but he looked around the barn as if he knew Hayden were there. He began to search for something rather cautiously, carrying his hammer in his right hand as he walked toward Hayden. Almost confused by the unfamiliar scent present in his barn, he called out, "who's there?"

Hayden looked up toward the loft, noticing a pulley mounted in the top of the barn. It was used to hoist hay in order to store it for winter. The rope hanging from it was what caught his interest. An evil glare was present in his eyes. Regardless of its intended purpose, he had other plans for its use, and it included Mr. Ferris's painful demise.

Death would soon be upon him, and he could feel it at that point. A cold shutter ran through his veins as Mr. Ferris walked to the barn door. Hayden circled around behind him holding the bailing hook in his left hand. Grabbing the rope which hung down from the pulley with the other, he walked up behind the old farmer as he tried not to make a sound.

The horses continued their odd behavior making even more noise. The old man had no chance of hearing Hayden slip up behind him, but a strange sense of danger was felt as he turned looking over his shoulder. The chill that surged up his back caused the hair on his neck to raise even further, seeing what was behind him. Hayden dropped the bailing hook where he stood as he rushed toward Mr. Ferris clasping the braided rope in both hands.

Taken by surprise, the old man hardly had time to react at all. He raised the heavy hammer he was carrying in his hand in an unsuccessful attempt to defend himself against the evil which had him dead in its sights. Hayden reached up stripping the hammer from his hand as he kicked Mr. Ferris's leg out from under him, using his steel toed boot. He let out an unexpected groan as Hayden knocked him off balance. The hammer fell to the ground along with Mr. Ferris. Neither he nor Hayden had control of it.

Hayden straddled his body as he placed the rope around the old man's neck. Pulling it tight, he pressed his knee into Mr. Ferris's back to keep him from reaching the hammer which laid several feet in front of him. The bailing hook that Hayden had dropped on the ground, just mere seconds earlier, was almost within reach as Mr. Ferris struggled to place his hand on it. His unsteady hand shook as he reached for it. Unable to grab it though, his face was turning red, and it became difficult for the old man to breathe as Hayden applied more force to the rope, stretching it tighter and tighter.

Controlling the flow of oxygen to Mr. Ferris's brain by constricting the blood-flow, he subdued the large man to a point where he was nearly unconscious. Hayden tied the rope securely around Mr. Ferris's neck. He then ran the rope under each of his arms before binding them together behind his back. With unrestrained wrath, Hayden forcefully drove the old man's face into the dirt by kicking him in the back of the head with the heel of his boot as he stood.

Looking down at the old farmer, Hayden placed his boot directly on Mr. Ferris's head. He leaned forward shifting his weight to his victim's skull, firmly applying more and more pressure, while Mr. Ferris struggled to breathe. Blood began to trickle down his face at that point, and Hayden had just gotten started.

The horses stamped their hooves in fear of what was taking place. They only quieted some when Hayden stared directly at them, before pulling his boot away from Mr. Ferris's head long enough to get a clear look at him. That's when he spat on the old man before turning to reach for the other end of the rope which was hanging down freely from the pulley above. He began to pull the rope taunt, retrieving it through the pulley, and Mr. Ferris's body slid toward him with each forceful tug. Hayden hoisted Mr. Ferris to his feet before tying off the loose end of the rope to a cleat, mounted on one of the support timbers, inside the barn.

He ordered Mr. Ferris to look at him as he bent over picking up the bailing hook, and the hammer which were lying in the dirt. Hayden delivered the first of many blows to Mr. Ferris's body, first using the steel hammer. As Mr. Ferris started to lose consciousness, he lowered his head a little. Hayden carried a smug look on his face as he said, "it's about dinner time, isn't it. Do you know where your wife is right now?"

Mr. Ferris looked up yelling at the top of his voice, "Emma!"

Hayden's fiendish grin appeared as he said, "I don't think she can hear you." Using everything he had he yelled out again calling her name, and Hayden took that opportunity to strike him once more. This time he pierced his stomach with the bailing hook as he slowly took him apart piece by piece. Hayden relished every second of it, seeing him suffer as he hung there.

Helplessly lying there, Emma Ferris could hear some of what was going on in the barn. Unable to speak, her eyes just filled with tears as she listened to her husband being tortured, and there was nothing she could do to stop it. She could hear him yell out her name, concerned for her well-being more so than his, and several tears trickled down her bloody cheek. She laid there asking herself why anyone would do this to God fearing people such as she and her husband.

Back in the barn, Hayden pulled the rope taut, hoisting Mr. Ferris into the air slightly as his feet dangled inches above the ground. The grueling pressure Mr. Ferris felt on his arms at that point was immense. Picking the hook and hammer back up, he put them both to use one more time.

The pain that was present in Mr. Ferris's eyes brought pure pleasure to Hayden Keller, and his thirst for vengeance was temporarily quenched as he watched the life leave Mr. Ferris's body. Hayden derived as much pleasure from killing his victims psychologically as he did physically, and this was just the start of things to come.

Tossing the hammer aside, he listened to the final sound Mr. Ferris made before giving up his ghost. Total silence was present in the barn as Hayden dropped the bloody bailing hook at Mr. Ferris's feet. He then calmly turned, walking out of the barn, and back up to the farmhouse, to see how Mrs. Ferris was fairing.

Chapter 3

A Good Bloody Meal

Upon entering the back door, he walked over to where she was lying on the floor. He looked down at her saying, "see, here I am as promised." Uncomforting words to say the least as she struggled to keep from choking on her blood. Hayden asked, "where do you keep the plates?" Of course, Emma didn't answer him. That's when Hayden helped himself. He started opening the cabinets in search of one, then he took for himself a little of everything he saw. His face showed no sign of emotion as he spoke telling Mrs. Ferris, "I don't believe your husband will be joining us."

Emma gave up all reason for living at that point as she watched him take a seat at her kitchen table enjoying the meal she had prepared for her husband. Hayden's cheap form of entertainment was watching the life leave her body before returning for seconds. He stared at her with a content look on his face as he ate.

Cleaning his plate of food for a second time something caught his eye. He looked over at a small decorative plate which hung on the wall in the kitchen. It read, **Cleanliness is next to Godliness**. Hayden smiled twisting his head a little as he read it aloud to himself. He nodded his head, almost as if he agreed with the simple statement, as he took the plate he held in his hand and threw it against the refrigerator. It shattered into numerous pieces, adding to the mess already present on the kitchen floor.

The expression on his face changed quick. Infuriated, he then stood, looking around the room. In a sudden fit of rage he reached for the chair he had chose to sit in, and he grabbed hold of it firmly with one hand. Violently snatching it using only one arm, he quickly pulled it from the floor maintaining his grip. Hurling it up in the air he brought it over his shoulder and down on top of the kitchen table, slamming it hard enough to break it into, the chair itself also busted into pieces. He took only a second to admire what he had done to the place. It was messy, bloody, and splintered. Then it was time for Hayden to check-out the rest of the house. He was fairly certain he wouldn't find God hanging out there.

Making his way into the living room, he took it upon himself to try out the comfortable looking leather recliner, which had belonged to Mr. Ferris. Picking up the remote on the table next to him, he turned on the television just in time to catch the last part of the evening news as he sarcastically questioned, "what's going on in the world today?"

With a satisfied look upon his face, he sat there staring at the TV screen, seeing the mayhem which was unfolding before his eyes. Startling statistics were reported about the increase of violent crimes taking place in what were once quiet parts of the country. He knew he was a part of it, and it reminded him of his purpose for being. That evening Hayden Keller made himself at home inside the Ferris' house. He saw no reason not to since they would no longer be needing it.

Chapter 4

The Smell Of Death

It was in the wee hours of the morning when Hayden awoke to the smell of death which filled the air inside the small farmhouse. No doubt, that particular smell did not faze him a bit. He had experienced it many times before, more than he could count. It was merely part of the fruits of his labor which he savored long after a kill, and Emma Ferris was ripening on the kitchen floor where he left her to die.

Hayden's face showed no sign of emotion whatsoever as he laid there pondering how long it would take authorities to arrive. It was a game he often played after a fresh kill, and he was quite good at it. His guess was days with them being out there in the middle of nowhere, but either way he figured his work was done at the farm. A little more rest, and he planned to hit the road. After all, he was a busy man with places to be, and people to kill. It was his perpetual destiny.

He had chosen his path long ago, and for him there was no other life. No life existed for Hayden Keller without bloodshed. A price had to be paid for his time spent on earth, and he was more than happy to wage war on others regardless of who they were. His killing had a specific purpose though. What spurned him to go on was Satan himself, and he knew him well. It was God he remained separated from for all eternity, and he was perfectly okay with that. He knew without question, God had written him off a long time ago. In a realm where the battle of good and evil raged on continually, Hayden had chosen sides.

As he closed his eyes, lying back in Mr. Ferris's comfy leather chair he took in a deep breath, enjoying the pungent gut wrenching stench that hung in the air. The resemblance of a satisfying smile spread from one side of his face to the other as he drifted back off to sleep. The gruesome foul odor coming from the kitchen stung the inside of his nostrils a little, and that sense alone made Hayden Keller relish being alive at that point, knowing others were not so fortunate.

When the sun finally did rise, he got up out of the chair, and walked to the bathroom to rinse off his face. He still carried a remnant of blood on it from his previous victim. Hayden wore it well though, it only helped distinguish his true character. Looking straight into the mirror as he lifted his head, he locked eyes with his revolting reflection.

Turning his head slightly toward his right shoulder, never taking his eyes off the mirror, he reached up with his right hand, placing the tips of his fingers on the scar which covered his left cheek. Tracing its path, he slowly ran his fingers down it. He almost appeared to be admiring the jagged line that marred the side of his face as he wiped off the dried blood with water, using his hand. After that, he took a razor to it.

Hayden could be rather meticulous at times when it came to his appearance. Image is everything in today's world - he was simply trying to keep pace with it. Pulling back his hair, he looked into the mirror once more. The crazed look he carried in his eyes intensified to the point it would scare the shit out of virtually anyone, and the chilling image he presented to others right before he ended their life was clearly captured in the reflective glass covering the face of the medicine cabinet.

He didn't gawk at his reflection for long though before a determined scornful look filled his detestable face as he told himself, "you never looked better." Hayden then destroyed the image in one swift blow, ramming his fist into the medicine cabinet mirror, watching it crack and shatter into pieces. Releasing his pent up anger, he calmed some as he turned away from the broken glass which had landed on the vanity filling the washbasin.

Hayden exited the bathroom ready to leave the Ferris home for good, but no good would be found there whenever law enforcement officials did arrive. Evil had originated right there just beyond the wheat field. That would be made clear soon enough.

Chapter 5

Leaving The Scene

Hayden was quite content with the way he left the place. Walking through the living room on his way to the front door, he picked up his jacket without looking back to consider doing anything to cover his tracks.

A wooden plaque hung on the wall next to the door which read, **Praise God. For this is the day the Lord hath made**. Hayden looked at it with distain. His face became twisted as if he smelled something rotten. At that point he truly wished to set the house ablaze, but he didn't want to destroy his handiwork that he left lying in the kitchen. He wanted to make sure Mrs. Ferris was found that way. He even went so far as shoving the fork in her back to show that she was done.

With the TV still on, and the front door left standing wide open, he stepped foot onto the front porch. His attention was directed to Mr. Ferris's truck parked out by the barn. The morning air felt bitterly brisk, but that didn't stop him from taking in the view for a moment. He then made his way out to the barn slipping on his jacket as he walked toward it. Mr. Ferris was hanging right where he left him with nothing to say, and Hayden found amusement in that thought as he walked over to the rusty old Ford pickup Mr. Ferris once called his. Looking inside Hayden saw the key in the ignition, and his transportation dilemma appeared to be solved for the moment.

He climbed inside the old rust-bucket, and he cranked up the truck, giving the engine a minute to warm up, before taking off down the lonesome stretch of road that happened to pass by the farm. The gas gauge read full, and Hayden continued to drive with no expectations of stopping until he reached another town at least a hundred miles away.

Keeping count of his most recent kills, he planned his next move as he sped down the road in search of his next victim. Pushing the old Ford to its limits, he topped it out, touching the pedal to the floor before backing off of the accelerator. The damn thing looked worn, but it still had plenty of horses hard at work under the hood.

Hayden stared out at the road in front of him as he turned on the radio. Dialing in a station, he felt the old truck start to sputter a little. Looking down at the gauges, he saw no change on any of them. The battery had a charge, and the engine temp was in midrange. The gas gauge itself hadn't budged a bit since he left the Ferris place. He began to question if the damn thing worked at all as the truck lost power once again, this time shutting down altogether.

He coasted to a stop, shifting it into neutral, and he tried to crank it again. That time it wouldn't even turn over. "Son of a bitch," was all he had to say as he hit the back of the bench seat hard with his elbow and fist. Looking in his side view mirror at nothing in sight for miles, except plenty of trees, he realized his transportation problems had only worsened. Leaving the old truck in neutral, he pushed it off the road, letting it follow whatever course it chose. Hayden watched as it rolled down the steep shoulder into the trees. Turning his back on the truck, he looked in both directions. Hayden was now on foot and he didn't like it one damn bit, but he knew what he had to do at that point.

Chapter 6

Hitting The Road

Hayden started to walk in the direction from which he came, knowing it would be miles before he could hope to pick up another set of wheels. He hadn't passed anyone on that road since he left the farm that morning. Chances of him seeing someone before reaching the farm were slim on such a desolate country road, but fate would bring him the unexpected, and Hayden would surely take full advantage if only given the chance.

Just a few miles into his foot trek, he heard a rumbling noise coming up fast behind him. It was the unmistakable sound of a large vehicle approaching. Hayden stuck out his arm, holding up his thumb as he continued walking, never looking in the direction of the RV, which was heading straight for him. As it rounded the curve, the driver saw Hayden up ahead, and he questioned if he was the driver of the wrecked pickup he saw miles back. He couldn't imagine who else would be wandering along that road on foot.

The old guy behind the wheel slowed down, applying the brakes as he neared Hayden. He rolled down his window as he slowly pulled up alongside him to see if he could give him a lift to wherever he was going. Sticking his hand out the window, he raised it slightly saying, "hey there. You wouldn't happen to own that truck I saw back there in the trees would you?"
Hayden looked over at him as he said, "not anymore."
The old fellow chuckled just a little before asking, "you okay?"

Hayden replied, "that depends on what you mean by okay. I'm not hurt if that's what you're asking."

Bringing the RV to a complete stop, the old guy grinned saying, "I guess you could use a lift about now. Huh?"

Hayden sarcastically said, "I'm not holding my thumb out for my health mister."

That made the old fart laugh too, it seems just about everything did. He introduced himself saying, "my name's Roy. Come on and hop in. I can use the company."

Hayden took him up on his offer. Roy opened the passenger door, and Hayden walked around to climb inside. Obviously, Roy wasn't the best judge of character. He was from a time gone by, where people did what they could to help one another, but basically what it came down to was Roy just liked to talk a lot. Before Hayden could even take a seat, Roy added, "you could probably use a drink about now I imagine. Why don't you reach in the frig there and grab us both one." That's when he noticed the large scar on Hayden's face. He wanted to know where he picked that up, but it seemed too forward a question to ask at that moment. Still, it caught Roy by surprise, and Hayden could tell it had his attention. Hayden had grown accustomed to wearing that scar on his cheek. So much so that he would feel naked without it.

Hayden tried to tune out Roy's jovial chatter as they cruised along in the RV. It was difficult though, he had never run up on such a happy character in all of his lives put together. It was disturbing how damn happy Roy seemed to be, and Hayden certainly couldn't figure him out. All he wanted was for Roy to quit his incessant yapping. That wish never came true though as Hayden endured a never ending barrage of bullshit, which Roy seemed to have no trouble delivering. Referring to the truck he saw off the side of the road, Roy said, "Ford, I guess it really does stand for found off road dead." He laughed at his remark, and Hayden smiled a little as well. Hayden was picturing in his mind where police would find Roy's body, of course. He kept that little secret to himself for the time being as he listened to Roy say, "yeah, I've always been a Chevy man myself, have been ever since I bought my first one back in 1968. Now that was a hell of a car I tell you. No, they don't make 'em like that anymore. I think, I only paid about two thousand for her. You can't hardly get a piece of junk nowadays for that, you know."

Hayden knew he had heard enough of Roy. He didn't care if he was breathing thirty seconds from now, much less what kind of car he bought back in yesteryear. Still, Roy's gifted ability to carry on a single-sided conversation left Hayden speechless, questioning if he should allow the old bastard to live for that reason alone. It was obvious Roy could spread misery to others simply by being so damn irritating, using only his mouth, and his boring-ass recollections.

Hayden imagined what kind of look Roy would have on his face, walking out of a convenience store seeing the RV was gone. In his mind, he told himself *that would surely give him something to talk about*. Never missing a beat Roy said, "I guess today was your lucky day, me coming along when I did. Hell, I don't think there's anything around here for close to fifty miles. I'm not sure what's up ahead." Hayden was, but he wasn't telling. Roy talked about everything from baseball to the leaves in fall. He even got on his soapbox babbling about how important it is to have a plan for your life. "Yep, you got to have a plan for your life," Roy said. He then asked Hayden if he had a plan for his, but Hayden never responded to that. Then he said, "you don't say much, do you." Hayden just cut his eyes at him as he continued to ramble on.

Hayden had a plan for his life alright. He developed it long ago, and never deviated from it for the most part. He planned people's deaths, the more horrid the better. For many he was the grim reaper in the flesh, and he loved that role with a passion. His simple plan consisted of killing in order to keep living.

Chapter 7

Deadly Highway

A long story cut short, Hayden had heard about enough from old Roy. That's when he excused himself to use the head. Roy continued talking as Hayden walked to the back of the RV. He looked over his shoulder at Roy, wanting nothing more than to reach out with both hands and strangle the life right out of the bastard. Hayden figured that was the only way to shut him up. He stopped dead in his tracks as he turned facing Roy's back. At that point, Roy raised his voice a little to be sure Hayden heard him. Hayden used that opportunity to slip up behind him without making the slightest sound as Roy brought up another topic, saying, "you know, I actually worked for the company that made the tires on this vehicle." Then he started yammering about different tire models and sizes.

As Hayden's hands moved closer to Roy's neck, he looked out the window accepting that now was probably not the best time to take him out since he was zipping down the road at sixty miles an hour. Roy said, "I worked for them for twenty-eight years before I retired. That's a long time working in a tire factory. Sometimes that place was hot as hell. Do you have any idea what that's like?"

Hayden just leaned forward planting both of his hands on Roy's shoulders. He quickly placed his mouth close to Roy's ear saying, "I believe I know perfectly well what that's like."

Roy was truly startled, so much that he swerved a little upon hearing Hayden's voice right next to his ear. Hayden jokingly said, "be careful Roy. You're liable to kill us both."

Hayden laughed a little at that as he returned to his seat.

Roy replied, "I thought you were back there taking a piss. You damn near scared the hell out of me. Surprised I didn't have a heart attack. You ought not slip up on someone like that."

Placing his hands behind his head, Hayden stared out at the road in front of them. He tried to tune Roy out as he muttered, "we all do what we're good at Roy."

Roy looked over at him. For a single brief moment there was silence. To Hayden's ears it was truly golden. Roy looked at the scar on Hayden's cheek as he continued to drive. Curiosity was getting the best of him, and finally he just had to ask. Hayden's eyes were now closed as he imagined being somewhere else other than in Roy's company. When Roy did ask, "how did you end up getting that scar you have there?"

Hayden never flinched a muscle. In a serious tone he said, "if I told you, I'd have to kill you." Roy obviously thought Hayden was joking, even though he seemed to sell that line pretty well with the inflection in his voice. Hayden wasn't joking, of course. He was dead serious about that. Opening his eyes he looked dead at Roy asking, "so, how bad do you wish to know?"

Roy just kind of twisted his head, trying to shake off the growing uncomfortable feeling which had been building between them over the last several miles. He told Hayden that was the most he heard him say all day, and then he began to talk about the weather. He couldn't just comment on the weather outside the RV, and leave it at that. He had to bring up the worst storms he had ever seen firsthand, and what he was doing way back when. Hayden finally shouted, "damn Roy! Do you ever shut the hell up?"

Roy's happy grin just kind of faded away slowly as he took in Hayden's words. Roy realized he could carry on sometimes, but he also felt Hayden could have chosen better words to call his attention to it. Either way, they had both had enough of one another at that point. Not a word was spoken between them for miles until Roy noticed a gas station up ahead.

Breaking the awkward silence, Roy said, "well, I guess you can get to where you're going from here," as he started to pull into the parking lot. Hayden looked out the window and back at Roy before nodding his head. He had nothing to say other than, "take care of yourself Roy."

Roy brought the RV to a stop, and Hayden climbed out disappearing into the passing traffic. Gassing up the RV, Roy decided to pick up a couple of hotdogs from inside the store just to tide him over until dinner. When he returned to the motor home minutes later, he saw no sign of Hayden anywhere. Roy got back on the road never suspecting he would ever see him again.

Hearing a noise in the rear of the RV in one of the sleep compartments, he looked over his shoulder. There was nothing he could see to cause alarm from the driver's seat where he was sitting. Figuring it was just something jarred loose that was now rattling around unsecured, he paid it little attention for the moment. He had just turned onto another unfamiliar stretch of road, and he pulled over to check his map real quick.

With the motor idling and air blowing hard, Roy couldn't hear Hayden's footsteps as he crept up behind him. He had company ever since he pulled out of the gas station, he just didn't know it. Hayden had been lying silent in one of the sleep compartments, just waiting for the right moment to strike. Sadly for Roy, this was that long awaited moment. As he looked down at his map, he positioned his finger on his exact location. That's when he felt the thud of something metal forcefully bludgeoning his skull. After that, he felt nothing as he fell forward against the steering wheel, and then to the floor.

Hayden stood over him holding a fire extinguisher in both hands. He tossed it toward the rear of the RV. Then, leaving the RV in park he immediately lifted Roy dragging him out of the vehicle as the motor still continued to run. Using a cord he had yanked off Roy's portable TV set, he bound his hands securely behind his back. He wanted to strangle him with it since the old coot just never could seem to keep his mouth shut. However, Hayden knew of a more fitting way for Roy to meet his maker. He was a master when it came to demise.

As he drug Roy in front of the RV that sinister grin came over his face once more. Hayden said, "live by the tire, die by the tire Roy. That's just the way it goes." Roy was still unconscious though, and he remained that way for several minutes. Hayden climbed back inside the RV, taking a seat behind the wheel. He leaned his head out the window as he looked down at Roy lying on his back in the dirt with his hands tied behind him. Hell, he already looked dead, but Hayden knew he still had a breath of life left in him. The old windbag had a lot of air in him actually. Hayden was hell-bent on remedying that though.

Waiting for Roy to come to, Hayden tossed the map aside. He didn't care where he was or where he was headed as he switched on the radio, tuning it to a rock and roll station. Hearing the words to "Tumbling Dice" by the Rolling

Stones, he began to sing as he stuck his head back out the window. He hollered at Roy sarcastically asking, "how does that tire pressure look down there Roy?"

The old man regained consciousness. He lifted his bloody head looking straight at the RV's tires and undercarriage. Hayden yelled, "look who's in the driver's seat now," as his turned up the volume on the radio. Hayden shifted the RV into drive yelling, "you got to have a plan Roy. What's your plan now?" He sadistically laughed at the old man's situation as he inched the RV forward just to toy with him.

Roy tried to move out of the way using his feet as best he could. He resembled a fiddler crab, scurrying across the sand in search of safety, but Roy was out of luck. Hayden pressed the gas making sure to take the front tire over Roy's foot, then his leg. The old man's eyes got big as he watched the tire from the motor home pop his ankle into as if it were a brittle old stick. Gritting his teeth, and tightly shutting his eyes for a moment, he tried to cope with the pain he felt in what was left of his leg.

As Hayden turned the wheel, the old man let out a yell that could curl one's hair, and Hayden nodded his head with extreme satisfaction before running the tire over Roy's abdomen. Breaking several of his ribs, he squeezed the life right out of him. Hayden put the RV in reverse pointing the tire in the other direction as he backed up. The RV rocked as he drove over Roy's chest. Shifting it back in drive, Hayden positioned the tire next to Roy's head. In an extreme measure of overkill, he mashed the gas. He rolled right over it, smushing his skull like a ripe melon of some sort. Roy didn't look like himself at that point.

Hayden pulled the vehicle back on the road, Roy's body remained lodged under the carriage of the motor home. The pavement started tearing away at his clothes and skin as Hayden drove down the road without a care in the world for the time being. He just kept singing, "you got to roll me. Keep on rolling." Hayden Keller's mission in life was to see to it that no good deed went unpunished. That was his plan, and he was diligent about carrying it out. A trail of blood lined the road as it ate away at Roy's corpse, which was pinned underneath the RV. It was undeniable proof, Hayden Keller was serious about his intensions.

The stream of torn skin mixed with Roy's blood and the occasional detached human appendage strewn over the road made it vivid to anyone seeing it, especially law enforcement officials. It was easy for them to label Hayden Keller as some sick psychopath, but it would take them a fair amount of time to identify Roy. Hayden knew that, but when they did, they would discover he had a motor home registered to him. Hayden would then, have to seek out new living arrangements.

Chapter 8

Inside A Black Heart

The moon was full, and the evening seemed much too tranquil for Hayden's taste as he enjoyed one of Roy's overpriced cigars while sitting outside the RV at a nearby campground. Knowing the remains of Roy's body were already discovered somewhere along the highway, he knew it was only a matter of time before police started searching for his RV. He now felt it best to make other transportation arrangements.

It was a simple strategy really. Changing course was one of the ways he avoided being captured, changing vehicles in which he traveled was another. A dead body or two here and there in no particular logical pattern made it impossible to predict where he would strike next.

At that moment authorities had no idea where he was or in which direction he was headed, and Hayden was kind enough to leave a blood trail for them to follow, right on the pavement. He also took the time to spray down the tires and the underside of his newly acquired RV before he doubled back. He was just toying with police at that point. Hayden was used to making it up as he went along, and he had been at it a long time.

If there was anything he had down to a science, it was dealing out death and living to do it another day. With Hayden it was almost an art form of sorts. He killed then walked away leaving all the evidence in the world for investigators to find. He didn't care in the least. In fact, he wanted them to discover it because he feared no man, and with good reason.

Some time had passed since Roy's demise but not enough. He knew his next victims would present themselves to him given time. However, Hayden didn't like to wait. If they didn't come to him at the appointed time, he would hunt them down, and make them curse the day they ever laid eyes on him. That was a certainty. He found nothing more satisfying than exacting his revenge upon the innocent, and this particular evening was no different. However, even Hayden was bound with limitations. They were not necessarily rules he wished to play by, but he made sure to never cross them - only because his life depended on it.

His body count for the week was filled thanks to Roy, and it would be after midnight before he could enter the hunt once more. As that glorious hour approached, his anticipation grew. His mouth even watered thinking about his next kill. This is what his life had come to. Taking the lives of others was the one thing which made him feel most alive. As he stepped back inside the RV snuffing out the cigar, he couldn't wait to experience life once again. He laid down unable to sleep, repeatedly looking over at the clock to see what time it was. He looked through some of Roy's things just to pass the time, and he became even more familiar with his latest victim.

Even after learning more about him, Hayden didn't miss Roy in the least. He never regretted killing a soul. That's what made him so damn great at it. He told Roy, "we all do what we're good at," and he proved it to him. Hayden's talents were just revealed to people in their final moments of life, that's all. He truly was the reaper in the flesh. Consequently, killing was part of his job description no matter how he sliced it. It was a morbid career path unlike any other he had chosen for himself, and it came with its own unique benefits.

Hayden did the devil's work in order to avoid the fire himself, and his appetite for blood was greater than a lion's. Maybe that's why he carried that crest tattooed on his arm, where everyone could see it, as a way of forewarning others of his most basic instinct.

Rummaging through one of Roy's bags, he pulled out a Beretta. It was a finely crafted semi-automatic pistol with a thirteen round clip. It was a rare piece indeed making it extremely hard to come by, and there was no doubt in Hayden's mind that Roy probably bragged about having it, more than he actually fired the damn thing. Still, he had to admire Roy's taste in weaponry as he took the time to appreciate its unique design.

Inserting the loaded clip into the gun, he pulled back the slide. Chambering a round, he couldn't help but think, *Roy probably carried that pistol for protection, and when the time came to use it, he had not planned for it.* The irony made him smile as he wiped off the firearm. Softly under his breath Hayden said, "good ole Roy," and he started to laugh a little making no sound at all. He was a hollow man with virtually no soul to burn. As black hearted as they come, that's Hayden Keller.

Now thanks to Roy's poor planning, that weapon would not only fail to protect him from a would-be attacker, it would almost certainly be used to send another victim to an early grave. All of a sudden Roy was growing on Hayden. He laid the gun in the passenger seat as he climbed behind the wheel of the RV, pulling out of the campsite in the dead of the night. He knew he had less than twenty-four hours to change course and find a new ride in order to stay a few steps ahead of the state police.

Chapter 9

Past Kills

Without much to do as he drove down the highway, he thought about some of his previous victims. He enjoyed recalling their final words or their facial expressions. Something about it almost made him feel warm inside, but his black heart was incapable of holding onto any true emotion other than rage. Still, he found humor momentarily in other peoples' pain, although his eyes could never show it.

He carried that dismal stare that was demonic in nature, bordering on insane, looking possessed most of the time. Tonight was no different, it was ever present as he recounted places he had visited, each of them bringing back images of people he had killed. Just reminiscing about the time he spent with them made him feel as though he was doing them a favor. After all, so many times in life the living forget about the dead. Hayden certainly didn't wish to see them fall into that category.

Some of the people he thought of, no one in the world would ever miss. The homeless guy in Philadelphia, probably no one even knew he existed until they found his dead body in the very dumpster he used to climb into to forage for food. Hayden looked at that one as a mercy killing. In his twisted mind he had done the old guy a favor.

After all the killing over the years, it still amazed Hayden just how much people wish to go on living even if they had miserable lives. Somehow, at the brink of death suddenly life started to look like something worth hanging onto. Some literally begged to go on eking out their pitiful existence, but that never prevented Hayden from paying the devil his due. He had a quota to fill and he never came up short. The price to pay for missing the mark was too high even for Hayden. He knew one day he would have to square away his debt, and account for all the evil he had done, but today was not that day. Hayden was substituting other souls to burn in his place, endless steady stream of them in fact.

Hayden thought about the little girl he watched burn inside an old clapboard house just outside of Centerville as he stood out in the front yard waving to her. He then thought about all of the disappointments in life he spared her from experiencing by taking her life at the perfect age of seven. It was moments like those that made him question if there wasn't a little goodness hiding deep down inside him somewhere, but Hayden knew good could not exist in the presence of evil. They were one in the same, evil was Hayden Keller, no question about it. He proved it to each of his victims time and again, and he certainly had his favorites.

Perhaps the two best recollections he had of his victims were that of Theresa Fitz and Dennis Cantrell. It was a cold winter night when he arrived at Theresa's house. She was wrapped up in a blanket, talking on the phone as she watched *Entertainment Tonight* while sitting on her sofa. She was discussing the latest Hollywood gossip with her longtime friend Cheri Tomlinson.

Hayden could hear some of what she was saying as he watched her through the window at the back of the house. Staring at her through the glass, he observed her every mannerism, from the way she twirled her dirty blonde hair when she spoke, to her obsession with admiring her nails on both her fingers and her toes. She would hold them on display where she could see them, and delight in their perfection as she changed the topic of conversation to skincare products.

Hayden entered through the backdoor when she set the phone down for a moment to run to the bathroom. He moved about the house as if he owned it himself. Following her into the bedroom he could see the door leading to the bathroom. The light was on and Hayden was at home. He stood inside her bedroom waiting patiently by the bathroom door, listening to every sound she made, and just as she flushed the toilet, Hayden heard a broken hissing sound behind his back. It was Theresa's cat, Felix, and he did not care for Hayden at all.

Hayden turned looking at the frenzied feline. He gave it a look which expressed severe displeasure. Making a slight move toward it, the cat screeched as it shot off the bed, longing to get as far away from Hayden as possible. Oddly enough, Hayden cared nothing about skinning the cat. Theresa, however, was another story. *Maybe he would amputate her lovely fingers and toes, keeping them for himself*, he thought. Right at that moment, Theresa shut off the faucet and opened up the bathroom door. Hayden moved out of her line of sight placing his back to the wall.

All Theresa saw was her cat's tail exiting the bedroom exceedingly fast. She assumed she had frightened Felix, all on her own. She called him by name in an attempt to put him at ease. The image of her cat fleeing the scene gave Theresa a small laugh as she criticized him for being such a scaredy-cat. She was quick to walk back into the living room, never noticing Hayden as she picked up the phone to continue her conversation. She sat down on the sofa saying, "Felix is so funny sometimes, I swear." She had to take that opportunity to tell Cheri how Felix is afraid of his own shadow. Then she said, "I don't know where he ran off to, probably hiding under the bed. Now what were you saying?"

Hayden listened to her chatter away about what was wrong with the guy she quit seeing recently, and then she had to complain about one of her co-workers saying, "it's not like she does anything. All she really does is suck up to Barbara, and I just don't like her attitude." Theresa's world was full of problems. Hayden planned to nix them all for her. She wouldn't be complaining about shit when he got done with her.

He was now standing at the end of the hallway. He leaned his head forward slightly looking over at Theresa as she continued talking. Feeling somewhat uncomfortable, she looked into the decorative mirror which hung on her living room wall. Her eyes became wide and suddenly she stopped speaking halfway through a sentence. She could see Hayden's horrifying reflection, and he could see her petrified facial expression. She started to scream, but Hayden grabbed the phone cord pulling it to her throat as she gasped for air. Quickly, wrapping it around her neck, he slowly strangled the life out of her. She tried to fight back using her perfect nails, but it was no use. She couldn't reach Hayden's face, and the scratches she made on the back of his hands merely served as a trophy of the kill in his twisted mind.

Cheri could be heard on the other end of the line saying, "Theresa? Are you okay? What's going on?" She could hear Theresa choking and she knew she was in distress.

Once the struggle ended, Hayden took the receiver in his

hand and said, "Theresa is all tied up right now."

Knowing something was wrong, and not recognizing Hayden's voice, Cheri threaten him by saying, "I'm calling the police."

Hayden always smiled whenever he thought about the remarks he made over the phone to Theresa's friend. He calmly said, "good, tell them to hurry up and get here, and I'll kill them too. Better yet, I'll come to you. What's your address?" All that was heard at that point was an abrupt click followed by a dial tone.

Hayden left the phone cord wrapped around Theresa's neck as he walked to the refrigerator in search of something to eat. Taking his sweet time, he emptied the contents of her purse on the coffee table taking what money she had in her wallet, and the car keys he found lying on the dresser. He left long before anyone showed up to investigate the scene. What they found was Hayden's masterful handiwork. Ironically, he had allowed Theresa to keep all of her nails. Her fingers were very attractive to the point she could have been a hand model. It was her tongue Police found lying on a shelf inside the refrigerator. It was cut-out post mortem, but in Hayden's sick mind that was part of the makings for a great late night news story.

His encounter with Dennis was every bit as enjoyable since it resulted in an overabundance of pain. However, the location and duration of Dennis's demise was quite different than that of Theresa's. It was a pleasant Sunday afternoon, tailor-made for watching a ball game, and that's what Dennis was doing while finishing off another beer in his garage. As Dennis turned to grab another one, he noticed a man standing on the other side of the road just staring at him. It was Hayden, of course, and he had located his next victim. He said nothing, he just stared locking eyes with

Dennis as he cracked open another cold one.

Dennis wasn't in the mood to invite him over to watch the game. He found it extremely odd that some man he had never seen before was looking straight into his eyes as if to stare him down for some reason. He had to question who the hell he was as the situation grew more uncomfortable. When Hayden said nothing in response to his aggressive line of questioning, Dennis raised his voice a little asking, "you got some kind of problem?"

Hayden found that part laughable even though he refrained from showing it. He hadn't done a thing to this character, and he was already under his skin, figuratively speaking of course. When Hayden was done with Dennis it could truthfully be said he literally got under his skin.

Hayden took that opportunity to step across the street and introduce himself to the asshole, holding what was left of a six-pack in one hand, and an open Budweiser in the other. Dennis didn't look near as intimidating in his sandals, Bermuda shorts, and tank top as Hayden did swaggering across the road all dressed in black. As Hayden approached he turned his head to see if anyone was within eyeshot.

He carried a disgusted look on his scarred face, and it was genuine. Looking back at Dennis he made sure to look him directly in the eye, and there was no doubt the situation was going to become confrontational. Dennis held his ground as Hayden stepped foot on his property. Feeling a bit bold from the beers he had consumed and overly territorial, he warned Hayden not to come any closer. In fact, he shouted, "get the hell out of my yard," but Hayden paid him no attention whatsoever. He continued walking right up to him placing himself in Dennis's personal space as they stood toe-to-toe, face-to-face.

Dennis started to step back, Hayden quickly reached up with both hands grabbing his shoulders to prevent him from pulling away. Hayden then lowered his head slightly, ramming his forehead into Dennis's nose busting it wide open, and blood starting running down Dennis's face. It was on Hayden's face as well, and he licked his lips tasting it as he watched Dennis reach for his nose with both hands, never stopping to think what's going to happen next. He should have. Hayden knew exactly what he was going to do before he ever crossed the street.

Dennis had no plan at all, except to shoot off his mouth in hopes of getting rid of a weird onlooker he had never seen before. Now, he was in complete shock. His nose was broken, and it hurt like hell. All he could do at that point was yell, "what the fuck man!" In his mind he questioned if Hayden was insane. Seeing his own blood drip onto the concrete floor of the garage, he didn't have to ask that question. He still had no idea, Hayden's horrible face would be the last one he'd ever lay eyes on.

Hayden reached over picking up a full can of beer out of the cooler. He forcefully plowed it into the side of Dennis's head. Dennis tried to defend himself with one hand while holding his nose with the other. His feudal attempt failed miserably as Hayden rendered him unconscious with a single blow. Hayden looked over his shoulder to see if anyone saw what was going on, and closing the garage door, he turned grabbing the power cord which was hanging on the pegboard next to the hedge trimmer. He used it to bind Dennis's feet and hands. Then, he looked over at the work bench in Dennis's garage, and he smiled. He had found the perfect place to conduct business.

Looking down at Dennis lying helpless on the floor, he cranked open the vice which was mounted on the corner of the tool table. Hayden was ready to undertake another project, but Home Depot didn't have a course to teach people how to do this one. No, this one was classic psychopath 101, 'How To Dismantle A Human Body.'

Hayden grabbed Dennis's bound arms hauling him over to the workbench, and he placed his skull in the vice tightening it to the point Dennis could not move his head without causing extreme pain. Hayden then, walked over to the television set turning up the volume in an effort to mask his screams from anyone that might happen to pass by, and he turned noticing Dennis was now aware of his tight fitting surroundings.

In an effort to add some levity to the moment Hayden said, "looks like you're just in time for the second half." Dennis couldn't make much noise at all, without the teeth on the vice tearing into his skin on each side of his face. Hayden mocked him as he walked over sitting down next to him on the stool. He cracked open a beer saying, "you don't mind, do you."

Hayden twisted the handle on the vice tightening it even more. Dennis cringed as he felt the pressure increase to a point where it was unbearable. Hayden tapped the open beer against Dennis's head saying, "don't worry. This buds for you." He drizzled some beer on Dennis's head before taking a long sip. All the while, he admired Dennis's tool collection, thinking, *it would be a shame not to put some of those tools to work*. He offered Dennis a choice by asking, "which one shall we start with, the hacksaw or the pliers?"

Suddenly, it dawned on Dennis he may not survive this ordeal. No one ever accused him of being bright though. Hayden picked up the saw and said, "I think we'll leave the ears for last, that way you can hear me." Dennis was now living a nightmare that was made real by the pain he felt coursing through his body.

Hayden clinched his hand tightly around Dennis's pointer finger, and he touched the edge of the saw blade to his knuckle. Then, he tested the blade for sharpness. One push forward and one pull back, Hayden was hard at work. Ten seconds later that finger was gone. Moving to other parts of his body using the saw, he slowly ran the teeth of the blade across Dennis's shin, pushing it deeper into the bone with each downward stroke. Merely wanting to inflict pain, Hayden played a game he liked to call, "let's see what we can sever next."

Dennis yelled, but no one could hear him other than Hayden. He tried to wrestle his way loose, but it was no use. Hayden laid his severed finger on the work table right in front of his eyes where he couldn't help but see it. Tears welled up in his eyes as Hayden said, "this is going to get messy. I think you see my point."

Hayden took another drink of beer as he picked up the grinder. He plugged it into a nearby receptacle as Dennis's body moved in disapproval of what was about to take place. To the best of his ability, he managed to scream, "no, God no!"

Hayden was able to make it out, but that didn't slow him down any. He just callously said, "I was wondering when you would bring him into this." Revving the power tool he added, "I don't think he can hear you." That's when he touched the abrasive disk to the bloody stub, which was once Dennis's forefinger. He began grinding away what was left of it. The pain was so intense Dennis passed out. This went on for several hours until Hayden became bored. Whenever Dennis would regain consciousness, Hayden would have a new tool in his hand ready to dismantle him further.

Dennis prayed for it all to end when Hayden began the tooth extraction using a rusty pair of pliers he found one day laying in his yard. He was now wishing he had never picked those up. To make things worse, Hayden felt compelled to see how well Dennis's weed-eater worked. With Dennis's head still in the vice he tightened it again for good measure, and the pressure on Dennis's brain became immense. His eyes were now bulging to the point his vision became blurred. What happened next was almost indescribable as Hayden cranked up the weed-eater and tried it out on Dennis's legs. As Hayden flipped the switch shutting it off Dennis collapsed, and his neck was broken by the weight of his body, his head still held in the giant vice. Dennis could have ended it long ago, but the thought of snapping his neck with the help of the vice and gravity never crossed his mind.

Hayden quickly jerked his head to the side, admiring the weed-eater's ability to inflict tremendous damage. Hayden grinned as he said, "now, that brings a whole new meaning to being taken to the tool shed, don't it." Hayden drank the last beer Dennis had as he slapped him on the back saying, "we'll have to get together and do this again sometime." He then, borrowed Dennis's trailblazer, and blazed a path to parts unknown.

Whenever Hayden thought about Dennis, it certainly brought back memories of good times in front of the TV, and the sports highlights were definitely not the most memorable moments from that afternoon. When it came to Dennis, Hayden would always chuckle a little thinking, *that guy probably wasn't the sharpest tool in the shed, but he was one tough son of a bitch.* He had to give him that much.

Never taking his eyes off the road, Hayden reached over to flip on the radio, catching the tail end of "Free Bird" being done only the way Lynyrd Skynyrd could do it. He started moving his head to the rhythm of the hammering guitars as he sang, "oh, I can't change. No, I can't change." That was the honest to God's truth as they say, and for Hayden Keller the night was young. What he would find on the highway would remain to be seen, but you could rest assured it would resemble hell when Hayden was through with it.

Chapter 10

Road Rage

The road was dark and the RV was nearly full of gas. Hayden had to dump it though. He had already held onto it longer than he anticipated. It was only fitting that he should be listening to AC/DC screaming out, "Highway to Hell," as he ventured down the road in search of his next unsuspecting victim.

Hayden didn't pray for what he wanted, he simply took it. If he had been a prayerful man, his prayer would have been answered as he made a turn onto Highway 35. Less than two miles down that stretch of road, he saw a set of taillights up ahead in the distance. Not knowing whether or not it was law enforcement, he hung back a ways until he could determine exactly what kind of vehicle it was.

Inside the moving vehicle was Edward Pennington and his wife Sandra. They were traveling with their two children, heading to Sandra's mother's house for the holidays. Ashley sat in the back seat nearly half asleep listening to her iPod, while Brandon played a video game tuning out everything his parents were saying. They were arguing mostly, but in a civil tone for the moment.

Sandra had suggested they leave earlier that day, but Edward's work didn't make that possible. Sandra emotionally stated, "I told her we would be there by now, that's all I'm saying."
Edward wished that's all she was saying as he tried to refrain from losing his temper. Immensely frustrated at this

point, he said, "then call her and tell her we're running later than expected. Better yet tell her we'll see her in the morning."

He had resigned to just getting a hotel room for the night. He had already experienced an extremely stressful day at work, which was not unusual for a hospital administrator, and the ride in the car hadn't improved things much. After putting in more than a full day at the office, he had rushed home to load up the car for their trip.

All he had heard since leaving the house was how they were going to be late. His wife was more than a little putout with him. Paying no attention to her critical comments, Edward continued to drive noticing headlights coming up fast from behind. They reflected off his rear view mirror making it difficult for him to see the road ahead. He looked up wishing the approaching vehicle would switch off their high beams, but he was forced to adjust his mirror so the lights wouldn't hit him right in the eyes.

Sandra tried to phone her mother, but she couldn't pick up any signal on her mobile phone. They simply weren't close enough to a cell tower for her to make the call. Exasperated, she closed her phone and looked over at her husband. Even in the dark Edward knew what that look meant, and he said, "I guess that's my fault too, huh."
Sandra just shook her head as she said, "I didn't say a thing."

Edward turned his head looking over in his side view mirror at the vehicle behind him. Whatever it was, it was big and it was riding right up on him. He pressed the gas to try and put some distance between him and the RV, but Hayden followed suit. Unable to put the least bit of space between his rear bumper and the front fender of the RV Edward let off the gas. His wife asked, "what's the matter?"

Thoroughly agitated he replied, "this son of a bitch behind me." Sandra looked over her shoulder through the rear window at the RV. She turned warning her husband to just be careful. Edward raised his voice a little as he said, "come on around you asshole."

Sandra remarked, "I wish you wouldn't talk like that." Her husband lifted one of his hands from the steering wheel turning his palm up as if to question what he did wrong now. Edward's response was, "do you see this guy? He's right on my ass." In a sarcastic tone he said, "evidently he likes riding it as much as you do."

Suddenly, what was going on in the front seat became much more interesting than any videogame or song on one's iPod. Both Brandon and Ashley were now paying attention to what was being said. Something didn't feel right. Ashley touched her necklace holding the crucifix between her thumb and forefinger as she turned to glance over her shoulder at the vehicle behind them.

Hayden could see her face for a moment before she turned away. He saw Brandon's as well as he looked in Hayden's direction. Hayden laid on the horn before moving over into the other lane to pass. He blew by the gray sedan almost sideswiping it in the process, forcing it to come off the road a little to avoid having an accident. Edward cursed as he heard the right tire leave the pavement.

Hayden immediately swung back over into the other lane cutting him off, and he tapped the brakes several times. Edward said, "oh, now this bastard is just trying to piss me off," as he gave Hayden the finger.

Brandon said, "way to flip that bastard off dad."

Sandra turned damn near in shock at what her twelve year old son just said and she started to scold him by saying, "you watch your tongue Mr."

Edward cut her off by saying, "it's alright. That guy is a bastard, and if I see him, I'll tell him that to his face."

Ashley remained quiet as her mom said, "just find us a hotel. I'll call her from there so she won't be worried."

Hayden raced up the road rounding a slight curve and disappeared into the distance. Finding a place to pull over along the edge of the road, he cut the lights off never shutting off the engine. Hayden sat and waited as he watched for the gray town car in the big side view mirror of the RV. It was rounding the curve behind him and picking up speed as it neared. As it moved closer, Hayden pulled out onto the road blocking both lanes.

By the time Edward saw the RV, he was right up on it. There was nothing he could do to avoid hitting it head on except jerk the wheel hard to the left while slamming on the brakes. The lights were still out on the RV. Hayden shut off the engine, and he reached over picking up the gun he had placed in the passenger seat. Tucking the weapon inside his waistband behind his back, he exited the vehicle using the passenger door. His jacket and the night itself concealed the gun from plain sight. He looked toward the rear of the RV as he stepped out of the passenger side door. Wasting no time whatsoever he walked to the rear of the motor home.

The back end of the gray sedan sat caddie-corner in the road, almost parallel to the RV. Its' front tires were off the road completely with virtually no way of getting around the motor home. Edward had very few options. If he took the town car off the paved road altogether, he risked becoming stuck on the soft, uneven shoulder. Infuriated by the entire situation Mr. Pennington looked at his wife. He then glanced in the backseat to check to make sure the kids were alright. Shifting the car into park he automatically reacted by hastily reaching for the door handle.

Calling out his name, his wife reached over to grab his arm in an attempt to stop him from getting out, but Edward was moving fast as he exited the car. He was livid. Ashley watched her father as he walked toward the driver's side door of the RV and Brandon asked, "what's going on?"

A little hesitant to say anything, his mom replied, "your dad is just going to check things out. That's all."

Brandon reached for his door handle saying, "I'll go with him." Sandra instructed Brandon to stay put as his father went to open the driver's side door of the RV, only to find out it was locked. It was too dark to see who was inside.

Sandra had a feeling something bad was about to happen as she watched Edward beat on the door of the motor home yelling, "what the hell is your problem?" Hayden rounded the rear of the RV, and headed straight for the back of the car. Walking up behind the gray sedan in the dark he approached on Ashley's side of the vehicle.

As Edward walked in front of the RV to the passenger side of the vehicle, he vanished from sight. Everyone's attention was focused on the motor home at that point. Hayden carefully slipped up behind the town car without making a sound. Just as Brandon started to open his door, his mother turned in her seat to tell him to stay put once again. The words never escaped her lips before the screams of both she and Ashley alarmed Edward. He turned looking back at the car only to see a tall shadowy figure pulling his daughter out of the car by her hair. His wife was screaming, "no," at the top of her lungs as she and Brandon both reached for

Ashley's legs trying to save her from Hayden's clutches.

Edward ran toward the car concerned for his family's safety. A look of life or death was etched upon his face. Hayden placed his knife next to Ashley's throat as he held her hostage, and Sandra screamed out to her husband, "no he has a knife."

Ashley was still in shock by the whole ordeal. All she could do is yell, "daddy!" Suddenly, Edward stopped dead in his tracks. He couldn't risk losing his daughter. He tried to think of what to do next in order to assure his daughter's safe return. Very little came to mind though. He could offer to give Hayden anything he wanted in exchange for her, but he figured that would do little to sway him. Struggling to remain calm himself, he carefully approached the car as he moved closer to his daughter and Hayden. With authority he shouted, "let her go!"

Hayden informed him, "you're not in control here. How does it feel?"

Her mother pleaded for Hayden to let her baby go as Edward moved closer, but Hayden was hardly moved by her hysterical request. He just shook his head slowly as he looked down at her. With his next step Edward took a more aggressive approach saying, "let her go now. That's all I ask of you." He then added, "I'll give you whatever you want. I mean it, just let my daughter go."

Hayden smugly said, "you still haven't answered my question," as he quickly jerked Ashley's hair causing her head to snap back, forcing her to look straight up at the stars. She tried to look at her father using her eyes, but she could not see what he was doing. She let out a small scream of terror before starting to cry a little, fearing for her life.

Her mother pulled her hand to her mouth, praying it would all end, and her father told Hayden in no uncertain terms, "you really don't want to do this." Truth be known, there was nothing more Hayden would have rather done than kill them all, and swap rides, but making Ashley's father squirm a little bit as he stood there in the headlights made it all the better. Hayden said, "I tell you what, you want to be in control. So, I'll let you decide who lives and who dies."

With his left hand pressing the sharp blade of the knife against Ashley's jugular, Hayden reached behind his back with his right hand gripping the Beretta he had tucked in his pants. He drew it aiming it at Brandon through the open rear car door. Hayden then said, "the boy or the girl, which one will it be?" Seeing their father stand there in the headlights speechless was priceless in Hayden's book. He'd never forget that image as long as he lived. Hayden also knew what was penned on the next page of that book, and it was sure to be written in blood.

Sandra clung to Brandon in an effort to shield him from the bullet as Hayden waited for Edward's answer. Impatiently, Hayden demanded an answer from her father saying, "come on now, some of us don't have all night. Besides, your kids are dying to find out which one lives to tell the tale."

"You son of a bitch," was all Edward could say at that point. Sandra screamed out Ashley's name fearing the worst, and Hayden squeezed the trigger firing two rounds into the backseat of the town car. One of them struck the boy in the chest, the other pierced his mother's hand, and Brandon's shoulder. She screamed, "oh my God! He shot him!"

She pulled her bloody hand away from her son's shoulder looking at it in disbelief before placing it back in an attempt to limit the blood loss. She wept as she tried to tell her son he was going to be alright. Edward had no choice at that point, all negotiations were off the table. His son needed immediate medical attention, and his daughter was still the hands of a mad man. He came over the hood of the car lunging toward Hayden as he ordered his daughter to run. Hayden turned the gun on her father firing once hitting him in the side as he almost came within striking distance of Hayden. As the adrenaline rushed through Edward's veins he continued his efforts to stop Hayden from harming his family any further. In a last ditch effort, he grabbed Hayden's arm as he fell to the ground, all the while trying to take Hayden down with him.

Hayden's grip on Ashley eased, and she broke free of him fleeing just as her father instructed her to do, not knowing those would be the last words she would ever hear him utter. Hayden's focus was now entirely on Mr. Pennington. Ashley's mother screamed out her husband's name in horror, and Hayden snarled saying, "to tell you the truth, I didn't think you had it in you."

He took his left hand which was holding the knife, and he slashed Edward's cheek leaving a long gash across it like the one he sustained many years earlier. Blood spattered on the outer part of his hand as he sliced open Mr. Pennington's face. Hayden pulled his hand to his mouth. Dragging it across the lower part of his face he wiped the blood off his sleeve and hand. He relished the taste of blood and he was about to have his fill. He watched Mr. Pennington try to stand in one final attempt to defend that which God had given him.

Hayden didn't want to waste another bullet. As far as he was concerned it was cutting time, and that's what he proceeded to do. Edward looked over at his wife telling her to go as he fell to the ground beside the open car door. He used his last bit of strength to slam the door shut hoping his wife would get out of there, and get their son the medical care he so desperately needed at that point. The keys were still in the ignition, but Sandra was paralyzed with fear. She held onto Brandon shielding him from seeing his father being brutally stabbed.

Hayden forcefully plunged the knife into Edward treating him as though he were a human pincushion. Sandra saw the damage Hayden was inflicting driving the knife deep into her husband's back repeatedly burying the entire blade all the way to the hilt. Each time he stabbed him he used greater force. Sandra was in utter shock.

Seeing Edward die at the hands of a vicious murderer, Sandra Pennington knew her only chance to save herself, and her children was to get help immediately. Brandon's face started slowly losing color. Letting go of him for a moment she slid over into the driver's seat as she cranked the car. She looked out the window at Hayden as he raised his gun. He sadistically tapped the tip of the muzzle against the glass as he grinned.

She panicked as she tried to shift the car into reverse. She slammed on the gas sending her forward, and she nearly ran into the ditch. Hayden took that opportunity to bust out one of the rear windows using the butt of the Beretta. Unable to open the door before she found reverse, he dove into the car through the window. Sandra looked up in the rear view mirror and screamed.

Hayden was now a passenger in the backseat right along with her son who was now losing consciousness. Hayden slowly brought an eerie smile to his scarred face as he placed his arm around Brandon's neck as if they were best of friends. Sandra turned around lashing out at Hayden with her fists as the car continued to roll backward with no one in control of the wheel. She shouted at Hayden ordering him to get away from her son, but he just delivered a sick laugh saying, "no need to yell. After all, I'm right here."

The words that came out of Sandra's mouth at that point were filled with venom as she screamed, "let go of him, you fucking bastard!"

Hayden liked this side of her. It seemed that both her and her husband rose to the occasion when push came to shove, but it was now time to end it. There was a girl out there somewhere who could possibly describe him to authorities, and Hayden couldn't afford to let that happen. It was dark, of course, but all she had to do was mention the scar he carried on his left cheek, and anyone could spot him at that point.

Hayden liked to choose the moment when he revealed his real personality to those he happened to meet. He figured Mrs. Pennington knew him well enough at that point to refer to him as bastard, which he was, but he went ahead and made the formal introduction telling her, "my name is Hayden Keller." Hayden also saw no reason for them to spend a great deal more time together. Holding his knife where she could see as he waved it a little side to side he said, "your son isn't looking too well, but don't you worry I'll be sure to take real good care of his sister for you."

Hayden grabbed one of her wrists, and he twisted her arm as he pulled her toward him in the backseat. He began cutting on her arms and then her face. He wanted to see her facial expression as he sliced her into pieces. As she watched the blood flow freely down her arms, out of her cuts she became silent. Hayden knew the look she had on her bloody face. It was the look of someone that had accepted what was about to happen next.

Sandra knew there was no way of changing fate at that point. Not for herself anyway, she was going to die. There was no question about that. She had already lost her husband and her son to this wretched son of a bitch that was sitting so content in the backseat of her town car. Her only thought at that final moment was *God please be with Ashley.* It was a final prayer without the formality of bended knees and folded hands. She asked nothing for herself, just for God to somehow save her daughter.

She never doubted that dying wish would be granted, even with some hell bent demon like Hayden in pursuit of her. That's how strong her faith was. Her mother had taught her that faith can move mountains, and at the moment she was asking God to place one between this demented psychopath and her daughter. It was a mother's dying wish never spoken out loud. She knew Hayden was the antithesis of anything holy or righteous and she would not give him the satisfaction of hearing her final thoughts prior to leaving this world.

Hayden took in a deep cleansing breath as he ran the bloody blade of his knife across her throat. Pulling her carcass into the backseat, he swapped places with her to gain control of the vehicle. As it rolled off the road he applied the brakes bringing the car to a complete stop. He looked over his shoulder as he placed his right hand on the passenger headrest. He had to take the time to admire his carnage filled handiwork, and he flashed a devilish grin as he said, "let's go pick up dad. What do you say?"

Sandra nor her son could say a word obviously, but Hayden sometimes enjoyed talking to the dead. It was usually a morbid comment he liked to throw their way for his personal amusement. As he pulled over to the other side of the road he drove over Edward's arm. He got out of the car laughing as he said, "good thing you won't need to be using that anymore, I guess." He felt better than he had in a long time after damn near killing an entire family.

Killing was Hayden's gift and also his curse. He had to take a life in order to feel alive, and although some may say the devil made them do it, in Hayden's case it was true. Hayden knew what was expected of him, and he lived to kill. Normally, Hayden was filled with rage as he was when he first rolled up on them, but now after momentarily quenching his thirst for blood he felt at ease. This was as close to happy as Hayden ever came. That feeling, of course, would wear off soon enough unless he found another victim to provide the temporary high he received every time he took a life.

As he shoved Edward's corpse into the backseat, he placed Edward's broken arm around his wife's shoulder. He looked in the direction of the RV for any sign of Ashley, but she was nowhere to be found. Hayden liked a challenge and he was hoping she would not disappoint him.

Hayden climbed back inside the car, and he looked in the rear view mirror at the once perfect family. He cocked his head as if he were trying to figure something out and he said, "something is missing. Oh yeah, that would be Ashley." He held up one finger as if to gesture hold on, and don't interrupt me as he said, "don't you worry I will find her." He drove off leaving the RV straddled across the road for some unsuspecting driver to find coming around the curve. He hated to miss the collision, but he had a girl to chase after, and Hayden wanted nothing more than to catch her. He drove slowly into the night in search of the one that got away.

Chapter 11

Let The Hunt Begin

Ashley ran along the side of the road hoping to find someone who could help her. She had no idea what had happened to her family, she just knew they were in danger. She was scared and she started to hyperventilate as she ceased running. That's when she heard an engine in the distance. She couldn't tell what direction it was coming from, but it sounded low and heavy like the RV Hayden was driving. Frightened it might be him she backed away from the road just to be safe. Taking cover in the trees she heard music blasting as headlights appeared on the road no more than two hundred feet from where she was.

It was an old beat-up pickup truck filled with a couple of locals out making another beer run. They were hollering at the top of their lungs as one of them beat the dash as if he were the drummer for REO Speedwagon while the other two sang "Keep On Rolling." They scared Ashley almost as much as Hayden did, but she needed help. She decided to run toward the road to try and flag them down, but the only one that saw her was La Don, and he was the drunkest one of the bunch. Still, she had caught his attention. He stopped beating on the dash a minute as his head turned watching her wave her arms in the air hoping that they would stop.

Bruiser looked over at him and said, "you ain't getting sick, are you? If you do make sure you roll down that window."

La Don muttered, "I ain't sick. Did you just see a girl?"

Clay looked over at him saying, "hell I've seen lots of

them," and he laughed.

La Don turned with a puzzled look on his face as he looked directly at Clay and Bruiser. He slowly shook his head and said, "I saw one right back there and she was waving at me."

Clay said, "shit," as he glanced over at Bruiser. Pointing his thumb toward La Don he said, "tell me this boy hasn't had way too damn much to drink."

Bruiser laughed as he continued to drive, adding, "I know one thing, he damn sure don't need to be behind the wheel. He'd kill us all."

That brought another laugh as Clay asked, "what did she look like?"

La Don said, "it was dark. I don't know. I just saw her for a second."

Clay started shaking his head and tilted as he leaned forward saying, "you are so full of shit, it ain't even funny."

La Don said, "I swear she's there."

Bruiser settled the argument by saying, "hell we'll just pick her up on the way back after we get the beer. Who knows maybe she's got some friends."

Clay hollered out, "I get the one with the big boobs," and they all started laughing.

Hayden couldn't help but see them approaching, flying down the road like a bat out of hell, and he couldn't resist seeing them plow right into Roy's RV. He was traveling slow in search of Ashley, but he stopped, waiting for the pickup truck to blow past him before turning around to follow them. After Bruiser zipped past the stationary gray sedan he looked in his side view mirror. Clay questioned if it was a cop, and Bruiser said, "I don't know, but the son of a bitch is turning around."

Clay hollered out, "punch this mother fucker," and a huge smile came across Bruiser's face as he floored it.

La Don let out a howl that would knock the rust off the front fender and they all joined in with him as they attempted to leave Hayden in the dust.

Hayden knew he was about to witness these dumb sons of bitches bite the dust, and he couldn't wait for it to happen. He literally chased them to their death. As they got closer to the RV Hayden backed off the gas, and Bruiser started pulling away. Clay looked out the back window yelling, "you're losing him man," and Bruiser looked over in his side view mirror smiling with a great deal of satisfaction plastered on his drunken face. La Don took it upon himself to roll down his window and stick his hand out giving Hayden the finger. Just at that moment, the headlights of the truck landed on the RV and none of them saw it coming.

Bruiser turned his head as he started to say something, but the last thing he spouted was, "oh fuck," as he managed to hit the RV almost head on. He barely had time to search for the brake pedal with his foot before the collision.

When the shattered glass and smoke cleared, Clay was no longer in his seat. He had flown right through the windshield and bounced off the hood of the truck after plowing headfirst into the RV. He was killed on contact. Bruiser and La Don were not so fortunate. Metal shrapnel from the passenger side of the truck had pierced La Don's chest entering his right lung. He was still breathing, but losing blood fast when Hayden got out of the car and walked up to the wreckage.

La Don's lung was slowly filling with blood, and he found it increasingly more difficult to breathe as he said, "you ain't no cop." Hayden had to laugh at that remark. He noticed the blood trickle out of La Don's ear and steadily drip onto his shoulder. Eventually, he would drown on his own blood if he didn't bleed out first. To make matters worse he had crushed several vertebrae, and he was unable to move from the neck down. There was no coming back from this one, not for any of them.

Bruiser found himself pinched between the steering column and the front seat. His head was busted wide open thanks to the hit it took upon impact, and there was no doubt he had sustained a serious concussion.

Hayden walked around the truck surveying the damage. He made a clicking sound with his tongue as he walked up to the driver's side door of the pickup. He looked inside saying, "damn, I couldn't have done better myself." Then he asked, "you haven't seen a girl around here anywhere have you?"

Bruiser's eyes got really big as he looked over toward Hayden. Blood covered his face as he tried to say one word. That word of course was, "help."

Hayden just mocked him a little by saying, "I'm sorry, but I can't seem to make that out, try again." Bruiser made his best effort to speak clearly, but his speech was more garbled and slurred than before. Hayden said, "I can't understand what the hell you are saying man. You need some help." Then in a surprised tone Hayden said, "oh, that's what you mean, help." Shaking his head rather regretfully, Hayden said, "I'm sorry, but I seem to be fresh out at the moment."

He turned walking over to where Clay's contorted body laid, and he reached down long enough to relieve him of his cigarettes and wallet. He held up the pack of smokes saying, "watch out man these things can kill you." That joke never got old to Hayden no matter how many times he said it. He skimmed over his driver's license noticing he was an organ donor. Hayden couldn't resist making an inappropriate comment that displayed his morbid sense of humor as he placed the wallet inside his jacket pocket. It was something along the lines of "people are going to be happy to see pieces of you coming my friend."

Hayden then did an about face and strolled on back to the gray town car as if he hadn't a care in the world. Halfway there he pulled a cigar from inside his coat pocket. He stopped and turned to look back at the mangled mass of metal and glass one last time, while lighting the cigar with the lighter that read, ***Congratulations Roy, on twenty-eight great years. Enjoy your retirement.*** At that moment Hayden thought to himself, *life is good*, as he took a long drag off the stogie.

Bruiser's eyes had answered his question regarding the whereabouts of the girl even if Bruiser himself was unable to express his thoughts in words. Hayden knew Ashley was out there probably searching for help, and he knew he would find her. He also had a feeling they were going to get to know one another well over the next several days. There was only one problem, time was no longer on Hayden's side. He was only permitted to take six lives, in order to deliver six souls, in six days, and he had already reached his limit. More time had to pass before he could kill again. Hayden hated it, but he dared not bend that rule.

Hayden found a consolation prize lying on the road behind the pickup truck as he made his way back to the gray sedan. It was a chainsaw that had bounced out of the bed of the truck on impact. Hayden picked up the saw holding it in both hands for a moment eager to try it out on something or someone. He felt more powerful than ever clinching it in his hands. Imagining the mess he could make with it, he turned slinging it over his shoulder, and walked to the car. Once there, he tossed it in the passenger seat before heading out in search of Ashley.

He motored down the highway looking on both sides of the road for any trace of the girl. Seeing something move in the trees up ahead he slowed to a near stop. Hayden knew she was close, he could sense it. Pointing the headlights in the direction of the movement, he saw what appeared to be a young deer standing just inside the trees on the side of the road. Hayden whispered under his breath, "you're not what I'm looking for," as he continued his search.

He felt betrayed by his senses for a minute or so until he heard the faint sound of Ashley's voice calling out to the passing car as she yelled, "here I am!" She had seen the gray town car and assumed it was her family searching for her. That was her first mistake, her second was flagging it down with Hayden Keller behind the wheel. She had no idea what really happened to her family. Hayden couldn't believe how trusting she was. He had expected a challenge, and she had almost come running right to him. He put the car in reverse and backed up to meet her.

Hayden got closer, and Ashley got that sick feeling in her stomach, not knowing why just yet, but she began to feel something wasn't right. She stopped where she stood as she waited for the car to come to her. She didn't hear her father or mother's voice when she called out to them. She started to back away from the car as Hayden watched her through the rear view mirror. He stopped the vehicle altogether. The red brake lights were all Ashley could see until Hayden opened the driver's side door, and the light came on inside the town car. She was horrified at what she saw, and she screamed as Hayden exited the driver's side door. He grimly growled, "now there's the Ashley I know. I've been looking all over for you." He moved towards her chasing her off the road and into the woods.

She franticly used her arms to push away limbs blocking her path while running as fast as she could to get away from him. A true look of horror covered her face as she literally ran for her life. No one escaped Hayden's clutches once he had them in his sights, but she had no idea how long he had been masterfully crafting the art of killing. All she prayed for at that point was to survive her encounter with him. Little did she know that was asking for a miracle.

He followed her until he lost sight of her and that's when he called out to her again saying, "come on out wherever you are." She remembered what it felt like to be held captive by him, and now she was all alone. She never wanted to feel his cold hands touch her skin ever again, and she certainly didn't want to be captured by him. Fear welled up inside her as she kept telling herself to just stay put and maybe he won't find you. As he got closer, she honestly thought he would be able to hear her heart beating. She couldn't control it pounding hard within her chest. Even her breathing became heavy in an attempt to calm herself down.

She was panicked to the point she could not think clearly. She began running once again. Hayden could hear her footsteps as she ran from him, and he lived for a good chase from time to time. He knew she wouldn't disappoint him now as he yelled, "I'm right behind you!" The scent of her perfume made it easy for Hayden to stay on her trail.

Trying to get away she was repeatedly pelted by limbs and low hanging branches. She looked over her shoulder to see if Hayden was close behind, but she couldn't tell where he was. Barely able to see a few feet in front of her she tripped over a large rock causing her to fall forward hitting the ground face first. Scared to move at all, she stayed right where she was and she closed her eyes tightly praying Hayden would not find her. Tears streamed down her cheeks as she tried not to make a sound. That's when she heard the rustling sound in the leaves off to the side of her. She dared not move an inch, but she had to see if it was Hayden. Holding her body perfectly still, she slowly turned her head in the direction of the sound. Opening her eyes, she saw nothing. A relieved look came over her face as she began to breathe again, and at that very moment she felt Hayden's hand grab hold of her hair as he yanked it hard snatching her up off the ground. Her eyes opened wide and she let out a terrifying scream while struggling to get away. Hayden pulled her ear up close to his mouth and candidly he said, "don't worry. I got you babe."

"Oh, God no," she screamed.

He growled, dragging her in the direction of the car. Ashley tried to grab hold of anything she could reach in an effort to break the grip Hayden had on her. He drug her through the woods as she kicked and screamed, but soon Ashley knew there was no escaping him at least for the moment. She hadn't the strength to run any further, and she knew she had no chance of getting away from him without having a considerable head start.

Nearing the edge of the woods, Hayden looked for passing traffic, and the gray sedan itself. He peered down at Ashley telling her not to drag her feet before pulling her by her hair all the way to her parent's car. She tried to stay on her feet to avoid the pain she felt whenever she fell. Whenever she did stumble, she could feel the full weight of her body pulling at her scalp as Hayden maintained his grip on her hair. Once at the car, Hayden forced her to get on her knees. He told her to close her eyes, and if she opened them he would surely kill her. She didn't doubt his words for a second.

She lowered her head slightly, and she began to pray. Hayden saw the crucifix hanging on her neck, and he paused a moment not quite sure what to do with her just yet. He opened the trunk removing two large suitcases in order to make room for Ashley. Then he told her, "stand up," as he lifted her by her hair before shoving her into the trunk. Looking down at her all scrunched up inside the trunk, Hayden told her to stay put before slamming the damn thing shut. A shiver ran through Ashley's body knowing without question she was in the hands of a madman. She had no way of knowing why she was still alive, or how much longer she would be breathing.

Hayden quickly climbed back inside the car. He cranked up the vehicle, and Ashley started to cry once again. Now mourning the loss of her family, she heard music coming through the rear speakers inside the car. It was Pink Floyd's "Another Brick In The Wall." Hayden knew that song by heart. Pulling back onto the road, he whispered the words to it under his breath, "all in all, you're just another brick in the wall."

Chapter 12

A Dark Path To Follow

Hayden drove most of the night putting plenty of distance between himself and the wreckage, which was once Roy's recreational vehicle, and a 1978 Chevy Silverado. As he cruised down the road Ashley remained confined to the trunk. She feared what would happen whenever Hayden stopped, but she also feared never being let out of there as well. She was living a horrible nightmare, and all she could do was pray for someone to come and save her.

After being cooped up in the confined space for several hours she became unable to move at all. She was exhausted by that time and sick to her stomach. The fact that she had very little oxygen left, and a problem with motion sickness didn't help matters any. Just before sunup, Hayden did stop the car in order to dump the bodies on what was normally a very busy stretch of highway. He pulled off the road and made sure no vehicles were approaching before exiting the car to dispose of the corpses filling the back seat.

Ashley could hear him pulling her parents bodies out of the car. She cried once more, but no tears left her eyes. She was nearly dehydrated. She remained silent as she kept saying in her mind, *please don't let him kill me* over and over again. Hayden hauled each of the bodies into the trees off the side of the highway. He worked quickly, constantly checking to make sure no one was coming down the road. He wanted the bodies to be found in the condition he left them in, but he wanted to be somewhere else when they were discovered.

He had not yet decided what to do with Ashley. He knew she had to die. Everyone that saw his face met their death in some horrible way, but now was not the right time. The backseat was covered with blood and broken glass from the window Hayden had smashed, but he didn't care in the least. He knew he would find other transportation soon enough, but he unfortunately had to wait out the day before taking another life. That being the case, Hayden knew in the meantime he'd have to lay low until he could do his thing once again, which was stealing another soul in an attempt to appease Satan. He also had to observe the Sabbath in the process, but that was just one of the rules which bound him.

Hayden got back inside the car, and pulled back onto the highway. At the next exit he pulled off to change course as he drove in another direction altogether. He had this part down cold. Where he would turn up next was anyone's guess. What he was traveling in was a mystery too. It would be damn near an entire day before the bodies were discovered. By then, he could have been several states away, but Hayden chose to switch things up a little from time to time.

Ashley felt her prayers were answered when Hayden started back down the highway, but her fear never lessened no matter how many miles he drove. No matter how hard she tried she could not get rid of the images she had in her head of what had taken place. Hayden made one more stop using the credit card he found in Edward's wallet to gas up the car, and grab some food out of a local Stop and Go. Pocketing a map and some duct tape on the way out of the store, he got back inside the car and drove to a secluded reservoir several miles off the main road. Once there, he got out and walked to the rear of the vehicle. He wasn't in the business of taking hostages, and this was undiscovered territory even for Hayden.

He opened up the trunk as Ashley squinted trying to see where she was, but unable to open her eyes much at all with the sun's rays blinding her. It was cold, and it was morning. That's all she knew. Hayden said, "you can get out now if you want." His voice sounded different almost to the point of being considerate, but it still scared the bejesus out of her. She tried to climb out of the trunk, but she had trouble standing. She sat down on the ground with her back resting against the rear bumper of her dad's car, and she pulled her knees to her chest clinching them tightly with her hands. She had no idea what Hayden was about to do to her. She couldn't look at him. She kept her head pointed down looking only at the ground. She was covered in dirt where she fell in her attempt to escape from Hayden the second time, and it was a reminder to her that barring a miracle taking place, she would never be able to get away from him. Still, she held out a little hope that God would deliver.

She clinched the crucifix in one of her hands as she prayed silently. Hayden just watched her knowing what she was doing even though she never spoke a word out loud. He asked Ashley point blank, "what has God done for you?" That was a question she did not wish to answer. She had just prayed the Lord's Prayer expecting to be killed in much the same way her family had been. She never expected to see another sunrise, and she certainly never expected to receive any kindness from Hayden.

Perhaps, the most kind thing he could do for her at that point was kill her quickly without her seeing it coming. Over a minute went by without either of them saying a word, and then Hayden finally said, "nothing. That's what I thought. That's what he did for me." Then he reached inside a plastic bag and dropped a cold sandwich wrapped in foil down beside her feet. He ordered her to eat it, informing her she was going to need her strength. She was confused by his actions as she listened to his gruff voice say, "it's going to be a long day for both of us."

She reached down slowly picking up the sandwich, afraid Hayden was just playing some sick, twisted game with her in order to torment her further. The question ran through her mind as to why he had not killed her, but she didn't dare ask him. Instead, she unwrapped the sandwich taking a large bite out of it, and started planning her next move. If he truly was going to let her live for now, that meant she possibly had enough time to get away. Suddenly, hope of escaping death at Hayden's hands returned to Ashley, and she made up her mind to do whatever it took to successfully live through this horrible ordeal. She owed that to her family, and she wanted to see Hayden burn in hell for what he had done to them. That wasn't very Christian-like, but Ashley wasn't feeling very forgiving at the moment.

Bold enough to ask him two questions, she started with, "why do you kill?" She looked at Hayden's feet the whole time she spoke. Unable to see the look in her eye, he was stunned she would ask such a thing. She had definitely caught him off guard. Most people in her shoes would ask if he was going to let them live. Hayden responded to her question by asking, "why do you breathe?" Ashley didn't understand his response, and Hayden knew she wouldn't be able to solve the riddle.

She then asked, not about her family, but Hayden's, and that was a grave mistake. Hayden grabbed her arm snatching her up forcing her back into the trunk. She struggled to keep from being locked inside again, but she was no match for Hayden when it came to brute strength. Still, she had hit a nerve triggering something inside him to snap as he lost control of his temper, and this time just as she had prayed, she feared no evil. Hayden could sense that, and that enraged him all the more. He warned her if she made so much as a sound, she would never make it out of that trunk alive. She never doubted he would keep his word.

Hayden took that opportunity to step away from the car to get some rest. He thought about the obstacles he had to overcome in order to kill Ashley, and then he questioned if it was meant to be. He had never allowed someone to live before, after laying eyes on his scarred face. Either way, he looked at her as a challenge. They now had one thing in common. Perhaps, one day they would come to see things eye to eye. If they didn't, then he'd kill her.

Nightfall couldn't come quick enough for Hayden, but there was good reason for that. It wasn't time to kill yet, and he needed a new ride. These were the rules the devil made him live by, and there were no exceptions. He had to kill in order to live, and he could only do it on Satan's timeline. Hayden had made that deal long ago in the days of old, and he knew the price to be paid if he should break a deal with the devil.

Somehow, continually having the flesh burned from his bones didn't appeal to Hayden at all. If he killed before nightfall he would burn for all eternity with no chance of returning to wreak more havoc on mankind, and that would truly be hell for Hayden Keller.

Centuries ago, he had vowed to be a plague upon the earth, and a scourge to all men, wiping the face of the world of them one by one, laying their souls to waste. This is what he proclaimed as they burned him at the stake over three hundred years ago for practicing satanic rituals he was known to perform in the dark of night. His family was also slain right before his eyes, and the scar he wore on his face was given to him by the mob which sentenced him to death in the name of their faith. That mark was placed there to identify him to future generations in the event he ever did defy death and return. Superstitious origins passed down through generations had a place and purpose which many had forgotten. Still, Hayden carried the mark forever. That was also part of the terms he was held to.

Chapter 13

Wait To Kill

Shortly before dusk, Hayden heard the whining motor from some sort of dirt bike approaching, and he wasn't prepared for company. It was intermittent for the most part, but it sounded as though it was getting closer. Hearing it backfire, Hayden quickly got to his feet. Even though the sound was still in the distance he figured he had best make his way back to the car just in case someone happened to stumble up on it.

Walking toward the vehicle, he kept it within eyeshot staying hidden in the trees surrounding the reservoir. As he neared the edge of the tree line, he stopped in his tracks, and he watched intently without making a sound. A young man, probably close to Ashley's age, was racing along the upper bank of the reservoir. There was always the chance he would not notice the unattended vehicle, but that wasn't likely. Whether he would become curious enough to investigate remained to be seen.

Hayden watched him jump the bike over the berm on the other side of the man-made pond. He was fearless as most young men are at that age, but Hayden knew his bold nature would be the death of him someday. He landed with the front of the bike pointing toward the other side of the lake as he slammed on the brakes. A small cloud of dust rose from the ground where his rear tire rested. The young man remained motionless for a moment as the dirt he kicked up drifted away in the wind. He looked at the parked town car on the other side of the reservoir. Sure enough, soon as he lifted the visor on his helmet to get a better look, Hayden knew right then what his next move would be.

Without even thinking, the young man circled the reservoir intent on checking out the abandoned vehicle. He pulled up next to it, cutting off the engine, and he removed his helmet to gain a better look. Ashley could hear him from inside the trunk. She had no idea where Hayden was or what was actually going on. She listened closely trying to determine if Hayden was present before making any noise at all.

Hayden got as close as he could to the small clearing where the car was parked without being seen. Patiently he waited watching the sunlight disappear from the sky overhead. He observed the young man getting off his bike to take a look inside the vehicle. It was getting dark, and he couldn't see very well, but he could tell it was blood covering the backseat when he looked in through the busted rear window. "Wow," was all that escaped his lips as he opened up the driver's side door, and he couldn't help but see the chainsaw Hayden had confiscated from the scene of the collision the night before.

Suddenly, the young man became very uncomfortable. He knew he had found something important, and he knew authorities would want to know of his discovery. He backed away from the vehicle never taking his eyes off of the car as he moved toward his bike. Hayden moved in, closer and closer he crept up behind him, without him hearing a sound. It was dark and Hayden had mastered the art of the prowl. As Hayden slipped up behind him the young man started to turn around as he went to climb back on his bike. That's when he heard a pounding sound coming from the trunk, and he damn near pissed in his pants not expecting it. Startled himself, he shouted, "is anyone in there?"

Ashley's muffled voice could be heard as she struggled to get his attention. He responded by saying, "hang on I'll get you out."

As he hastily moved to the rear of the vehicle attempting to open the locked trunk, he was met with another startling surprise. It was Hayden standing right behind him, and he held the keys to the town car in his left hand as he jingled them to get his attention. He rhetorically asked, "you need these?" That's when the hairs on the back of the boy's neck stood on end, and he was afraid to turn and face the ominous voice behind him. Ashley heard it as well, and she knew her chance to escape was gone as all hope left her at that moment.

Hayden took the boy's helmet slamming it up against his head rendering him unconscious. He couldn't wait to kill him, but it wasn't time yet. However, that hour was fast approaching. Hayden opened up the trunk, and he allowed Ashley to see the body of the young man that tried to save her. A look of pain and despair washed over her face, she tried to hold back tears. Unable to do so, Hayden questioned her as he lashed out shouting, "is this what you asked God for?" She looked down at him shaking her head no, and Hayden stated sternly, "he's going to have to die you know, and it's all because of you."

Chapter 14

Hour of Death

Hayden bound her hands with duct tape, and he walked her to the passenger seat of her father's car. She saw him reach inside removing the chainsaw from where it sat, and she begged him not to use it. Hayden was dying to cut someone into little pieces with it, and that boy, in that location, seemed like the perfect opportunity, but it had been a long time since he had drowned anyone. He loved doing that as well. Toying with Ashley, he said, "you choose, the saw or the water."

Against her better judgment Ashley said, "you're crazy."

Hayden replied, "maybe so, but I'll still be breathing long after he is gone. Now, you decide his fate or I'll have to use this on you."

The choice wasn't easy, but she regretfully picked water. Her voice was weak as she said it.

Hayden knew she had done him a favor simply by choosing. There was less blood involved, and it seemed more humane to Ashley. That's when Hayden informed her he once took over two hours drowning a man in Michigan, and he enjoyed every second of it. Ashley became sick to her stomach again as she hurled while leaning her head outside the car. She had no idea where the chainsaw came from, she just never wanted to see Hayden use it on anyone.

Hayden ordered her to lie down on the ground. He bound her feet together seeing to it that she couldn't run away. Hayden then grabbed the boy by his ankles, and he pulled him to the edge of the water as stars appeared in the sky above. He looked up at the moon and back at Ashley to make sure she was watching. He knew exactly where the moon had to be positioned for him to have the freedom to take the next life, but Hayden wasn't much on patience. Still, he waited until he felt it was safe to take another soul in order to spare him from immediate eternal damnation.

When the time came, Hayden shoved the boy's face into the cold water just to wake him up. He callously said, "you're not going to want to miss this kid." Holding him under the water for close to a minute, the young man's arms began to move erratically in an effort to save himself from drowning, but Hayden was in total control. As he lifted the boy's head out of the water allowing him to regain his breath Hayden said, "don't die on me yet boy. It ain't time for that."

Ashley had no idea how long this would go on. She just closed her eyes tightly wishing it would all just go away, and end like some horrible nightmare, but this was real. She could hear the young fellow begging not to be killed, and she knew no matter what he said, it would do him no good at all. The last words she heard him utter were, "I won't tell anyone, I promise."

Hayden of course had to respond to that remark by looking the young man right in the eyes saying, "I know."

A look of lost hope came to the young man's face as Hayden cut off his oxygen supply once again. Ashley knew he was going to kill him. Now she was just praying that it would be quick and painless as possible, but that wasn't Hayden's style. His way of doing things usually entailed extreme pain and unspeakable terror. He looked up at the moon as he held the boy underwater. Deciding it was still too soon he lifted his head out of the murky pond.

After, dunking him underwater several more times and pulling him back out again, Hayden grew bored until finally the young man stopped moving completely. Jerking him out of the water again, Hayden shook him and he hit the boy on the back, helping him dispel the water lodged in his windpipe. "Any last words," was all Hayden said as he allowed him one final moment to rethink his every decision.

The young man spit water out of his mouth as he choked on the muddy water. Barely able to breathe at all, Hayden gave him time to remember all the best parts of his life, which he would no doubt miss soon enough. How he used that time mattered not to Hayden, but he liked to believe his young victim's life was flashing before his eyes. Something just felt satisfying to Hayden when he stopped to think about the future this boy would no longer have.

Hayden imagined the boy's heart was filled with regret at this point, as he looked over at a large river rock which sat on the bank. Half of it was sticking out of the water, and Hayden placed his forearm firmly under the boy's chin as he led him in that direction. Hayden said, "I don't know what I was thinking. Hell, don't worry. I'm not going to drown you." A look of relief showed in the young man's eyes just as his foot touched the bank. He was still struggling to breathe after ingesting so much water, but the thought of not drowning sounded pretty good at that point. Perhaps what he had said had gotten through to Hayden. Maybe he bought the fact that he would keep quiet.

Hayden released his grip around the young man's throat, and he instantly snatched hold of his drenched hair while kicking the boy's feet out from under him. As he fell to the ground, Hayden forced the boy's head in the direction of the rock. The front part of the boy's head struck it with such force that Ashley could hear his skull crack from where she was lying. A chill ran down her spine as she shook her head in complete despair. This guy was some kind of psycho that wanted her alive for some reason, and she couldn't make sense of it. Still, she had to question why Hayden chose to kill the boy and not her. There wasn't a merciful bone in Hayden's body, and that she knew.

Why Hayden decided to bash the boy's brain out instead of continuing to water torture him she'd never know. She opened her eyes to see Hayden push the boy's body out into the water. As his lifeless body drifted on the surface of the pond floating face down, Hayden took a deep breath savoring the cool night air. It felt liberating to take another life, especially one so young and strong. Hayden's spirit was renewed by the fresh kill, and he replayed the entire thing in his mind as he rolled the dirt bike into the reservoir.

Picking up the boy's helmet, he threw it out into the water trying to hit the floating corpse. However, he missed it by several feet. Hayden looked over at Ashley saying, "well, there's always next time." She looked away as Hayden lifted her off the ground, placing her back in the trunk. Slamming it shut, Hayden said, "what do you say we take a little ride." Ashley obviously had no say in the matter. She was just glad to still be alive as she thought about the young man floating face down in the reservoir. If he hadn't tried to help her, he may have cheated death by way of Hayden's hands, and lived to see another day. She thought about his family, and what they would do upon hearing the news. That, of course, brought back memories she had of her own family which Hayden had taken from her without remorse.

Ashley's sorrow turned to bitter hatred for Hayden, and she became furious as she pictured killing him herself. She wished to see him suffer the same way each of his victims did, but she barely knew the depth of Hayden's depravity. She could never come close to even imagining the misery many of his previous victims experienced before they begged Hayden to simply go ahead and kill them. That was a level of evil reserved only for Hayden's demented mind.

Chapter 15

Danger Ahead

Everyone has heard someone at some time say *the best is yet to come*. Whether or not it's true depends on who you are and where the road in front of you is going to take you. Ben Goodman was about to find out what that road had in store for him.

It was pitch dark, not a star visible in the sky above, due to cloud cover, and the moon was completely hidden from view. Headlights on the highway were fast becoming blurred. Ben continued to drive further though, against his better judgment, counting on the cup of coffee he held in his hand to keep him alert. He figured he could stay awake until he could find a suitable hotel to check into. A decent night's rest is something he hadn't had in over two days.

Taking a sip of coffee, he lowered the cup resting it on his leg as he drove. Each exit he approached had no lodging of any sort. It appeared he was out of luck, and his eyelids became heavy as he pressed on hoping to find some place to lay his head. Nine hours on the road with only short breaks to stretch his legs and gas up had taken their toll.

He questioned why he chose to take the trip in the first place. What was waiting for him on the Pacific coast was anyone's guess. Still, he felt compelled to find out for himself. He started reconsidering whether he had selected the right mode of transportation just as his eyes closed.

Drifting off, losing consciousness for a second on an unfamiliar stretch of road like the one he was on could turn deadly in the blink of an eye. Soon, that would become very apparent. What started out as the trip of a lifetime almost ended his life abruptly when an oncoming semi laid on the horn. Ben was headed right toward it. With both vehicles hurdling toward each other in excess of sixty miles an hour, Ben was given little time to react as he woke to find the headlights of the truck blinding him. The horn had caught his attention just in time. Instantly, his body twitched as he clinched hold of the steering wheel with a death-grip, his eyes were trained straight ahead at the lights of the oncoming truck. Without even thinking, he quickly jerked the steering wheel, spilling his coffee all over his lap as he changed course. Just as the truck blasted passed him, he could hear the rumbling noise coming from the tires of the semi. The driver of the tractor trailer was forced to use part of the shoulder to avoid a head-on collision. Ben swerved and slammed on the brakes just before hitting a ditch on the other side of the road, scared shitless, but still breathing.

The whole experience left him shaken causing his heart to race as he tried to catch his breath. *That was a freakin close call*, he thought, as he looked up in his rear view mirror watching the taillights of the truck fade into the distance. For a second, he felt as though his heart was going to beat right out of his chest, but Ben hadn't experienced true terror yet. That truck was nothing more than an attention getter.

Thankful to still be in one piece Ben thought, *thank God*, but as he looked down at the mess in his lap, and all over the steering wheel all he could say was, "damn." He couldn't complain much though. He was just lucky to be alive. He realized that as he wiped off his pants and his leather seat. Life is about decisions, and he had made a wrong one by choosing not to stop earlier when he had the chance. Now, he was paying the price for his error in judgment. He tossed the crumpled cup on the ground just outside the driver's side door before climbing back inside.

A brush with a near accident like that gave him something he didn't have when he started his journey. Suddenly, he had gained a new appreciation for what God had given him and allowed him to retain a little while longer - his life, but unlike most of us Ben was given two. He just didn't know it.

The trip, how tired he was, none of that seemed to matter. At that moment, sleeping on the side of the road even seemed like a viable option. He told himself he would do just that if he couldn't find a motel of some kind at the next exit. He turned up the air conditioning, and blasted the radio, hoping it would help him stay awake long enough to get to where he was going. He shifted the car into drive as he glanced into his side view mirror, and he carefully pulled back onto the road keeping a firm grip on the wheel using both hands.

Listening to the radio announcer, he caught the tail end of his banter before the next song came on. All he could make out of his closing remarks were, "that just goes to show some really bad things can happen out there, so be safe, and make sure you are extra careful if you are out traveling on the road." Ben saw the irony in hearing those words just minutes after what had just happened.

He looked at the radio, and back at the road shaking his head a little, sarcastically saying under his breath, "now he tells me."

Had Ben heard the news item mentioned before the DJ's closing remarks - he would have never considered sleeping in his car on the side of the road. Life is a fragile thing best not left to chance, and the road ahead would bring him face to face with destiny. The only problem is Ben had no clue as to what he would be confronted with, and even though he believed everything happens for a reason, sometimes putting those pieces of the puzzle together correctly is a little more challenging than one might think.

Chapter 16

Bad News

Nearing the next exit he saw what he had been searching for. A neon sign read, **VACANCY**, and he wasted no time finding a parking space. Grabbing his bag out of the backseat, he walked into the lobby of the Greenbriar Motel wiping his tired eyes as he approached the desk. The clerk took one look at him and asked if he preferred smoking or non-smoking. There was no question as to whether or not he needed a room. That was obvious by the worn look he carried on his face.

Ben looked up at him slowly opening his eyes as he said, "non-smoking please."

The place was a dump, but Ben didn't care. He just needed a bed and a shower. Making his way to his room he felt a cold chill touch his bones. It was a strange uneasy feeling which he had never really experienced before. He looked over his shoulder as he approached his room. All he could see was a passing shadow, which vanished into the darkness as it turned a corner at the other end of the building.

It was late and his mind was playing tricks on him. That's what he thought as he opened the door and entered his room. He tossed his key on the dresser, and picked up the remote flipping on the TV as he placed his bag on the bed. He looked back at the door as he walked to the bathroom to wash his face and grab a quick shower. He took the time to latch the lock on the door before walking into the bathroom.

The news was on, but Ben had no way of hearing it over the running water in the sink, toilet and shower. As he brushed his teeth the news anchor said, "and tonight we take you to an actual crime scene where our own Sydney Burns is reporting live. Can you hear us Sydney?"

"Yes Paula, I'm here at the scene where three bodies were found earlier this evening along a remote stretch of U.S. Highway 30. As you know, this is a heavily traveled interstate with numerous vehicles on it throughout the day. However, around 9:00 p.m. this evening the bodies of a man, and woman, and what appears to be their son were found brutally murdered, and left on the side of the road where a passing car noticed part of one of the bodies near this tree line right behind me. That's when he called authorities, and Officer Phelps with the Ohio State Patrol, who happens to be here with me was first on the scene."

Sydney then shared the microphone with the officer as she asked, "can you tell us anything at this point?"

The officer just glanced back over his shoulder at the bodies being carried out of the woods in bags. Crime scene tape was strung across the trees. He looked back at the camera, and his face was almost ghostly white as he said, "at this point we can't release the names of the victims. I can tell you each victim suffered multiple wounds, and there were also defensive wounds on their hands."

Sydney then asked if a murder weapon was found and what the possible motive was for the grisly murders.

As Ben flushed the commode before stepping into the shower, Officer Phelps shook his head no. He simply stated, "all I can tell you is this is the worst thing I've seen in over twenty years of law enforcement."

Sydney nodded her head with a concerned look that also expressed a sense of disappointment. Thanking the officer for his statement, she turned facing the camera as she said, "well there you have it. It's a real tragedy Paula. This is something this community may never really get over. I'm Sydney Burns reporting live for News Channel Nine. We're here first."

Paula looked over at her co-anchor Sam Sheffield, and she said, "wow, that is terrible. Of course, our thoughts are with the victims' families wherever they may be."

Sam nodded his head in agreement with her statement, and he added, "I couldn't agree more. It's just hard to believe something like that taking place, but you just never know. Do you?" He laid the papers down which he held in his hand, and he said, "well maybe Tim will have better news for us concerning the weather, and Chris is up next with sports. So, don't you go anywhere."

Paula flashed her pearly white teeth saying, "that's right. We'll be back in just a minute. So, stay with us."

Just at that moment the dark gray sedan pulled into the parking lot of the Greenbriar Motel. Ben showered off as the car slowly circled the building. The driver was Hayden of course, and he cruised past the front of the motel with his forearm resting on the steering wheel as he peered into the office to see if anyone was minding the desk. Pulling the car to the rear of the motel, he parked facing the rooms on the backside of the building. Sitting in the car, he surveyed his surroundings. He pressed some of the buttons on the console strictly out of curiosity. A black SUV with dark tinted windows was parked near the rear of the motel, and the only sound that could be heard was the noise coming off the highway as the large trucks flew down the interstate.

It began to rain lightly as drops collected on the windshield, and the mist sprayed off the pavement underneath the pressure of the passing truck tires. Pulling the keys from the ignition, he stared at a room on the backside of the motel. Suddenly, a noise could be heard coming from the trunk. It sounded like someone kicking the side of the car. Ashley's muffled cry of distress could faintly be heard outside the vehicle. Hayden looked up into the rear view mirror. He adjusted it slightly, and he stepped out of the car without blinking an eye. Wearing a black leather jacket and dark pants. He blended into the night like he was part of it as he casually made his way to rear of the vehicle. Taking his fist, he forcefully hit the top of the trunk. Leaving his fist firmly pressed against it he said, "don't make me come in there." Instantly, the noise coming from the trunk ceased, and only the sound of the falling rain could be heard as Hayden approached the SUV.

Ben stepped out of the shower reaching for his towel. He began drying off as he listened to the weather report. With the towel wrapped around his waist, he walked into the other room just in time to catch the five day forecast. The weatherman closed the news broadcast saying, "so, don't worry, it looks like things are going to get better over the next few days, and tomorrow should shape up to be an outstanding day." That sounded great to Ben. In fact, he felt that way himself. Slipping on his shorts, he figured tomorrow would bring with it a new lease on life, and seeing another day was part of the process. *It might as well be a perfect one weather-wise*, he thought, as he pulled back the covers to lie down.

He switched off the light next to the bed leaving the television on as he fell asleep. He was completely exhausted. Within minutes, he was snoring loud enough to wake the dead, and his mind began to wander into a dream state of sorts as his body tried to recharge itself. He laid there motionless for quite some time, and then, suddenly he started to toss and turn a little. Whatever he was feeling it certainly wasn't comfort, but it was a cheap mattress in a cheap motel. What do you expect? For Ben the morning couldn't come quick enough as he struggled relentlessly trying to find peaceful slumber without much success.

Chapter 17

Death At Your Door

Hayden looked inside the SUV, hearing the television blaring in the room next to it. The tinting was so dark on the windows he couldn't see much of anything inside the vehicle. Still, he had found his next set of wheels, and he figured he might as well break the news to the owner. He walked up to the door of the occupied motel room. Tilting his head forward so only the top of it could be seen through the peephole, he knocked.

Jamal heard the knock at the door, and immediately became paranoid thinking *it might be the poe-poe*. Leaving the TV volume turned up he carefully slid off the side of the bed, and stepped over to the window looking out the corner of it without moving the curtain whatsoever. He could see it wasn't the police. Who the hell it was, he had no idea, but he obviously had the wrong room. Jamal wasn't expecting company and he was pissed, but he tried to play it cool as he walked to the door. He looked out the peephole, but all he saw was Hayden's hair. He mumbled to himself, "what's this white mother fucker want," as he unlatched the door.

It was dark outside, but Jamal wasn't afraid to tell that son of a bitch to get lost. He opened the door saying, "yeah, what you want sucker?"
Hayden looked up concealing the scar on his left cheek as he said, "I want the keys to your Tahoe." Hayden didn't bother to add the word please. He just brandished a grisly smile which quickly faded away leaving only a hell-bent look of determination on his face.

Jamal thought to himself, *this bastard is crazy*. His temper got the best of him as he said, "you a damn fool, and you best get the fuck up out of my face."

When Jamal raised his voice Hayden turned his head slightly revealing the jagged scar which crested his face. Suddenly, Jamal stopped speaking. His eyes were focused on the scar Hayden wore on his cheek. His blood grew cold quick. Fighting to shake off that weird feeling, he started to close the door right in Hayden's face. However, Hayden had placed his foot inside the door preventing Jamal from doing just that, and he forcefully shouldered open the door all the way instilling a look of fear on Jamal's face.

In a frightened attempt to scare Hayden away, Jamal shouted, "I'll kill your ass fool," as he went for the gun he had placed under the mattress on the other side of the bed. No one could hear Jamal's threat other than Hayden. They were standing in the only occupied room on that side of the building. Jamal had requested a room on the backside so as not to be disturbed. His real reason stemmed from the fact that he was driving a stolen vehicle, and he wanted to avoid the cops.

Hayden came at him without flinching, kicking the door closed behind him. Before Jamal could retrieve the gun, Hayden lunged at him knocking Jamal to the floor. As he struggled to get to his feet Hayden placed him in a choke hold, steadily tightening his grip until he had cut off the blood flow to Jamal's brain. All the while Jamal kept reaching for his gun which he had stashed under the corner of the mattress.

Hayden could see the muzzle of the weapon as the mattress shifted during their struggle. He admired Jamal's tenacious attempt to defend himself, but he found his preparedness lacking considerably. Using his elbow, Hayden bumped the side of the mattress pushing the firearm further away from Jamal's limited reach. Hayden released his death hold on Jamal's neck saying, "who's the fool now mother fucker?"

Jamal laid there on the floor unconscious as Hayden reached under the mattress to retrieve his gun. Even though he was out cold, Hayden popped him in the head with the butt of the pistol for good measure. He pocketed Jamal's keys before sticking his head outside, and he looked to make sure no one was present. Hayden tossed Jamal's stuff in the SUV and he left his room key on the table next to the window. The last thing he took out of the motel room was Jamal himself as he dragged Jamal's body outside, and down the back of the building before stopping in front of one of the empty rooms. Kicking open the door he flipped on the light. He hurled Jamal's body into the tub, and he whistled an eerie tune as he went to the town car to get the chainsaw.

Chapter 18

A Painful End

Hayden soon returned with the chainsaw in hand, and he shut the door behind him. He picked up the remote and turned on the TV, running its' volume up all the way before cranking the gas powered killing machine. That's when Jamal woke to the terrifying sound of a revving chainsaw, and he attempted to crawl out of the tub as Hayden met him at the door of the bathroom. He wielded the saw waiving it close to Jamal's face as Jamal crouched forward with both hands pressed to the floor supporting his weight. This wasn't exactly as Hayden had planned, but life is full of surprises. Who would have ever guessed he would be in a motel room with a man he had never met, about to dismember him from head to toe? Certainly not Jamal, but he was fast becoming a believer.

Hayden knew this was going to get messy, and he couldn't wait to get started. Jamal tried to strike Hayden hoping to overpower him and take control of the saw or at least get by him in order to escape. What he found was he was not fast enough or strong enough to bring that plan to fruition. With one wave of the saw, Hayden damn near removed his entire hand as he cut into his wrist. In shear disbelief, Jamal looked at what was left of his hand and he screamed in agony. Defense was no longer an option. All Jamal could hope for at that point was a possibility of getting away and finding immediate medical attention. He refused to accept that this was how it was going to end.

Hayden raised his steel toed boot as he went to kick Jamal in the head. Jamal leaned back as he used his good hand to limit the blood loss from his other wrist. Bringing his arms up under Hayden's boot heel, he stood up hastily using all the strength he had in his legs. Hayden lost his footing and he fell backward on the floor still holding the saw in both hands allowing Jamal a chance of a lifetime. His only thought at that point was to prolong his life by getting the hell out of there, but Hayden ran the bar of the saw across his shin as Jamal leaped over him while fleeing the bathroom. He fell to the floor in front of the bed and he tried to crawl to the door. Hayden stood over him running the saw down his back and Jamal cried out, "what the hell are you doing this for!"

Hayden kicked him hard in the side wanting him to turn over so he could see the pain in his facial expression. Jamal continued crawling on his belly as Hayden began to sever his leg. The teeth on the chain kicked a little bit as they entered the bone, but that didn't stop Hayden from severing it completely. At that point, Jamal rolled over taking one last look at the hideous monster that was Hayden Keller. That's when Hayden put the saw right between Jamal's eyes in a final attempt to terrorize him. He knew it would all be over soon and he hated that. He could do this for hours on end if the human body would allow it, but Hayden knew Jamal would be dead in a matter of seconds. He also knew who would be left to pick up the pieces.

He never liked cleaning up after himself. That's why he planned on dicing that son of a bitch up in the tub to begin with, and now he had his hands full. Just for that, he took the saw and gutted Jamal as he looked down at what was his stomach. That was the last thing he saw before leaving this world. It was a hell of a way to go out. In fact, it was as close to hell as one might get on this earth. Hayden continued cutting on him even after he was dead severing him into little pieces. He painted the room a heinous shade of red using Jamal's blood as it splattered on the walls each time he cut into him. The last cutting remark Hayden made as he carved on Jamal's body was, "take that sucker." He grinned with delight and his eyes displayed the unquenchable vengeance of a madman.

When he was done, he picked up the severed body parts and tossed them on the bed. Hayden then showered off himself before carrying what was left of Jamal's body out of the motel room inside the spread which had covered the bed. He placed the chainsaw, and the bloody bundle of body parts in the back of the SUV before retrieving Ashley from the trunk of her parent's car. Placing a pillow case over her head, Hayden led her to Jamal's room where he allowed her to use the bathroom before forcing her into the backseat of the black SUV.

It was just before sunup when the black Tahoe pulled out of the Greenbriar Motel parking lot, and that's when Hayden told Ashley, "if you play your cards right you can ride shotgun next time." Ashley knew nothing of the cut-up corpse behind her seat. All she really knew was she was already closer to Hayden Keller than she ever wished to be.

Chapter 19

Premonition

The weather was perfect just as predicted. Ben had envisioned the trip providing plenty of scenery and adventure. So far, what it turned up was a near death experience and plenty of wheat fields for as far as the eye could see. Driving past an open pasture, he looked out the window at the rundown shack in the distance. A stone chimney was still standing, marking its prior existence. It had probably been close to a hundred years since anyone had stepped foot inside it - much less called it home. The dilapidated windmill behind it was no longer in operation. It stood there as a reminder of times gone by.

Some may say the landscape itself was filled with sights that stirred ones' imagination if they only opened their minds to consider all the possibilities. None of that really interested Ben though, to him they had no purpose. It was just another long stretch of deserted lonesome highway in the middle of nowhere. History markers aside, he couldn't care less about the old rusted silo he saw up ahead. He had California on his mind and nothing else as he flew past the fence posts lining the side of the two lane road to nowhere.

He reached into his pocket pulling out his cell phone only to find he still had no signal. Closing it shut, he tossed it in the empty passenger seat next to him. That's when he checked the gas gauge. Looking up, he noticed a road sign ahead which read, *Chanceville 20 Miles*. Immediately, his concern of being stranded was put to rest. He was glad to see that little dot on the map. Surely, the place had a gas station.

Crossing over the county line on the outskirts of town he could see a small café. There was nothing fancy about the place. It was just a little brick building with a large glass window which faced the gravel parking lot, and a portable letter sign stationed out front that would point you right to it. Directly across the street from it was a little white house with a large sign out front which had a giant hand painted on it. The sign read, *Sister Lee Palm Reader.*

He dismissed the fortune teller's sign at first glance with a halfhearted grin, which drew his mouth to one side as he pulled into the parking lot of the café across the street. Shutting off his engine, he sat there behind the wheel outside the café looking the place over, questioning if he should enter. He was famished.

A man exited the small café with a toothpick in his mouth. Folding his newspaper in half, tucking it under one arm, he lifted his hand to wave at a passing car. From where Ben sat, it appeared to be typical rural town America. This was obviously the kind of little town where nothing much ever happened. The people seemed friendly and unrushed. Why should they be? They lived in a place where nothing went on, and they had all the time in the world to tend to it.

Ben climbed out of his car making certain to lock the door before entering the little diner. Walking through the door, he sidestepped a gentleman leaving the cash register. He then took a seat at the counter as he glanced over his shoulder. He helped himself. Reaching over the counter, he picked up a menu as he overheard the waitress talking to her only other customer.

The man seated at the table behind him folded up his newspaper and laid it on the chair next to him. Something he read apparently caused him to groan, "damn." His voice carried a serious tone as he spoke, and that drew Ben's attention.

A disturbed look came over the waitress's face as she said, "I know. That's so awful, isn't it?" She paused as she poured him some coffee, and she looked up saying, "I just don't understand how someone could do something like that."

The guy seated at the table spouted, "well there are some crazy damn people in this world, that's for sure." Ben observed the waitress as the customer added, "you know, they don't even have a clue who this guy is. Hell, it could be anyone."

The waitress shuttered as she shook her shoulders, trying her best to fend off the eerie chill she felt at that very moment. Touching her hand to the side of her head, she pulled the pencil from behind her ear nervously professing, "I don't even want to think about it." That's when she turned her attention toward Ben, preparing herself to take his order. She dug in her apron pocket for her pad, and the guy seated at the table behind him continued speaking to himself as she walked away.

Ben overheard him say, "yeah, that's a damn shame," as he shook his head a little before taking a sip of coffee.

The waitress's face cringed as she tried to clear her mind of something gruesome before asking Ben, "what can I get you?" He pointed to one of the specials on the menu still not absolutely sure it was what he wanted. He always seemed to have trouble making snap decisions. Ben had settled on going with the chicken sandwich plate, and he started to ask if it came with onion rings, but he didn't. Instead, he paused shivering a little himself as he tried to place his order. That's when the black SUV passed right by the diner.

Ben's train of thought immediately drifted, feeling that cold chill once again which he had felt back at the Greenbriar Motel. The waitress couldn't help but notice, and she looked up at the air conditioning vent admitting, "I know it's cold in here. Half the time I have to wear my sweater. You better eat it quick if you want it hot around here."

Her candid remark made the feeling seem justified in a way. Ben tried his best to brush off the chill yet again as the waitress placed his order in the window for the cook to fill. She then turned to pick up the dirty dishes off the counter just a few stools over from where he was seated. Ben just stared at the dirty pile of plates, and he started to question if he was coming down with something. He had a tendency to worry too damn much about crap that really didn't matter in the end, but this was different.

Doing what came natural, he rearranged the salt and pepper shakers making sure to use a napkin to avoid actually touching them. He had once sought help to overcome his greatest fears and compulsive tendencies, but a year in therapy did little in the way of fixing him. He stopped seeing his shrink months ago believing his anxieties and compulsions were just a part of who he was. He couldn't change it, but now he could explain it. Ben now knew that was the way he was programmed, and it was up to him to learn how to deal with it. What he found was his compulsive nature got the best of him though as he questioned what germ he picked up and from whom.

The other customer stood laying several dollars down on the table to pay his check. Looking over at the waitress as he walked toward the door, he left his paper in the chair telling her, "I'll see you later Sandy."

She looked up from what she was doing saying, "alright Tom, be careful out there." The man nodded his head as he opened the door to exit the café.

Ben reached over picking up the paper to see a headline that read, *Family Killed, Girl Still Missing*. He thumbed through it reading as he ate, and eventually he turned to the horoscope section. Using his finger he scrolled down the page until it stopped under the sign Virgo. The words read, *Today is a new beginning. You have much to live for. Prepare for the road ahead. You will face your demons in the next life. This life depends on it*. Disturbing to say the least, a curious and confused look came over Ben's face.

He looked up from the paper, and he stared at the sign across the road. Unsettling questions filled his head. Pulling his hand to his face, he rubbed his chin before resting his head on the lower part of his palm. Ben sat there contemplating the words he just read, and he looked back down at the paper with an uneasy feeling in his gut. Wishing not to ponder it any further, he folded up the paper as the waitress asked, "is everything alright?"

Ben answered her telling her everything was fine, but his face conveyed something else entirely. He was in very deep thought as he spoke, that was clear as he stared back out the window before picking up the check on his table. He couldn't help it. Through some unseen force, he felt drawn to the palm reader as he continued pondering what his horoscope said. It all seemed stupid on the surface and overly superstitious to say the least. Still, he kept trying to make sense of it as he walked over to the cash register. He had merely checked it for fun as all of us do at times, but this one was haunting in nature. Usually, he didn't put much stock in horoscopes, but this one was anything but typical. Grappling with concern based on its words, he tried to block it from his thoughts, but found it virtually impossible to simply brush aside for some reason.

He exited the café the same way he entered, without saying a word. Walking to his car he wished he had never picked up the paper to start with. Reaching for the door handle with his keys in hand, he was compelled to look across the road once more. He wasn't dismissively smiling when he stared at the sign this time. Ben didn't even bother opening the car door. He just walked to edge of the parking lot looking both ways before crossing the road in front of him.

Steadily, he approached the small house belonging to the palm reader, and the sign in the window clearly showed she was open for business. Just as he reached out to knock on the front door, he heard a voice command him, "come in."
That voice issuing him instructions came through a tiny speaker mounted on the porch. Slightly startled, he looked up at it. Somewhat relieved seeing it, he smiled. Holding back a laugh almost, he looked down slowly shaking his head, knowing his thoughts had gotten the best of him.

He opened the creaking door, and upon entering Ben looked around the room. The walls were covered with bookshelves and tapestries. In the center of the room was a large round table with four chairs, but no sign of Sister Lee anywhere. A tapestry of the yin and yang symbol laid draped over the old wooden table. His anxiety level rose once again as he called out, "hello. Is anyone here?" Ben grew a little more nervous as he patiently waited for a response. However, no one answered. He questioned himself asking, "what the hell am I doing here?"

Hearing what sounded like boards creaking somewhere else inside the house, Ben stood in one place almost frozen, it seemed. His mind raced as he looked over the room and up at the ceiling. A few seconds later, a slender Asian woman entered the parlor through a side door. She stared at Ben studying him carefully with her pitch black eyes as she calmly walked over to the table in front of him. Her face remained stoic, and her eyes were ill, discerning, and distant.

She took a seat in her chair placing her hands on the table, and looked directly at him. Uncertainty displayed itself in his face as an ominous shadow fell upon the room, and her black eyes stared at him intently. At first no words were exchanged at all. Ben didn't know what the hell to say, but then the woman gracefully motioned with her hand for him to pull up a chair. She told him, "come, take a seat."

Ben walked over to the table pulling out the chair closest to him, and did just as she requested. Something about the whole encounter felt odd as soon as he entered her parlor. Now, it was even more strange just being in her presence, and his thoughts quickly became disjointed. She nodded her head slightly toward the table feeling no need to introduce herself. That's when he placed his hand on the table with his palm up for her to read. The woman looked at him and then at his hand. Her head leaned forward slightly as she placed her hand under his. The other hand she placed next to his palm. She then said, "twenty dollars please."

Ben slowly reached into his pocket pulling out his wallet.

Retrieving a twenty, he handed her the bill. She placed it in her cashbox next to her chair then she looked down at Ben's hand. Using her hand she made some kind of mystical sign in the air right over the center of the table. Ben had no way of understanding its significance. He just assumed it was part of the show.

Again her head leaned forward, she focused on the lines engrained in Ben's palm. Using her index finger she carefully traced his lifeline. Her finger slowly moved over it before pausing completely. Her motionless forefinger pointed to a place along his lifeline, a divide of some sort. Her finger remained perfectly still, pointing to the center of his palm as she turned her head slightly toward her shoulder, her eyes still trained on his hand. The look of concentration on her face soon turned to a look of question as she thought intently. Her brow then furrowed.

Ben tried to read her face sensing something was wrong. His own face at first carried an ever increasing sense of curiosity which quickly turned to grave concern. With his hand still resting in hers, he moved his head back away from the table trying to gain a clear picture of what was actually going on. His feeling of uneasiness became overwhelming as he asked, "what is it?"

Sister Lee's head didn't move at all just her eyes as she looked up at Ben, and this time her eyes appeared fearful. Looking back down at his hand, she began to breathe again saying, "your lifeline, it is very unusual. It's broken in half, like you have two lives to live."

She looked up staring directly into Ben's eyes as she placed her hand on top of his palm. She then said, "yet you are not a Gemini."

Ben admitted, "that's right. But how did you know that?"

She replied, "I know more than you can even imagine, but

your hand holds many secrets for me to discover."

Her grip tightened on Ben's hand. Focusing on his eyes, she closed hers. Sister Lee's face looked somber as she raised her chin. She gently turned her head to the side while her eyes remained closed. Suddenly, her head began twitching uncontrollably, then it became more pronounced. Jerking without restraint, she appeared as though she was elsewhere, possessed by some other entity even.

The whole thing startled Ben, it scared him half to death. He wanted his hand back, but her grip remained firm with her fingers pressing into his skin as she saw horrible images in her mind. With her eyes still closed, her head sharply snapped in the opposite direction as if what she was seeing she was trying to avoid. Her grip on Ben's hand became painfully tight as she clinched his hand in hers. She looked as if she was having a seizure as her head continued to twist from side to side violently. Ben asked, "what's going on? Are you okay?"

Suddenly her head stopped moving. Her eyes popped wide open with a crazed look sewn deep inside them as she stared directly at Ben. She appeared to be in a trance-like state. Looking as though she was being electrocuted, her head jerked back as she envisioned several violent images flashing before her eyes. One of them showed Ben's blood covered hands, and a look of severe pain upon his face. The first flash image she saw showed a body forcefully hitting the windshield of a moving car. The second showed a gun being held to someone's head, and the finger applying pressure to the trigger. The third image was Ben's bleeding shoulder which he was grasping with his hand. She convulses as the next image appeared in her head of a man violently beating someone to death with a tire iron. Blood spatter flew everywhere. She couldn't bare anymore images, and Ben could feel some kind of force surging through his hand that stung like fire. He wanted out of there quick. "Fuck! Keep the twenty dollars lady. Just let go of my damn hand!"

Breathless, she released her grip on Ben's hand as she envisioned an explosion engulfing a gas pump. Her hands started to shake uncontrollably. She closed her eyes tight while shaking her head, trying to remove herself from what was revealed to her through her third eye. Ben was scared shitless, but his nightmare had just started. Now free from her grip, he looked down at his hand yelling, "whoa, what the hell?"

Fearfully, he jumped to his feet pushing himself away from the table. Just at that moment, she reached out grabbing the outer edges of the table. She took several deep breaths as she tried to regain control of her breathing, and she opened her eyes pointing straight at Ben. She forcefully warned him saying, "beware the scarred lion with cancer. Touch him and you die."

Hearing that, Ben knocked over his chair, and it made noise hitting the hardwood floor. He hastily retreated toward the front door with his back turned to it trying to keep his eye on the palm reader. Franticly, he reached behind him in search of the door knob. His final words were, "man, forget this shit," as he managed to open the door planning to haul ass to his car parked across the street.

Sister Lee stood, using one hand to support herself, resting it on the table, and the other one still pointed at Ben as she spoke. "Listen to me, this life depends on it. Evil has a face and it will reveal itself to you," she proclaimed. Those were the last words Ben heard as he exited the small white house leaving the door standing wide open.

Sister Lee lowered her hand placing it in the center of the table on the yin and yang symbol. Holding it there, she looked down at the tapestry covering the table which her hand rested on, and she spoke ominous words in a language few would understand.

Ben looked back at the palm reader's house across the street as he scrambled to pull his keys from his pocket. He wasted no time in opening the door, and he climbed inside looking in his rear view mirror as he fired up the car ready to get the hell out of there. He quickly backed out of the parking space, and shifted the car in drive as he peeled out of the gravel parking lot.

Hearing the sound of Ben's squealing tires hitting the pavement from inside the restaurant, Sandy walked over to the window to check it out. She could see the taillights of Ben's car getting smaller as he flew up the road toward town, and she wasn't the only one watching.

Across the street in the little white house, Sister Lee had made her way to the window as well. Her left hand rested on the window casing, and it was marked with a mystic symbol. Using her other hand, she reached for the curtain moving it with the back of her hand. She too peered out the window watching as Ben's car disappeared in the distance. Looking over at the old phone which sat on a small table next to her, she reached down placing her hand on the receiver. She paused before picking it up to make a call. Standing there, she looked back outside, raising the phone to her ear.

Ben glanced in his rear view mirror as he raced away from Sister Lee's house. Approaching the edge of town he passed a pawnshop and several other stores. He kept looking in both directions as he came to each intersection, hoping to find a gas station somewhere in that Podunk town. All he really wanted to do was put some distance between himself and the palm reader. Passing by the grocery store, he figured he must be getting close to a gas pump.

Ben had calmed some as he slowed the car down on his way through town, but he almost felt as though he was being watched by people walking along the sidewalk. They all seemed to stare at him as he cruised by without waving. Some of them wore perplexed looks on their faces as if they had never seen a stranger before. Others just seemed overly interested in his presence there on the streets of Chanceville. Either way, it was weird.

The entire town freaked Ben out. Maybe it was just what he had been through that was leaving him with an uncomfortable feeling. That aside, he knew something wasn't right about that place by the way people stared at him as he drove down the street. The experience he just had with the palm reader was now replaying itself again and again in his mind, thanks to them. He couldn't help but recall the words she spoke and what he had read in his horoscope.

Chapter 20

A Killer On The Loose

It was an unusual day inside the sheriff's office. The phones continued to ring with panicked people demanding answers. Most of them were calling to complain about their particular situation, or the fact the sheriff just didn't seem to be able to get the job done. For some reason, a few of them even felt compelled to give their two cents to the deputy answering the phone.

It seemed almost everyone had some idea of how to go about putting an end to a madman's killing spree. A rash of murders across the state had come to their neck of the woods, and that's the kind of thing that gets the folks in Jefferson County all worked up. It was the kind of place where only once in a blue moon would someone turn up dead. Half the time it was gun related. An occasional hunting accident would inevitably occur without fail, or someone having too much to drink would pull the trigger in a drunken state, and somebody would cash in their chips as a result. The rest of the time old age was usually the culprit when it came to someone pushing up daisies in Jefferson County.

Today was different though. A longtime member of the community found brutally beaten to death hanging in his barn changed everything. What was done to his wife was unmentionable in their little local county paper. The sheriff refused to release the details regarding what he found at the crime scene. Only he and his deputies saw the carnage out at the Ferris farm and they weren't talking. In an attempt to limit some of the hysteria, Sheriff Baker made the county coroner swear to secrecy when he arrived to pronounce the time of death and retrieve the bodies for autopsy. Fred Hicks had no problem with that.

He had seen a lot of bad things in his eight years as coroner, like the time Willie Miller ended up crushed under the weight of his tractor, but this was truly horrid. What made it worse was someone intentionally did it. This wasn't some kind of freak accident as it was in Willie's case. Fred Hicks would have gladly forgotten he ever saw what he did on that farm, but the fact was he could never forget it no matter how hard he tried. There would be nights he would wake up remembering that crime scene for years to come. It made him reconsider his career choice, that's for sure, and he was the coroner for Pete's sake.

Determining the actual cause of death was more difficult than one would think. The sheer number of lethal injuries Mr. Ferris sustained made it difficult to determine which one actually ended his life. The bloody bailing hook which was found in a pool of blood beneath Mr. Ferris's dangling feet was repeatedly used to inflict extreme damage to his legs and body. It was later determined that his crushed windpipe was what put him out of his misery. Judging from the other wounds he sustained during the torturous bludgeoning, the brutal blow to his throat which left him feudally gasping for air had to be a gift at that point. His wife was not so fortunate. She was left to bleed out on the kitchen floor with plenty of time to lay there wondering why.

After finding their butchered bodies, the sheriff had to ask himself who could inflict so much pain. All he could come up with was this must have been done by Satan himself. It was almost impossible to even imagine what kind of evil existed inside the person that actually tortured and killed Mr. and Mrs. Ferris. Sheriff Baker wanted to see that son of a bitch dead though. He never spoke those words out loud in front of his deputies. He didn't have to. They knew what he was thinking. They were thinking the same thing themselves. This was Jefferson County after all, and the only real question was which one of them would be given the chance to put a bullet through this sick bastard's brain.

Mr. Ferris had never been known to harm anyone, his wife either for that matter. He was the kind of man you could take at his word, and Emma Ferris was one of the sweetest people you'd ever meet. She was one of the best cooks in the county, and she consistently took home some kind of prize at the county fair each year for her baking abilities. Her husband's size alone was a testament to her skills in the kitchen. They were good people, and there wasn't hardly a Sunday that passed when you couldn't find them seated on the sixth pew inside the Church of Christ just a few miles from their quiet little country home.

One thing's for sure they deserved better than what they got, and Sheriff Baker took this one personal. He refused to speak to anyone about it though other than law enforcement officials. He had been made well aware that something sinister was headed his way. A trail of bodies were forming a path to his jurisdiction. That's why he didn't hesitate to ride out to the Ferris' farm to check on things when he got the call from Clay over at the Feed and Seed. It seemed that Mr. Ferris was expected to pick up a large order he had placed first thing Wednesday morning, but no one had seen or heard anything from him. The fact that no one could reach either him or his wife by phone was a little odd. Mrs. Ferris usually answered the phone within the first few rings without fail.

Sheriff Baker had no idea what he would find as he drove out there. He had just hoped for the best like their phone line was out or maybe Mr. Ferris was just a little under the weather. Obviously, what he found turned his stomach inside out. His mission at that point became catching this twisted killer who was clearly a true menace to society, and sending him straight to hell where he belonged. Nothing else mattered after seeing that first hand.

As Deputy Ratley answered the phone, he paused listening to the voice on the other end of the line. Once he was finally able to get a word in edgewise he stated, "I understand Mrs. Harris. We're doing everything we can to find who did this." He paused again looking exasperated as he tried to calm the old woman down. Holding the phone to his ear with one hand, he raised his other hand which was resting on his desk up in the air, not knowing what to tell her at that point. Using his feet to push himself back from the desk, he placed his free hand on the armrest of the chair as he told her, "just keep your doors locked, and don't open them for anyone you don't know. If you see anything suspicious - you call us right away."

Mrs. Harris didn't appreciate the dismissive tone in the deputy's voice. He didn't intend to offend her, it just came across that way after answering as many calls as he did that day. She told him point blank, "I want to speak with Sheriff Baker."
Ratley couldn't even bring himself to smile at that point as he thought, *you and everyone else in this town.* He just said, "I'm sorry, but he's tied up at the moment. I assure you we're following every lead we get. I can take your number and have him call you back."

Patience was never a virtue of Mrs. Harris. Everyone that knew her would have to use the word "feisty" in their description of her to others. She was a small woman with a lot of grit, and she had no trouble speaking her mind. Even though she barely weighed a hundred pounds soaking wet, her abrasive nature was a large part of who she was. Fed up with the runaround as she so eloquently called it, she said, "don't bother, I could be dead by then," and she hung up the phone without saying another word.

Ratley was once again left stymied by the whole situation. He knew the phone would ring again with another loose nut on the end of the line that felt the need to vent their frustration using him as their sounding board. This damn sure wasn't why he went into law enforcement. He joined for the badge, the gun and the bi-weekly paycheck. Like all law enforcement officials, he longed for the day when he could put that gun to use, but today wasn't that day. Instead, he was playing phone receptionist, and in his mind *this part of the job was for the birds*.

Listening to the dial tone through the phone he looked over at Deputy Singer. He couldn't help but shake his head as he hung up the phone. Venting his frustration, Ratley exclaimed, "damn, I swear these folks are going to drive me crazy."

Singer avoided looking over his shoulder at Ratley as he spoke. He placed a folder back inside the filing cabinet offering, "you better get used to it. We got a growing body count and until someone makes an arrest these folks are going to keep on calling." What Singer said made sense. Ratley shook his head though. He dreaded taking another call. Propping his elbows on his desk, he rested his head in his hands. Wiping his face with both hands, he rubbed his tired eyes and took a deep breath, then he stared straight ahead at the window in front of him. Singer turned walking over to his desk adding, "face it they're scared. Hell, I don't blame them. This is one sick son of a bitch we're after."

Ratley deliberately nodded, accepting what Singer said with a clear understanding of what they were up against. That's when he said, "hell, I know. I'll just be glad when the state police get here. We need help." Just at that moment the phone rang again interrupting Ratley's confession. He cut his eyes toward the phone, then he looked over at Singer prior to answering it. Now thoroughly disgusted with the whole situation, Ratley said, "shit, here's another one."

Singer told him, "just try to calm 'em down. Tell them we have help on the way."

Even tempered as possible, Ratley answered the phone saying, "Sheriff's Office, this is Deputy Ratley." He listened in almost disbelief as his adrenaline started to rush. He heard the words "dead body" which woke him right up. His total look of surprise caught Singer's attention, and he watched Ratley from his chair as his eyes grew big. The young deputy quickly leaned forward grabbing a pencil out of the tray on his desk. He then reached for his notepad, which happened to be laying on the floor next to his desk. That's where he had dropped it while speaking with Mrs. Harris. Within seconds he started to write something down as he listened close to the person on the other end of the phone. He looked over at Singer then back at his notepad as he anxiously questioned the woman asking her, "where did you see it, ma'am?"

Responding to the unusual commotion, Deputy Singer immediately walked over to his desk. Ratley looked up at him, and without saying a word he used his eyes cutting them in the direction of his notepad. Singer tilted his head, looking down at it as Ratley finished scribbling out, ***man hit by a black SUV, body on Highway 80.***

Reading what Ratley had written on his pad, Singer's facial expression changed from mildly curious to deadly serious in an instant. He turned in the direction of the sheriff's office and he hollered, "damn! Sheriff you better get in here."

Panicked, Ratley began scratching down more notes as he asked, "alright ma'am, where are you now? Are you in any immediate danger?"

He wrote down a street address and Singer read it saying, "I know where that's at. It's right outside of town." He looked over at Sheriff Baker as he approached Ratley's desk and that's when he informed him, "looks like we got another one."

A painfully concerned look came over the sheriff's face. Ratley turned his notepad around where the sheriff could easily see it. Looking down at Ratley's notes, the sheriff read over them as he leaned forward placing both of his bald up fists on the deputy's desk. Within seconds he carried the same serious look Singer did. He didn't want to see another body turn up in Jefferson County, but if that's what it took to nail the psycho they were after then so be it. On the surface, from what Ratley showed him, it appeared the bastard was still hard at it, planting dead bodies in his backyard. Ratley had jotted down everything he thought to ask, but several pieces of critical information were missing. The deputy looked up at the sheriff as he hesitantly asked, "okay ma'am, what is your name?" He wrote down, ***Sister Lee***, as he told her, "I'm going to stay on the phone with you until Deputy Singer arrives to take your statement. Is that okay?"

Sister Lee responded, "your concern for me is not

warranted. I will be here when you arrive."

Sheriff Baker looked back at Singer with a doubtful look on his face. He had a gut feeling, nothing more. Turning his attention back to Ratley he said, "ask her if she can take us to the exact location where the body is now." The sheriff knew if she was telling the truth, time was of the essence. Ratley did as he instructed, and the sheriff turned to Singer telling him, "if this is for real, I want an accurate description of this guy right down the mole on his ass. I want to know what he's driving, where he's headed - you make sure you ask her everything." Singer nodded as he and the sheriff waited to hear a yes or no answer from Ratley, but that's not what they got.

Ratley just sat there listening in disbelief. He looked up at the sheriff with a lost sense of confusion masking his face. The twenty-eight year old deputy looked the sheriff right in the eye as he explained, "she says she doesn't know where it is now, but she can take us to where we'll find it." As he spoke his facial expression became even more perplexed. Listening to her words were confusing enough. Relaying what she said in her exact words sounded even more odd coming from his mouth.

Sheriff Baker held out his hand and Ratley gladly gave him the phone. Clearing his throat before he spoke the sheriff introduced himself. "Sister Lee, this is Sheriff Baker. I understand you witnessed a murder on Highway 80. Is that correct?" He paused as he listened to what Sister Lee had to say. He questioned her asking, "alright what was the man wearing?" The sheriff gave a slight pause as he listened.

Ratley and Singer glanced at one another and then back at the sheriff. Confirming what he just heard Sister Lee say on the phone, Sheriff Baker said, "okay, it was dark. When did you see it occur?" Another split second pause and he said, "a few minutes ago. I see." Sheriff Baker looked out the window and the sun was still shining. A little putout he pressed his lips together tightly before speaking. He then said, "alright. You can take us to where we will find the body? Are you in your car?" He listened and repeated what she said. "You don't drive. Okay, may I ask how you got from there to your house then?"

Sister Lee tried her best to explain the unexplainable, and a skeptical look came over his face. Again for his deputies' benefit, Sheriff Baker repeated Sister Lee's words, "you never left, I see. So, you saw it in a vision of yours. Great! Oh, that explains a lot." Sheriff Baker slowly shook his head up and down as he said, "ah, huh, I see." He looked over at his deputies with a disgusted look on his face. They smirked at each other as they listened to Sheriff Baker's retort. "I guess you got all this from your crystal ball."

The tone of Sister Lee's voice changed almost immediately, rendering an obvious contempt she had for those with no understanding of the supernatural forces that surround us all. She deliberately pointed out, "you do not believe in the power of the third eye."

Almost flipped, the sheriff replied, "oh, I'll believe almost anything at this point Ms. Lee. So, what you're saying is the murder hasn't happened yet."

Sister Lee informed him, "that is correct. Only the one with two lives can stop the evil I have seen through my inner eye."

Trying to process what he was hearing, the sheriff had to ask himself if this was some kind of sick joke or just the ramblings of a delusional woman. Whatever it was, it couldn't be real. Trying his best to get to the bottom of things he repeated, "the one with two lives? This is a person you know?"

Sister Lee simply replied, "I have seen him, yes, and I have seen through his eyes in the future."

Unable to refrain from using a sarcastic tone, Sheriff Baker remarked, "well that's wonderful. We can still prevent this from happening. All we have to do is track down this guy with two lives. That ought to be easy enough. What's this guy look like?"

Ratley sat glued to his chair in utter shock at what he is hearing. Singer managed not to laugh, but he couldn't help but smile shaking his head as he looked away. It was the first bit of humor any of them had been able to muster since finding the bodies on the Ferris farm the day before. It was unfortunate it came to them under these circumstances, but the crazy claims of the fortune teller at least provided them with some amusement. This whole ordeal had given them a very clear understanding that she was not the only crackpot in Jefferson County. With some of the calls they received, they would have sworn half the County had fallen off their rockers so to speak, but this nut-ball was different than all the rest. That's what Sheriff Baker thought anyway. He tried to take her seriously since he was investigating a double homicide, but Sister Lee knew he didn't put any stock in what she was saying. She became angry as she scornfully said, "you mock powers you do not possess. Death is a high price to pay for lack of faith."

The sheriff had no idea how to take her remarks, but it certainly got his attention. His reply was, "what I believe in is not important, but I'm going to have one of my deputies come out and take your statement. If you can show him where this body will be found, by all means amaze us."

Sister Lee didn't mince words as she said, "I have nothing more to say to you sheriff. I will only speak with the deputy that took my call."

Sheriff Baker looked at Ratley handing him the phone with a serious look in his eye. His face harbored resentment as he said, "you tell her you will be out to take her statement personally."

The sheriff turned placing his hand on Singer's shoulder. Speaking directly to him under his breath as they walked away from Ratley's desk, the sheriff said, "I want you to go with him. See if she can take you to a location on Highway 80 where she says the body will be found." Deputy Singer questioned the sheriff asking, "you don't believe any of this crap do you?"

Without blinking the sheriff said, "no, but I believe she believes it. I want you to write down everything she says word for word."

Singer admitted, "this ought to be interesting."

All the sheriff had to say at that point was, "you both just act like she's the most intriguing person God put on this earth."

He turned looking back toward Ratley's desk as Singer replied, "she might be."

Just at that moment Ratley hung-up the phone. He grabbed his hat and notepad, ready to hit the road as he quickly headed toward the door informing Singer, "I'm ready, let's go." He actually looked eager. Singer on the other hand was going to have to act as if he were. He was under orders.

Chapter 21

Interview A Psychic

Deputy Singer climbed in the driver's seat as Ratley flipped through his notepad. He read over some of the strange words Sister Lee spoke over the phone, trying to make heads or tails of it with no luck whatsoever. All he really understood it to mean was someone is going to die according to her, but Ratley had a hard time believing anyone could predict what's going to happen in the future with any accuracy. Still, it intrigued him to think she could actually do such a thing. Sister Lee's belief in her ability to do so was what fascinated him most, even though he assured himself this was all a hoax of sorts. He looked over at Singer asking if he had ever gotten a call like that before, and he simply shook his head no as they drove off.

Within less than a mile of the sheriff's office they passed a black SUV headed west with Virginia Plates. Neither of them paid it any attention. They were focused on their mission, and that was questioning the only eyewitness they have to a murder that had yet to be committed. Talk about feeling stupid. This topped the list in Singer's mind, but he never questioned Sheriff Baker.

Ben approached an intersection with a blinking yellow light, and he blew right through it in his shiny BMW not thinking a thing of it. Only after noticing the oncoming squad car did he apply the brakes a little to decrease his speed. Ratley didn't even see him. He was intent on making something of what he had written down on paper as he stared at his notepad in deep thought. Singer's head turned as Ben passed them, and he looked over in his side view mirror at the brake lights on the BMW. "Did you see that," he asked, but Ratley never bothered to look up from the page he is staring at.

He just responded by asking, "what?"

Genuinely disgusted with their current assignment, and the missed opportunity to ticket the shiny silver beamer which blew by them like a bat out of hell he says, "some folks have no respect for the law, that's all. If we didn't have to take this damn woman sightseeing, I'd be writing him up about now."

Ratley looked up with a lost look on his face as he questioned, "who?"

Singer started to explain, but quickly gave up the effort seeing the puzzled expression on Ratley's face. "Oh, never mind," he muttered. As they approached the county line, Singer told Ratley he had best forget about making any sense out of what the woman told him on the phone. When Ratley questioned why, Singer said, "she's a loony tune that's why. The only thing we're going to get out of her is more incoherent B.S. that's all."

Ratley responded saying, "I guess you don't believe people can see into the future."

Singer looked at Ratley with a questionable expression on his face. He was somewhat stunned to have to explain what he did and didn't believe in especially to Ratley, but he made no bones about where he stood on that matter. Singer said, "I don't believe in things I can't see." Ratley then asked if he believed in a higher power, like God for instance. Singer said, "sure, I believe there is a God." Ratley asked, "have you ever seen him?"

Singer replied, "that's a little different."

"How's that," Ratley quipped.

Singer arrogantly said, "for one thing, I didn't hear about him through a phone line with the help of a crystal ball.

Perhaps, that's why I put a little more stock in him than this damn palm reader broad."

Ratley said, "I understand, but do you believe it's possible for God to give people the ability to see into the future, if only for a brief moment?"

Singer's eyebrow raised slightly as he pondered Ratley's words. He had never really thought about it until then. He chewed on his words as he said, "I guess if it were his will for some reason anything is possible." Ratley pointed out this may be one of those times, but he wasn't holding his breath. Singer said, "we'll find out soon enough" as they approached the large sign in the distance which stood out near the road in front of Sister Lee's little white house.

Sister Lee watched them through the window as they pulled up the drive. Ratley followed Singer to the door carrying his notepad, and just as Singer reached to knock, Sister Lee opened the door. Singer introduced himself, but before he could finish saying his name Sister Lee cut him off by saying, "I know who you are." She looked at Deputy Ratley and said, "you are the one I spoke with on the phone."

The deputies shared a look of disbelief at her intuitive abilities as they both become speechless for a moment. Sister Lee opened the conversation by saying, "you have things you wish me to tell you. Ask your questions." Ratley swallowed before asking her several questions pertaining to her vision. He asked her to describe in detail what the victim looked like and exactly what she saw occur.

Singer rolled his eyes as he wandered into the parlor where the wooden table sat in the middle of the room. He had to ask if that was where she did her readings, and Sister Lee stood with her back to him as she said, "yes. Do you wish to have one?" She knew his answer before she ever asked, just as she knew what he would ask her.

Singer replied, "no thanks," leaving it at that, but Sister Lee knew his inner wishes just by standing in the same room with him.

She proclaimed, "you say no, but deep inside you wish to know. The future can be long or short. I can tell you, and that is what you fear most."

Singer looked over at her in denial as he said, "not hardly." He did want to know, but like she said, part of him was unwilling to give into his curiosity.

He turned looking at her bookshelves as Ratley began asking one question after another. Singer paid close attention, pretending not to listen to the interview whatsoever. Sister Lee was very descriptive to a point, but when questioned about the color clothes the victim would be wearing, she called the deputy's attention to the fact that what she saw took place in the dark.

When asked about the killer her description of him was even more vague. Sister Lee said, "his hair is dark and so are his clothes like the night itself. That is where he belongs." Everything she said had a weird unsettling feeling which came with it almost to the point of being ominous in a way.

Ratley tried to stay focused on getting the information the sheriff wanted without offending her in some way. He wrote down every word she said as if it were gospel. He looked up clarifying what she had said. It all sounded farfetched and confusing to him, a man with two lives and a scarred lion description of the man thought to be their killer. Ratley reiterated Sister Lee's statement word for word and questioned, "is that correct?"

Sister Lee delivered an uncomforting nod as Ratley's stomach started to become a little uneasy. He glanced around the room as Singer read over some of the book titles Sister Lee had in her collection. His attention became diverted for a moment when he heard Singer read one of the titles out loud.

Ratley made mention of the man with two lives, and Sister Lee gave him a perfect description of Ben. Ratley nodded his head trying to accept what she was telling him as her honest interpretation of what she saw.

Singer looked over the room that Ben recently fled from in fear. He was searching for any sign of proof he had actually been there. He questioned if he really existed, as the waitress across the street looked out the window at the deputy's car parked in the driveway of Sister Lee's house. The only description she could give of Ben's car was its color. She knew nothing when it came to makes and models.

The chair Ben had turned over on his way out the door was now seated upright where it was when he first entered the room. A scuff mark was all that remained on the floor providing proof he was actually there. Sister Lee pointed to the chair as she explained, "the man with two lives entered and sat in that chair."

Singer wasn't buying it, although the part about Ben running out the door seemed plausible enough. He found the place fairly spooky on the surface himself. She had an assortment of old leather bound books filled with incantations on her shelves, and astrological maps with vectors and sketches pointing to shit Singer had never heard of. God only knows what she had in the back rooms. Singer had his suspicions, but he didn't feel the need to check it out.

Chapter 22

No Joy Ride

Sister Lee's place aside, Singer didn't enjoy being there. He had heard her answer enough of Ratley's questions to know they couldn't get any more useful information out of her since there actually was no body at that point. All he really wanted to know from her then was where they could expect to run up on the corpse in the near future. It was crazy to run through his mind even accenting it with Singer's classic sarcastic tone, but that didn't stop him from blurting it out just like that.

The palm reader paid very little attention to him up until that point. She was somewhat put off by his snide demeanor, but that was something she had grown accustomed to in a world of non-believers since she first discovered her spiritual gifts. Her face remained stoic as she said, "I will show you the place, and you will see what I tell is for real soon enough. Today you doubt and cling to only that which you know is true. Tomorrow all that will change." With that she walked outside with Singer and Ratley following her out the door.

As Ratley closed the door he asked her if she was going to lock it. With a killer on the loose now certainly seemed like a good time to do so. Sister Lee didn't see the point as she turned her head in his direction saying, "I see no need. I am not the one in danger."

Singer looked over at Ratley and tried to make light of the situation as he said, "you heard her. The only people that have something to fear are the ones that wander in there."

Ratley agreed with that statement in his mind, but he dared not utter a sound in an attempt to remain on the fortune teller's good side, if she happened to have one somewhere under that black gown she wore. He opened the door for her to get in, and she looked at Singer as he walked around to the driver's side of the vehicle. Before climbing in she candidly remarked, "you must have been a very lonely child." Ratley found humor in her statement at Singer's expense, but again he said absolutely nothing.

Singer looked over the top of the car at Ratley before climbing in the driver's seat. He boldly asked, "what does that mean?"

Ratley had no trouble making sense of those words as he closed the rear door securing Sister Lee in the back seat of their cruiser. His smile pulled to one side of his face as he shrugged his shoulder a little while opening the passenger door. Once inside, he radioed the sheriff to tell him they were in route to the suspected crime scene.

The mere sound of the sheriff's voice annoyed Sister Lee to no end, but she remained quiet as they drove out her driveway. Ratley looked over his shoulder at her as she stared out the window of the cruiser. They continued to drive several miles before turning off onto a desolate stretch of two lane road. Sister Lee's expression had not changed in the least. Her eyes appeared to be focused on the terrain outside the vehicle, and they gave the impression that her mind was in a faraway place at that moment. Her blank stare caused Ratley to speak in hopes of getting her attention. "Does any of this look familiar to you," he asked. Sister Lee shook her head no.

Singer looked over at Ratley. He continued driving as he asked, "you think you can show us the exact place you saw in your vision?"

Sister Lee confidently replied, "I will know that place. We are close." She then closed her eyes and a look of deep concentration came over her face.

Passing another mile marker, Ratley looked over his shoulder again, this time stunned to see her with her eyes closed. Refraining from saying anything, he looked at Singer as he shrugged his shoulders. Singer glanced at her using his rear view mirror. That's when he asked, "are you praying lady?" Sister Lee replied, "yes, that you will be quiet for a minute. So, shush."

Ratley started to smile, suppressing his laughter as Singer stopped the car right there in the road. The older deputy turned looking over his shoulder saying, "wait just a damn minute. This ain't no joy ride for me either, and I can…"

Before Singer could finish his sentence, Sister Lee opened her door and stepped out of the vehicle. She began to walk down the middle of the road with her eyes still closed. With her arms at her side, bending them at the elbow, she held her hands out in front of her at waist level keeping them close to her body.

Singer and Ratley watched her from inside the car. Singer muttered, "hey, where is she going?"

Ratley responded, "wherever she's going, she can't go too far."

Sister Lee continued to walk a little ways with the deputies following close behind her. Singer had to point out, "if she doesn't get out of the middle of the road, her body is going to be the next one we scrape off the highway." He was tempted to shout at her to get back in the car, but Ratley held up his hand in an attempt to stop him from picking up the microphone as he watched Sister Lee intently. Like Singer, he was trying to figure out what was going on. Just at that moment Sister Lee stopped. She paused, standing there in the center of the oncoming lane without flinching a muscle. The wind blew through her black hair as she turned to her left. Suddenly, her body jerked as if she received a jolt of electricity yet there wasn't hardly a cloud in the sky.

Startled by the whole thing, Singer uttered, "did you see that shit? What the hell just happened?"

Ratley admitted, "I don't know, but this is getting weird."

Singer informed him, "we passed weird ten miles back when we picked this woman up."

Ratley started to get out of the vehicle. Laying his notepad down on the front seat, he picked up a small roll of crime scene tape. Confounded by the entire situation, Deputy Singer spoke only to himself asking, "now what?"

Leaving the passenger door of the car standing wide open Ratley walked toward Sister Lee. Singer called out to him, but Ratley yelled, "stay here! I'll be right back." He never took his eyes off Sister Lee for a second. He just hastily made his way to where she was standing in the road. The whole thing felt like something he had seen right out of the Twilight Zone, but this was actually weirder. Maybe that's because it was real. As the deputy approached her, she held up her hand warning him to stop. Her eyes remained closed. Ratley was startled, he halted on her command with a look of confusion covering his face. Forebodingly, she warned him saying, "stay back, this is the place. This is where you will find him."

Ratley looked around trying to find a landmark of some sort to distinguish that particular point on the road. Singer watched him walk over to the tree line beside the two lane stretch of highway. Ratley placed a piece of yellow crime scene tape around the trunk of one of the trees nearest the road. He left plenty making sure it could easily be seen.

It felt odd wrapping the tree with tape when no body was present, but the entire situation was odd right from the get go. It became weird for Ratley as soon as he took Sister Lee's call. He couldn't explain it. For some reason she had taken a liking to him, at least over Singer, and she had brought him face to face with the supernatural. He didn't understand her even though he tried, but in his mind, it certainly beat answering phones. Honestly, Ratley was curious. Foreboding warnings, cryptic speech, and her uncanny ability to confound others whenever she spoke made Sister Lee an interesting person to get to know. Ratley's curiosity would soon change into something else though.

As he tied the crime scene tape to the tree, he heard Sister Lee make a horrifying sound. Ratley turned to see what was wrong, and looking in her direction, he froze in his tracks as he watched the blood pour from her nose. It had bled the same way when she saw the bloody images for the first time through Ben's eyes back at her house. It was proof she was at the right place, but only she knew it.

Ratley didn't know what to do. As drops of blood fell to the pavement where she stood, Sister Lee's face showed extreme signs of pain. Ratley had not seen her express much emotion at all up until that point, but the pain she felt at that point belonged to another. Her body spasms again, this time even more violently. That's when the wind began to pick up and Ratley called out to her, "whatever you are doing, stop!"

Singer watched from a distance inside his patrol car. Just about scared shitless himself, he couldn't help but notice the increasing cloud cover forming up ahead. He looked up at the sky and back at Sister Lee as she convulses standing there in the middle of the road. It was like she was connected to the storm in some weird way. In utter disbelief he groaned, "you gotta be kidding me. I ain't believing this."

Seconds later a large flash of lightening appeared in what was a peaceful sky just minutes earlier. The lightening storm was fast approaching Ratley and Sister Lee. Singer wasted no time pulling the car closer to pick them up before they were overtaken by the developing storm. Rolling down the window as he pulled up beside Ratley he ordered him, "get in." He then looked over to see Sister Lee forming some sort of mystic symbol with her hands as she touched the tips of her thumbs together and crossed her two index fingers. The rest of her fingers were clinched tight as if she were making a fist. The shape of a pyramid or triangle could be seen as well as the symbol of an "X" or the cross itself depending on how you viewed it.

She recited something neither Singer nor Ratley could understand. Singer leaned his head out shouting, "what's she doing?" Just at that moment, she fell to her knees on the hard asphalt in front of the patrol car. Ratley rushed over to help her to her feet. She was having a difficult time breathing, almost as if someone were chocking her. Ratley did everything he could to assist her to the car as she experienced several more spasms on the way there. Ratley told her to open her eyes, but when she did all he could see was the whites of her eyes, the black iris fully hidden. Freaked out by it, he called her by name shaking her a little trying to pull her out of the trance-like state she was in.

Singer shouted, "come on, get her in the car. Let's go!" He had never been more serious.

Ratley yelled, "wait just a minute," as he draped Sister Lee's arm over his shoulder. He lifted her, carrying her to the car and placed her inside. Singer looked at her and then back at the approaching storm. Once Ratley climbed in the car himself, he franticly asked Sister Lee, "are you okay?"

Now able to breathe she said, "this is it. This is where the lion will show his fangs. He is blood thirsty and he will shed much."

Singer has heard enough. All he said was, "yeah, well that doesn't sound good. So, let's get the hell out of here. How about it?" He immediately turned the car around to take Sister Lee back to her house. That's when he and Ratley observed a lightening strike make a direct hit right where Sister Lee stood in the middle of the road.

Ratley questioned her again asking if she needed to see a doctor. Sister Lee just shook her head and she assured him she was alright. Ratley noticed her condition improve as more distance was put between her and the place she identified on the road. Ratley was compelled to ask her, "what was going on back there?"

Sister Lee wiped the blood away from her face telling him, "I am there in my mind. For me it is real. The man you seek is pure evil. He feeds on it through soul transference."

Ratley didn't understand everything she was saying, but he knew something supernatural took place back there.

He informed her, "you stopped breathing."

Sister Lee confessed that even she gets scared sometimes when faced with death, but the man they will find on the side of the road will be battered and strangled. She then told Ratley, "blood will flow from his eyes, ears, and nose and the lion shall have his feast. Another body will be found in pieces."

Singer continued to drive as Ratley asked, "this man you refer to as the lion, why do you call him that?"

She answered his question by explaining, "this man seeks prey and he wears the mark of the beast on his arm. His purpose for being is to deliver death, nothing more, and he will not stop, not ever."

Ratley hastily wrote down her words on paper as he said, "tell me what he looks like. Did you see his face this time?"

Sister Lee responded, "all I can tell you is he is tall, dark hair, with a scar on his left cheek. I can't see his face clearly, it changes. Only his victims see his face. I can only tell you what he looks like through their eyes, but he has a tattoo on his right arm of a lion."

The sun was almost ready to set as the patrol car pulled up to the little white house which sat on the hill across from the diner. Ratley turned to Sister Lee as they came to a stop. He asked once again if she was alright but she said nothing. Pinching her lips together a little she just gave him a look which expressed gratitude for asking. She had answered enough questions for one day. She was tired and in need of rest.

Ratley got out to open the door for Sister Lee. Singer remained behind the wheel of the patrol car the whole time just shaking his head. He overheard Ratley ask, "is there anything else you can tell us?"

Sister Lee started to turn to walk to her front door but she said calmly, "only that you will be back here sooner than you think."

Ratley watched her make her way up the walk. She neared the front door as he turned to get back in the car, but he paused as he listened to her say these final words without bothering to look at him. "Today you do not believe. Tomorrow you will start."

Ten seconds later the front door closed shut behind her as Ratley slid back into the passenger seat of the cruiser and Singer mumbled to himself, "just what we need, another prediction from her."

They were both put on edge and left to think about what she had said and they had seen. Neither of them had answers though. Singer preferred not to ponder things too hard. He just turned the patrol car around saying, "let's get the hell out of here. This broad gives me the creeps."

Ratley's only words in response to that were, "yeah, no shit."

Chapter 23

Sense Of Danger

Ben had seen enough of Chanceville to last a lifetime, but he also needed gas in order to make it to the next town. *The further away, the better*, he thought, as he pulled into the Petrol Station to fill his tank. Parking next to the pump he felt the need to use the facilities. While he was at it, he thought he might as well ask how far it was before he came to some place worth being.

Just as he turned the key to shut off the engine, he had that strange feeling come over him just like he experienced back at the diner. This time it was even more intense. He was disoriented feeling the heavy chill course through his body. Something was wrong, but he couldn't put his finger on it. He figured it was nerves after getting the crap scared out of him at Sister Lee's place, but that didn't explain why he had the same feeling prior to meeting her.

Picking up his jacket, he went to put it on as he exited the car. His wallet was buried inside his right coat pocket, but he didn't question where it was. Turning toward the pump, he noticed a black SUV with heavily tinted windows parked several spaces over. It was the first time he had seen it, but he had trouble taking his eyes off of it. Why? He didn't know.

Perhaps he should have been more leery of what he would find inside the store. It was there that he would soon come face to face with the scarred lion Sister Lee spoke of in her vision. She perceived him to be a fearless psychopath with a sadistic soul, and she was right on target. Unfortunately, Ben was only armed with her warning, and its twisted interpretation left him lost. He knew nothing of the violent images she saw in her vision, and he had no real understanding of what any of it truly meant.

Ben thought Sister Lee was insane, maybe even possessed. He had never experienced such an encounter or really contemplated demonic possession, but what he saw take place at that table inside the palm reader's house was enough to open his eyes to the possibility. This was about to be Ben's wakeup call. He had no idea she was simply trying to save his life with what she had seen through her premonition.

The powers she possessed centered around a mystical world of supernatural forces he knew nothing of, and her ability to see into the future using her inner eye quite frankly scared the hell out of him. Ben didn't believe in that shit though. He had issues, but he wasn't crazy. He only understood what he could see and touch. Anything beyond that wasn't real in his mind, and that's why he saw Sister Lee as some kind of freak. That would soon prove to be a huge mistake on his part.

He was still dogged by the eerie chill he felt even through his winter coat, and that chill also seemed to increase dramatically whenever he looked in the direction of the Tahoe. Like everything in Chanceville, it was weird. He couldn't begin to explain it, but for some strange reason it had his immediate attention. Even as he went to close his door before going inside to pay for the gas, he paused literally staring straight at it, longer than he should have, in fact, but he wasn't the only one staring.

Hayden Keller was watching Ben, as well. Whatever his interest was in the black SUV, it didn't sit well with Hayden. He stood in the back of the store leering at Ben through the window from a distance with his head lowered and his eyes raised. He was silent at first, but then his breathing became heavy as he stared straight at his prey. Hayden carried evil intent with each slow weighted breath as his stomach growled. His foul tongue touched his lips. Hayden had a taste for vengeance, and it was dinner time.

He had planned to kill the store clerk manning the register and swipe the cash from the till on his way out, but suddenly his plan changed in an instant. Hayden had set his sites on Ben. Not only had he chosen him, he had found more than just his next victim. The plan he formed in his twisted mind was sure to end the life of Ben Goodman at some point, whether it be by his hand or someone else's. It didn't matter as long as Hayden kept his soul count balanced and delivered according to terms.

How would Ben die? That was really the question, not even Hayden could answer that just yet, but he planned on putting Ben to the test. The one thing Hayden enjoyed more than killing was the process by which it came about. Torturing his victims brought him pleasure. It was the only thing that brought him closer to those he killed, and he planned on getting to know Ben real well.

On his way inside the store, Ben was again compelled to look back over his shoulder at the Tahoe. He couldn't see inside the black SUV, but something felt off about it. In fact, his face displayed a look of measured concern as he stared at it. Nothing seemed right in Chanceville though, and Ben had to ask himself one question. Why should it start now?

Seldom did he ever question what lurked around the corner, but this was one of those times. He had no idea what was inside the vehicle, but it certainly overpowered his sense of curiosity to the point he could hardly look away. It was dark though, and he had no way of knowing there was a severed body wrapped up in the back of it, concealed in a blood soaked bedspread, and a girl taken hostage in the passenger seat with her hands and feet bound, head covered, and her mouth taped shut.

Still, he looked over his shoulder at the vehicle the entire way as he walked toward the convenience store. That chill he felt never left him either. It was Hayden's cold wicked stare producing a sense of imminent danger. Soon, Ben would see it up close.

Ben only took his eyes off the SUV for a second as he entered the store to pay for his gas and use the crapper. He never saw Hayden standing near the restroom in the back of the store, but Hayden managed to keep his eye on Ben watching him using the security mirror. It didn't take the scarred lion long to make his next move either. He had been at this game for many moons, and he relished the hunt almost as much as the kill. Lying and waiting for the appropriate moment to strike was all a part of it, but Hayden often preferred to torment his prey before devouring it.

Ben Goodman was about to pay the price Sister Lee forewarned him of. There's no doubt he should have stayed and listened to everything she had to say. Ben would soon pay dearly for all he did not know because Hayden's greatest pleasure was other people's pain, and he silently vowed to bring plenty of it upon Ben as he sized him up. He glanced outside at Ben's unattended car, and he planned on getting to know him personally before listening to his dying words and laying his soul to waste. He knew the measure of his soul, and knew what it would take to get it.

Hayden was gifted at reading people, and he also knew Ashley would only make things between them damned interesting. His evil mind raced with anticipation as he considered a dozen different ways to go about killing Ben. If he was lucky he would have the chance to try out several of them on him before he bid him farewell, but Hayden also planned to use him to cover his tracks if possible. All he needed was for Ben to be the unwitting participant in his diabolical game of death and mayhem.

Chapter 24

Touch Of Death

Ben saw no one but the clerk behind the counter when he entered the store. The guy paid him little attention since his back was turned. He just continued right on stocking the shelf with cigarettes as if he wasn't even there. That didn't stop Ben from asking, "can you tell me how far the next town is from here?"

The clerk never bothered to turn around to face him as he said, "yeah, Justice is about fifty miles up the road after you get back on the highway going west, but if you blink you'll miss it."

Ben understood that to mean it wasn't much of a town as he said, "it's pretty small, huh."

The clerk bent down to pick up another box of cigarettes as he said, "well, there ain't much of it to see. It's just a little junction town, but it will bring you to the crossroads you're probably looking for."

The store clerk had no idea how much truth he spoke with that statement. Ben just told him, "thanks. You have a restroom I could use?"

A bit put out, the clerk finally looked over his shoulder at Ben as he asked, "you plan on buying something other than gas?"

Ben thought nothing of it as he said, "maybe."

Hayden listened as he waited patiently near the bathroom door just around the corner from where Ben was standing. The clerk turned back to what he was doing with a disgusted look on his face. He slung his head in the direction of the restroom, and Ben started to head that way.

He neared the corner of the store where the hallway was which led to the bathroom, and Hayden stepped out in front of him. They collided as Ben rounded the corner.

Hayden could see the startled look in Ben's eyes as he said, "whoa."

Hayden abruptly placed his right hand on Ben's shoulder as he lifted Ben's wallet from his coat pocket using his left hand without Ben noticing. He then looked into Ben's eyes as he forced himself to smile. Hayden could see him begin to exhale as he let go of his shoulder. He stood there in Ben's way blocking his path to the door of the bathroom as he said, "I didn't mean to scare you."

Ben replied, "that's alright. You just caught me by surprise, that's all," as he tried to sidestep Hayden in order to get to the bathroom.

Hayden appeared to be in deep thought as he looked at him. He moved out of Ben's way, and he looked over his shoulder at him as if he were trying to place his face. That's when Hayden asked him, "haven't I seen you somewhere before?"

Ben glanced back at him saying, "I doubt it."

Hayden confidently shook his head a little as he said, "no, I never forget a face. I know I've seen you around somewhere. I just can't place where."

Ben couldn't help but see the hideous scar gracing Hayden's left cheek. Feeling a bit uncomfortable, he broke eye contact with him as he looked down at the floor. He was fairly certain he had never seen him in his entire life. Ben was sure he would have remembered him if he had.

Hayden just twisted his head slightly as he reached out to slap Ben on the shoulder. He turned taking a few steps, and

Ben opened the door to the restroom. That's when Hayden paused before turning back toward Ben halfheartedly saying, "I'll probably figure it out halfway between here and the next town." Ben just looked back at him nodding his head once and he entered the bathroom locking the door behind him.

Hayden walked out of the store looking over at the silver beamer belonging to Ben. He pulled Ben's wallet out of his coat pocket, and he opened it up as he walked toward the back of the black SUV. Hayden pulled the cash out, and shoved it in his front pocket as he read the name on Ben's driver's license. He even made a mental note of the address printed on it in case he needed it.

He made sure no one was approaching as he opened up the rear door of the Tahoe. He reached inside for a large toolbox which sat next to the bloody bedspread filled with Jamal's body parts. Truthfully, it was already becoming rather pungent, but Hayden had already figured out the perfect place to dump it. He opened the toolbox pulling out a large flathead screwdriver, and he carelessly tossed Ben's wallet in the bottom of the box. Hayden quickly shut the door and looked over his shoulder as he walked over to Ben's car. Standing in front of it, he leaned down jabbing the large screwdriver into the grill of the beamer. He punctured the radiator several times making sure Ben could not go too far. Engine coolant began to drip from the radiator falling on the ground underneath the car. Hayden grinned fiendishly as he walked away from the shiny BMW.

Ben flushed the toilet, thinking he couldn't get out of that place fast enough. He didn't care for the town or the guy he just ran into. That was another strange encounter that left him paranoid. At least he didn't hand the guy twenty bucks as he did with Sister Lee. That's what he thought as he looked in the mirror while washing his hands. Seeing his own reflection in the mirror, he couldn't get Hayden's piercing stare out of his mind.

Shutting off the water, he then flashed back to images of the palm reader jerking her head convulsing as she sat at her table. The mental picture he had of her grasping the table as her body shook uncontrollably was still unsettling. In fact, it was downright scary just to think about. He tried to block out those images, but his mind replayed the entire scene over again and again.

Ben started to become nauseous as he reached down cupping his hands together under the faucet. He then leaned forward splashing water on his face, and that seemed to snap him out of it for the moment. He ran his hand over his face as he looked back at his reflection. He made sure to check his appearance before drying off his hands and unlocking the bathroom door.

Outside the store, Hayden walked back to the SUV. He opened the driver's side door placing the screwdriver under his seat as he looked at Ashley. Her hands and feet were bound with rope and her head was covered so she could see nothing at all. Hayden smiled, and his eyes had a wild look about them as he removed the hood from her head. He sadistically asked, "did you miss me?"

Ashley just kept looking down at her bound hands and feet. She didn't even want to see Hayden's face because it disgusted her so. Hayden cranked the SUV and started to drive off as he said, "you know you really ought to learn to smile. Life is short." He then laughed a little at his remark as he pulled onto the road and began to drive out of town.

Ashley cut her eyes toward him without moving her head, and a tear ran down her tender cheek. Hayden pulled off the road leaving the gas station within eyeshot through his side view mirror. He cut off the lights as he looked over at Ashley. About that time, Ben walked out of the restroom and approached the counter where the clerk stood.

Ben reached for his wallet which he thought was in his back pocket, and a look of confusion took over his face. Not finding it there, he began to feel for it in his jacket. His mind raced as he considered all the possible places it could be. He thought maybe it was in the car or perhaps he dropped it somewhere like the bathroom or even outside. It never occurred to him that Hayden had it. Ben said nothing to the clerk as he turned walking back to the restroom to see if he left it there. Not finding it in the bathroom, Ben came out looking around the store and that's when the clerk asked, "can I help you find something?"

Ben responded saying, "I just seem to have misplaced my wallet, that's all. It's probably in the car." The store clerk's lips pulled to one side of his face, and he cut his eyes toward the door of the store. He watched as Ben walked outside to search for his billfold.

Hayden sat comfortably inside the SUV on the side of the road leading out of town as he watched Ben exit the store. Ashley had no idea what Hayden was doing. It was pitch dark in front of them, and she was too scared to say a word at that point. The last thing she wanted to do was enrage Hayden as she questioned in her mind what he planned to do to her.

While Ashley fretted over what would soon be her fate, Hayden watched Ben through his side view mirror. Ben walked around his car in search of his wallet and Hayden grinned. He looked back over at Ashley sitting next to him in the front seat and he reached over removing the duct tape from her mouth. He then glanced back at his side view mirror. Ben opened the door to his car. He leaned inside in an attempt to find his wallet which now happened to be secure inside Hayden's recently acquired toolbox. It was one of many accessories that came with the stolen Tahoe.

Ben walked back into the store, and Hayden waited to make his next move. He calmly said, "I like you Ashley. You have a sweet spirit about you. Maybe we can learn to trust one another in time. What do you think?" Ashley could not bring herself to say a word. This demon had killed her entire family without any sign of remorse, and she knew he would kill her to in time if she didn't manage to get away from him. Without saying a word she raised her bound hands, and Hayden asked, "you promise to do what I say?"

Ashley nodded her head while biting her lips just a little. Her face showed a glimmer of hope that she may be released from bondage if she mustered the courage to look Hayden in the eye and lie. She trembled, but she did her best to smile just a little hoping it would fool Hayden into trusting her. Hayden glanced at the ropes on her wrists and ankles, and he nodded his head firmly one time. "Let's see how this goes," was all he said as he began to untie her hands. As soon as Hayden removed the ropes from her wrists, she could feel the circulation in her hands improve almost immediately.

She couldn't believe he actually untied them. She looked down at her feet and then at Hayden, but he wasn't giving into that request just yet. He shook his head a little saying, "baby steps Ashley. Show me I can trust you and they come off." Hayden then cranked up the SUV as Ashley ran her free hands over her wrists, now appreciating that they were no longer lashed together.

Hayden turned the vehicle around and drove back to the gas station. Before getting out he asked, "do you want anything?"

Ashley just said, "I need to use the bathroom."

He looked down at her feet and then into her eyes. He didn't want to untie her, but he had little choice if she were to enter the store. Hayden warned, "I don't want to hurt you, so don't make me." He waited for her to visibly acknowledge his outright lie. A sorrowful look was present on her face and it was magnified by her watery emerald eyes. He gave her one instruction. "Wait here, I'll be right back." Ashley did as she was told not knowing what was going to take place inside the store.

Hayden entered through the front door and he could see the exasperated look on Ben's face as he tried to convince the store clerk to let him have some gas on credit. Ben pled with the gas station attendant promising he would send the money as soon as he got to his bank the next day, but the clerk kept telling him, "no money, no gas. I don't make the rules."

Ben started to lose his cool as he raised his voice some, and the clerk shook his head as he turned away from Ben saying, "what do you expect me to do?"

Ben turned toward the door seeing Hayden for a second time. His heart about stopped when he noticed the wicked looking scar covering his left cheek. Sister Lee's words didn't come to mind at that moment even though Hayden was obviously the scarred lion she had seen in her vision. She had tried to warn Ben about him, but he didn't have all the pieces to the puzzle just yet, and vision interpretation was something foreign to him.

Before another word was exchanged between the clerk and Ben, Hayden pointed right at him saying, "I got it, it's Ben isn't it."

A look of surprise overtook Ben's face as Hayden pretended to struggle to think of his last name. Ben said, "yeah. How did you know?"

Hayden confidently stated, "I told you I never forget a face. I just can't recall your last name or where I met you, but I knew I had seen you somewhere before."

Ben hastily admitted his last name was Goodman as if that would jog Hayden's memory as to where they had crossed paths.

Hayden just said, "yeah, I got halfway down the road and that's when it hit me."

If Ben ever needed a friend it was now even if that friend was someone he didn't recognize. The fact that Hayden gave Ben an uneasy feeling didn't really matter much at that point either. He simply wanted to get out of town, and if some rough looking character like Hayden could make that happen then so be it. Normally, Ben would have figured him to be a real lowlife, but suddenly he looked to be Ben's ticket out of that God forsaken place known as Chanceville.

Trying to shed that uncomfortable feeling he had in his stomach, Ben responded, "yeah, well it's a small world isn't it."

Hayden agreed with him and then he pointed out, "you don't remember me, do you?"

Ben admitted, "no, not right off hand."

Hayden was caught off guard with Ben's honesty. Most people in his predicament would lie, cheat and steal their way out of it. Ben was a good man just like his name stated, and Hayden knew right then it was going to be a true pleasure to kill him when the time came. Reaching for the door, Hayden casually waived his hand as he said, "awe that's okay, no big deal. You take care of yourself. It was good seeing you."

Ben couldn't let Hayden out the door without at least asking him for a favor. He explained he had lost his wallet and he could really use some help. Ben claimed, "I'm just trying to make it to the next town where I can get to a bank. I promise I'll pay you back."

Hayden looked at him and grinned as he said, "no problem man. What are friends for?" He reached into his pocket pulling out fifty dollars which once belonged to Ben. Hayden handed it to the guy behind the counter telling him to give the change to his new found friend.

Ben immediately assured him he'd pay him back, but Hayden told him, "don't worry about it," as he shook Ben's hand firmly before turning to walk back out the door. Ben said, "at least tell me your name."

Hayden paused as he held the door open, and he assured Ben he had faith in him that he would soon figure it out. Hayden's last words to him were, "just give it time. I'm sure it will come to you eventually."

Every encounter Ben had since pulling into town was beyond strange, and he thought to himself, *why should this one be any different*. He was just thankful to have gas money to move on down the road.

Hayden planned to follow suit. He removed the rope which held Ashley's feet together. He had waited until Ben pulled out of the Petrol Station seeing which road he took before allowing Ashley to get out of the SUV. He held her firmly by the arm as he escorted her inside, taking her straight to the bathroom. He didn't allow her much time or the chance to use it in private. Hayden's trust factor only went so far. As Hayden loaded her back in the Tahoe, Ashley sat in the back seat motionless as her eyes moved to one side catching a glimpse of the bloody spread which held what was left of Jamal. She was trapped with no way out.

Hayden had the childproof locks turned on and only he could open the doors. There was no way she could overpower him and she knew it. Seeing that he was armed, her only choice was to wait and hope for the right opportunity to present itself. That's when she would make a run for it. She knew when that time came if she was not successful she would die, and that raised the stakes pretty damn high for her. They were too high in fact for her to chance it unless she believed she could definitely escape. As for Hayden Keller, he was now on a mission and he wasn't being sent by God to get the job done. That task was reserved for Ben, and he alone, but at the moment he was in search of Justice.

Chapter 25

Stranded

Ben headed west making his way out of town. His immediate destination left much to be desired, but his eyes were focused on the dark stretch of road in front of him. The night itself was gloomy and wet. Ironically, he was pointed toward the small town of Justice, but he would find none there. He would never see the town on his own. It would take Hayden Keller to bring him to that place, and Ben had no idea at that moment his life would soon be placed in serious danger. Peril was the farthest thing from his mind after passing the sign which read, *Leaving Chanceville.* He glanced up into his rear view mirror bidding that little spot on the map good riddance. Ben figured that would be the last he would ever see of Chanceville, but things aren't always what they seem.

Sometimes there are forces greater than those we know of hard at work, ensuring fate has its moment in time, and Ben would eventually be faced with sudden death. Whether or not it was his death or someone else's remained to be seen, but Hayden had a pretty clear vision of who would die next.

Ben switched on the radio to keep him company as he drove down the dark stretch of two lane road. About that time a set of headlights came into view in the distance behind him. Those lights came into view and disappeared several times before they finally vanished altogether. Ben paid them little attention. Leaving Chanceville was all he had on his mind. Little else mattered other than finding a bank where he could get some cash, and reporting his debit card as lost or stolen. Of all the places for it to happen it was ironic he would lose it in a place called Chanceville. He suspected he dropped it while fleeing Sister Lee's house, but he wasn't about to go back and search for it at that point. That thought never entered his mind. He still hadn't put enough distance between himself and that diner where things just seemed to take a terrifying turn for the worse.

Someday, it would all make for an entertaining story perhaps. That's what ran though his mind as he drove down the winding stretch of two lane highway, but for now the situation held no humor for him at all. Several miles down the road Ben would soon discover just how bad things could really get.

It was growing cold outside, and fog began to fill the air all around the vehicle, impairing his vision the condensation clung to his windshield and windows. Yet, Ben continued to drive toward Justice a little slower struggling to see ten feet in front of him. He flipped on the wipers, and he noticed a temperature warning light come on as he questioned what could possibly go wrong next. Here he was on a deserted stretch of road in God knows where, and now his car's electrical system seemed to be going on the fritz. He knew nothing was wrong with the car because he had it inspected before he left town on his trip out west. He knew very little about cars, but whatever was causing that light to come on must have been some kind of false alarm. After all, his BMW was practically brand new and in perfect mechanical condition according to the mechanic that checked it out just days earlier.

Another mile or so down the road he looked down at the gauges on the instrument panel again. This time he heard a knocking noise coming from underneath the hood. He looked up with a stunned expression on his face as steam started to roll over the hood of the car. The engine had overheated somehow. Ben now questioned if that moron at the dealership that told him everything was fine after he inspected it knew his ass from a hole in the ground.

The knocking sound became more noticeable as Ben pulled off to the side of the road. Highly concerned, he turned off the radio listening closer to the knocking sound coming from under the hood. Not knowing what to do he quickly shut off the vehicle. He stared down at the gauges for a second before looking above his dashboard to see the continual stream of steam rolling out from the front end of his beamer. The check engine light was now illuminated and the temperature gauge showed nothing but red. The headlights were still shining bright, but the fog prevented him from seeing much outside the vehicle.

Ben looked up at the darkness in front of him pressing his lips together in total frustration. All he could mutter at that point was, "I'm not believing this." He sat there a moment looking out his window questioning what to do next, and he hesitated to even open the door to the car. He had little choice in the matter if he wanted to see what was wrong under the hood though. Flipping on the overhead light inside the car, he fumbled for the hood release.

He got out of his car feeling the cold damp air all around him, and he quickly walked to the front of his vehicle. Steam was still escaping from the edge of the hood as he reached down to open it. He saw it, but like a damn fool he still reached down to open the hood. He regretted that decision along with many others he had made as he stood there on that creepy stretch of road. Burning the tips of his fingers slightly as he reached down to open the hood he cussed as he quickly drew his hand away from the car.

Ben clinched his fist tightly covering his freshly blistered fingers in an effort to help extinguish the pain he felt as he backed away from the car. With the headlights still shining directly on him, he watched the steam vapor dissipate into the night air. He cautiously made another attempt at opening the hood, damn well realizing he wouldn't be able to tell the water pump from the master cylinder even if he knew what they were to begin with. He gave it the once over as he looked at some of the hoses and the top of the engine. He couldn't see much, but the steam was no longer present. That was a good sign he thought to himself as he looked over his shoulder in the direction of the next town. He knew he had quite a ways to go to get there. Either way he was determined not to go back to Chanceville. He had an awful feeling about that place even though the place where he was standing gave him the willies as well.

Ben closed the hood hoping for the best, and he climbed back inside the car planning to give it time to cool down before making another attempt to reach Justice. He knew it was pointless, but he picked up his cell phone just to see if he had signal. He wasn't surprised to see no bars present as he closed the phone laying it back down on the seat next to him. What choice did he really have? He could wait until someone found him out there or he could try to make it to Justice where maybe he could at least phone for help.

He turned the key and the car immediately cranked right up, but shifting it into drive he soon heard that knocking sound once more. The radiator was bone dry and the temperature gauge quickly climbed into the red zone again before he even made it a quarter mile down the road. The sputtering sound it made was followed by a steady hissing sound, and Ben knew that car wasn't going any further without the help of a tow truck. He was forced to pull off the road again, and now he was concerned about the damage he had done to his car simply trying to leave the town from hell.

Looking up at the angry sky above through his windshield, he sat there in the driver's seat feeling damn near helpless. Ben hit the steering wheel with the palm of his hand yelling, "shit, son of a bitch!" What else could he say under such conditions? He stared straight ahead considering his options, and then he just hung his head knowing he had a hell of a walk ahead of him in either direction. This was a hell of a place to become stranded like there's ever a good place for that to happen, but he had no idea this was all Hayden's doing.

Ben looked over his shoulder at his bag in the backseat. He reached for it pulling it into the front seat and he shut off the headlights. It was dark as shit outside the car. The moon was almost completely blocked out by cloud cover. Only minor glimpses of it could be seen as Ben looked up at the sky above him. He thought it best to turn on the hazard lights just in case someone did by chance happen to run up on him, but he wasn't holding his breath believing that would happen.

Truthfully, he was scared whether he wished to admit it or not. So scared in fact, he began to talk to himself in a unconscious attempt to calm his nerves. Ben just sat there for nearly twenty minutes almost motionless, and finally he voiced his inner most thought blurting out, "damn it's fucking dark. I can't see shit." Just hearing those words even though they came from his own lips made him feel a little less alone out there in the middle of nowhere.

He looked out his window but he couldn't see a thing. About that time he heard a noise outside the car, and he quickly reached over pushing the auto lock button on the car door. He waited listening to the sound of the coursing wind as it blew forcefully against the car. Ben thought this whole situation was like something right out of a horror movie he once saw, and the results for the guy inside the vehicle weren't good.

With his senses on high alert, he had to question whether he would be better off on foot or should he just stay put. That's when he heard something hit the car. It was just the wind which had blown something up against the rear of the vehicle making a small noise which had put Ben even more on edge. His head quickly turned in that direction, but he saw absolutely nothing as he confessed to himself, "that's great. I'm probably gonna fucking die out here." He was halfheartedly joking as he tried to face his fear head on, but that's when he made a bold decision.

Opening the car door he exited with his bag in his hand, and he closed the door locking it shut. Throwing the strap of his bag over his shoulder, Ben placed his keys in his pocket as he started walking in the direction in which he was headed never imagining all this was planned by someone for a single sinister purpose.

The wheels of fate were now set in motion. Ben had touched the scarred lion with cancer Sister Lee had warned him about. Now, he would have to pay the price. Ashley sat quietly staring out the window into the darkness with her hands and feet untied. She no longer had duct tape covering her mouth, but she had nothing to say to Hayden. She had seen how quick his temper could ignite, and for now she simply wished to continue living long enough to make her escape. That didn't stop Hayden from talking though as he drove down the empty rural highway. Uncharacteristically, he said, "I think we got off on the wrong foot, but I'm glad we've put that behind us." His face showed no sign of emotion whatsoever. Ashley knew he was insane, but she didn't know what to make of his words. She cut her eyes to the side as she avoided looking at him. Not knowing what to do at that point she simply nodded her head a little in agreement hoping that would keep him from going ballistic.

Hayden had been following Ben for miles keeping his distance ever since he left Chanceville. He also knew he would come upon him very soon. He could just about calculate which mile marker he would find him at when he happened up on him. Everything involving the hunt was game to Hayden.

Ashley knew nothing of what Hayden had planned, but she found his tone and words unsettling. Whenever he spoke, there was an evil edge present in each word that left his mouth which couldn't be overlooked regardless of what was said. Hayden just had a way about him that sent shutters through the spines of those unfortunate enough to meet him.

Ashley had seen enough to know he would soon kill again, and she wanted for nothing more than to be far from him when his vengeance resurfaced. He puzzled her though, there was no denying that. In another surprising remark Hayden suggested, "let's go give someone a hand in need." It was the nasty sound in his voice and the particular words he chose to use which made Ashley question in her mind what he was about to do next. She had no idea what was wrapped inside the bloody bedspread stashed in the back of the SUV. She would discover it soon enough, and when she did it would make her sick to her stomach, no doubt. Either way, she knew Hayden wasn't about to help anyone. Still, she silently prayed for someone to save her.

Chapter 26

Bad Moon

Ben continued his lengthy walk toting his bag swapping hands occasionally due to the weight of it. He noticed every little sound nature made all around him. A reminder he was not totally alone at that moment, but he didn't like nature much, and he was growing less fond of it by the minute. That's when he came to the conclusion things just couldn't get any worse. He was wrong of course. Hayden Keller was out to find him and when he did Ben would truly come to know the meaning of hell on earth.

The black SUV rolled up on Ben's car, and Hayden slowed to a passing crawl. Ashley recognized the vehicle from the gas station even though she never got a good look at the driver. What she knew was something not so good was about to happen. She was too spooked to say a word, but she knew Hayden was going to kill again. She thought about the young man Hayden killed at the reservoir. She didn't even know his name, and she preferred not to even think about her own family. She was still in shock from the tragic event. It was like she blocked it out for the most part. Her rush of adrenaline was the only thing that allowed her to focus on survival, but she would have chosen any thought to contemplate on other than what happened to those she loved. Forced thought control or FTC is what some like to call it.

Ashley had all the symptoms of an emotionally stricken captive, yet she did everything she could to vanquish the gruesome images occupying her mind. It was a defense mechanism victims often use subconsciously just to maintain their ability to focus and react under such horrid circumstances.

Hayden pulled over in front of the BMW and shut off the engine. He told Ashley to hop in the backseat, and he exited the vehicle locking her inside. She watched him walk over to check out the beamer but she did as he instructed. She couldn't help but notice the bloody bedspread in the back of the Tahoe. She preferred not to think about who was inside it, but she could see what looked like fingers right before she closed her eyes shut tight. She tried not to hyperventilate, but it was difficult. Regardless of what she thought she saw, she damn sure wasn't about to mention it to Hayden.

She tried to convince herself it was all just a torturous nightmare, but reality was psychological games couldn't overcome all she had seen. The blood she had on her hand was real. The rear doors were locked and Hayden was somewhere outside the vehicle. She had no idea what he was doing. From where she was sitting, she couldn't see a thing. That being the case, she figured now was not the time to make a run for it. Ashley figured she only had one shot, and this probably wasn't the right time to chance it. She was right. He was back inside the vehicle within seconds.

Hayden drove several more miles before he ran up on Ben who was glad to see any moving vehicle at that point. The headlights of the SUV illuminated the road right behind Ben. Hayden looked back over his shoulder at Ashley as he said, "I think I know this guy. What do you say we help him out." With a touch of a button Hayden rolled down the window asking, "Ben is that you?" Ben suddenly realized it was Hayden, but even he was a welcomed sight at that point if he could get him to the next town.

Hayden pretended to be surprised as he asked, "what the hell happened? Was that your car I saw back there?"
Ben walked over to the passenger side door of the Tahoe and tried his best to explain, "I don't know the damn thing just ran hot on me for some reason."
Hayden extended his helpful hand once again telling Ben, "well hop in, I'll give you a lift." That's when he went to unlock the door.

Ben climbed inside and noticed Ashley sitting in the backseat. She had a concerned look on her face when Ben introduced himself after thanking Hayden for coming to his rescue once again. Ashley knew something was up, and she knew Ben obviously knew nothing about Hayden. She kept her mouth closed for the moment afraid to say anything, and Hayden pointed out, "she doesn't talk much." She had something to say just not in front of Hayden. She desperately wanted to tell Ben what was going on, but she didn't know exactly how to do it without getting them both killed.

She didn't wish to see any harm come to Ben, but she had herself to think about as well. Anyway, for the moment, it felt much more comfortable just not being left alone with a psychotic killer, and even though it was all an act Hayden seemed almost normal for a change. Ashley wondered how long it would last before he showed his fangs. Whenever Ben would glance back at her she would cut her eyes toward Hayden and then at the bloody bedspread sitting behind her. When Ben asked her how they knew one another, Hayden switched on the radio as he said, "oh we've been through a lot together, haven't we Ashley." Pressing her lips together in despair she nodded agreeing with Hayden. That's when Hayden turned Ben's attention to his severe misfortune by saying, "I can't believe you got stranded back there."

Ben confessed that his entire trip seemed to be a disaster so far. Hayden calmly pointed out, "that's alright at least you got a ride to the next town. It's fate you know."

Ben responded by asking, "how's that?" He had heard enough talk of fate between his run-in with Sister Lee and what he read in his horoscope. Still he wanted to know what Hayden meant exactly.

The song playing on the radio was "Bad Moon Rising." CCR was delivering an omen through the airwaves decades long after the song was recorded and the irony in that was heavy. Hayden looked up at the sky. He slowly panned over it as if he were searching for something before focusing his attention directly on the moon. Hayden admitted, "that's a bad moon Ben. On a night like tonight anything can happen." He then looked over at Ben saying, "you know what I mean?"

Ben thought he had a pretty good understanding after the day's events, but he just took it that Hayden was a little on the superstitious side. Perhaps it wasn't a bad place to be, Ben was fast becoming a believer himself. He had certainly experienced more than his share of bad luck in the last several hours not to mention what took place earlier that day. In an effort to include Ashley in the conversation, Ben looked over his shoulder asking her, "do you believe in that kind of stuff?"

Still saying nothing, she deliberately nodded her head. There was no way she was about to disagree with Hayden on that note.

Trying to gain some kind of clue as to who Hayden was Ben asked, "so, what kind of work do you do?"

Hayden just kept driving telling Ben he was sort of in between right now, but he managed to get by. Hayden wasn't in between jobs, he was in between heaven and hell. He voiced his thoughts, "life is all about transitions Ben. Everybody's got to make them sometime."

Ben couldn't argue with that, but he promised to pay Hayden back as soon as he could get his hands on some money. Hayden gave it a halfhearted effort to reassure him, "I told you Ben don't worry about it. That's what friends are for."

Ben looked over at him trying to recall where he may have met Hayden before, but nothing came to mind. Looking at the road, Hayden tilted his head a little. That's when he said, "still hadn't figured out my name yet, I see."

Ben admitted he was working on it, and Hayden said, "like I told you, you'll figure it out." He then turned the topic of conversation to what Ben was doing now by paying him a compliment, "that's a real nice car you got there. You must be doing pretty well for yourself."

Ben didn't like to brag, but he told Hayden a little bit about what he did for a living. "Well, working behind a computer doesn't offer a great deal of excitement, but the pay is pretty good."

Hayden listened to every word Ben spoke before saying, "so you hit the road in search of adventure."

Ben replied, "yeah, well it looks like I found it alright."

Hayden's response to that was, "it could always be worse Ben. Take tonight for example. Where would you be if Ashley and I didn't happen to run up on you?" Ashley heard those words thinking *if Hayden hadn't found him he'd still be alive come sunup.* Still, she dared not utter a word of what went through her mind.

Ben shook his head agreeing with Hayden. He then confessed, "it's funny you should say that. I told myself it couldn't get any worse several miles back right after my car broke down."

Hayden glanced over at Ben looking at him out of the corner of his eye. That's when he said, "well you just never know how things are going to turn out, do you."

Ashley had a good idea of what was about to take place. Her mind raced trying to think of a way to alert Ben to the real danger they were both in. It was obvious Ben was clueless to the fact he was now riding next to a serial killer. She damn near wanted to strangle Ben herself just to get his attention, but she remained silent using only her head to motion toward the severed body behind her.

When Ben looked back at her he couldn't help but notice she was trying to tell him something each time she cut her eyes toward Hayden. That uneasy feeling really never left Ben, but it had lessoned a little during their conversation. Seeing Ashley's head motion to what was behind her, Ben quickly became uncomfortable sitting in the passenger seat. He now knew something was wrong.

Ashley didn't speak hardly a word yet she made constant eye contact, and something scared the hell out of her. Ben could identify with that feeling. The first time he ran into Hayden he felt that eerie chill surge through his entire body. That's when his mind started recalling all of the words spoken by Sister Lee. Hayden had a scar on his left cheek, but Ben had only seen it briefly inside the gas station. Even now where Ben sat he couldn't lay eyes on it. Hayden always seemed to have his right cheek turned toward him. About that time Hayden asked, "you alright Ben?"

Choosing to test Hayden, Ben answered him saying,

"yeah, I was just wondering if you ever figured out where we first met."

Hayden nodded his head stating, "a test, I like that. Do you like tests Ben?"

"Not really," Ben replied.

The tension was now building between them as Hayden said, "come on now a smart college boy like you. You got to enjoy a good test."

Ben claimed, "I've taken more than my share."

Hayden took that opportunity to enlighten him a little pointing out, "testing is good for the soul Ben. I think I'll give you one just to make the ride a little more interesting." Ashley closed her eyes fearing what was coming.

Ben became agitated and he firmly told Hayden, "I'm not into playing games."

Hayden looked over at him saying, "nonsense, all you need is the proper motivator." Hayden then looked in the rear view mirror to see Ashley's face.

They were miles outside of Justice when Hayden felt compelled to pose a question to Ben. He casually asked, "you ever watch those medical shows Ben? I find them down-right fascinating myself."

Ben answered, "no," keeping his eyes on the road in search of a mile marker.

Hayden informed him, "you can learn a lot about the human body you know. For instance, did you know the average adult has nearly twenty-five feet of small intestine alone?" Ben just looked at him. Hayden said, "it's true. What I find most interesting is the body only needs a portion of it to live." Ben really didn't know what to say to that so he just kept quiet as he looked out at the road. Ashley cringed as Hayden added, "the human body is an amazing machine. It's resilient, that's for sure."

Ben found his remarks to be out of place and unpleasant to say the least. He could have thought of a thousand other ways to start a conversation, and that's when he noticed the gun Hayden had tucked inside his coat pocket. Ben could see the butt of the handle protruding from his pocket whenever Hayden raised his arm a little while driving.

It was dead quiet inside the vehicle. Hayden actually enjoyed it, but he eventually broke the awkward silence by asking, "what are you looking at Ben?"

He paused for a second before answering not knowing if he should mention the gun at all. He was fairly certain Hayden knew what had caught his eye though. All Ben said was, "I see you have a gun."

A dismal look came to Hayden's face. He candidly responded, "yeah. You can never be too careful Ben. There's a lot of crazy people out there. You always have to be ready to protect yourself." Looking over at Ben he knew the answer to the question he was about to ask, "you got one of these?" Ben just shook his head never divulging that he really didn't care for guns at all. Hayden told him, "well I suggest you get one cause you never know when you're going to need it." Nearing the edge of town he said, "I'll tell you something else about the human body I bet you didn't know Ben."

Ben cut his eyes toward Hayden as he said, "yeah. What's that?"

Hayden said, "it has well over a billion nerves running through it. Each one of those serves a single purpose either to deliver pleasure or pain." He directed Ben's attention to a drunk man staggering along the side of the road up ahead in the distance saying, "but take this guy up here for instance, if I ran right into him he'd probably never even feel it."

Suddenly, Ben's blood started rushing through his veins. He raised his voice some without even thinking, questioning Hayden as he romped on the gas pedal. "What are you doing?"

Hayden calmly responded, "I'm going to prove it to you." He turned the wheel veering the Tahoe right toward the intoxicated man.

"You can't do that," Ben yelled, but Hayden just continued to apply pressure to the accelerator.

"Only you can stop me Ben. Whatcha gonna do," Hayden spouted. He leaned into the wheel knowing it was sure to get a rise out of his passengers.

Ben reached over jerking the wheel sharply before Hayden could regain control. His last second reaction saved the man's life, and Hayden looked over at him saying, "damn Ben, you almost killed us back there."

Ben spouted, "you could have killed him."

Hayden agreed with Ben's assessment, but then he pointed out that he didn't kill him. He went so far as to remind Ben of what he said earlier, "that goes to show, you just never know what's going to happen."

Ben didn't feel the need to take anymore life lessons from Hayden, but that didn't stop Hayden from toying with him, "I was testing you Ben, come on."

With a doubtful tone Ben responded with, "you mean you weren't actually going to hit him?"

Hayden let go of a grisly laugh telling him, "I figured you would pass that one Ben, but you had me guessing there at the end my friend."

Ben didn't appreciate Hayden's humor or his sick way of testing him. He informed Hayden he wasn't his friend and he damn near ordered him, "you can just let me off right up here."

Hayden replied, "that's no way to act Ben. You and I go way back."

Ben was certain he had never seen Hayden before except for bumping into him at the gas station in Chanceville. It was ironic Hayden was now giving Ben advice about etiquette. Ben figured the best thing he could do at that point was get away from Hayden and report him to authorities. He now had grave concern for his life and Ashley's. He lowered his voice saying, "just let me out."

Hayden responded with a flipped demand, "no problem, pay me my money."

Ben stared at him saying, "I don't have it, you know that." Hayden growled, "well you better get it, cause I'm not letting you out of my sight until you come up with what you owe me."

Ben started to reach for the handle of his door, and Hayden said, "don't be stupid Ben." He hit the power door locks and increased speed, leaving Ben with little choice in parting company. Ben came one step closer to determining Hayden's true identity. Hayden asked, "have you ever looked into the eyes of a dying man Ben?" Ben looked gravely concerned never answering him, and Hayden said, "I thought not. There's nothing quite like it. I'd even go so far as to say you haven't experienced living until you've done your share of killing Ben." Ben's look of disbelief never waned as Hayden told him he just might get the chance to really live for the first time in his life.

Hayden added, "I just might be the greatest friend you've never had. You never know Ben, tonight could be the night."

Chapter 27

Coming To Justice

They rolled into town and Hayden put Ben on notice. His face turned dead serious as he warned Ben not to push his buttons. Hayden told him point blank, "you don't want to mess with me Ben. I've got a real bad side, and I don't think you would like me when I'm angry." Only Hayden's lips moved as he spoke. His teeth were tightly clinched together, and Ashley could tell he was on the brink of losing control.

Being left alone with Hayden was something Ashley preferred not to think about. She didn't want to see any harm come to Ben, and she immediately tried to defuse the situation as she told Ben, "just do what he says." Those were the first words Ben heard leave her mouth, and they didn't sound comforting. They were weighted with distress.

Hayden's eyes were trained on her as she gave Ben prudent advice. She never looked at Hayden. She just stared out the window into the darkness. Her hope was fading fast. Hayden's tone changed when he looked Ben directly in the eye. All he said was, "that's good advice. I think you should take it Ben."

There wasn't much to Justice just like the guy back in Chanceville had said. One filling station and a blinking yellow light was all there was to it. What Ben would find there certainly wouldn't resemble justice. Hayden pulled into that gas station, and he had his first real test for Ben all laid out in his evil mind. He didn't need gas though, just a little running money. With his hands gripping the steering wheel of the SUV he peered straight ahead. Then he looked over at Ben saying, "here's your bank Ben. Now go get my fucking money."

Ben looked at him in disbelief as if he were insane. He didn't see anything resembling an ATM. Hell the gas pumps themselves weren't even setup to take credit cards. Parked next to the gas pump, Hayden unlocked Ben's door telling him, "go do your thing Ben. I'm waiting." He then added, "make it quick," as he got out of the SUV. Hayden opened the back door pulling Ashley from the vehicle, and using a death-grip he held her by the wrist as he reached over picking up the gas hose.

"What do you expect me to do rob the place," Ben asked.

Hayden's response was, "that's exactly how I would play it Ben. You do it however you see fit, but you got one minute to get my money or Ashley here won't look so pretty when I'm done with her."

Hayden held the nozzle over her head, and he squeezed the handle. Gas poured onto her hair, drizzling over her face, and she shut her eyes tight, knowing she would soon be a human torch. Hayden assured Ben he wasn't bluffing. Dropping the nozzle on the ground Hayden looked over at Ben and said, "you're not back in sixty seconds with the money, I'll turn her into the prettiest roman candle you've ever seen."

Ben froze where he stood. He didn't doubt Hayden would do just what he said. He couldn't take that chance, but he truly didn't know what to do. Ben shouted, "I don't have a gun," as if that would somehow get him out of it.

Hayden replied, "they don't know that Ben. Use your head, but if you yell any louder I'm sure you'll have your work cut out for you in there." Hayden tightened his grip on Ashley's wrist as she tried to pull away. He pulled out the lighter he had swiped from Roy after his untimely passing, and he said, "clocks ticking Ben, you got fifty-six seconds."

Ashley's face was filled with terror. Ben looked over his shoulder as he made a dash for the glass door of the filling station. Upon entering he looked around spotting the cash register. The old gentleman minding the store heard the bell ring above the door when Ben entered. By the time he got out front, Ben was franticly punching buttons trying to open the cash drawer.

The old fellow yelled, "what the hell are you doing? Get away from there!" Ben tried to explain he needed the money, and he would pay it back as he removed a fist full of cash from the drawer. Of course, the old man wasn't about to let him just walk out of there with it. Reaching for his Smith and Wesson, he shouted at Ben to stop. Ben never bothered to look back, he just fled out the door. The old man behind the counter raised his snub nose .38 and fired a shot which took out the upper portion of glass in the door as it closed behind Ben.

Hearing the sound of the shot, Hayden drew his gun. He pushed Ashley forcing her back inside the SUV. She was terrified but thankful she wasn't ablaze at this stage of the game. She really couldn't think of a worse way to die than to be burned alive, and she felt like she had plenty of time to mull it over as she waited for Ben to return with the money. It was without question the longest fifty-three seconds of her life.

The bullet which the old guy had fired managed to strike Ben in his left shoulder, but he barely stumbled upon being hit. Ben knew time was running out. His only thought centered on saving Ashley's life as he raced toward the

SUV. Hayden stood facing the store. He raised his weapon pointing it straight at the front door. As soon as the old guy stepped into view, Hayden squeezed the trigger placing two rounds in the old guy's chest. He watched the old man collapse on the concrete stoop outside the store. Then he hollered at Ben, "come on, move your ass Ben."

Ben grabbed the handle of the SUV as he looked back at the old guy lying on the ground. Some of the money fell from his hand as he attempted to open the passenger door of the Tahoe. Hayden saw him try to raise his gun one last time in a final attempt to defend himself, and Hayden fired another round into him for good measure. Ben watched the guy hit the concrete. The old man was dead and for now Ben was just wounded. He was fortunate just to be breathing. Hayden informed Ben he now owed him his life, and Hayden planned on collecting that in due time. Hayden climbed back inside the vehicle holding the gun on Ben, and he locked the doors as soon as Ben shut the passenger door. Ben and Ashley were trapped once again, this time fully aware Hayden was destined to kill them in time.

Hayden looked over at Ben who was sitting in the passenger seat holding his shoulder with his right hand. Blood trickled down his left arm tracing a path all the way to his hand which held the stolen money. He continued to apply pressure to his wound in an effort to halt the flow of blood from it. It hurt like hell whenever he pulled his hand away from it. Hayden could see Ben whence as the cold air entered the freshly made hole on his shoulder. Hayden showed his false concern for Ben by saying, "damn Ben looks like you did alright for an amateur." He reached down snatching the bloodstained cash from Ben's hand. Hayden held it up jovially commenting, "now, that's what I call real blood money."

It was Ben's blood that adorned the edges of the currency, and Hayden showed it to Ashley reminding her, "you are a lucky girl. I want you to know that. I don't think there's anything old Ben here wouldn't do to try and save you. Isn't that right Ben?" Ben didn't answer him. He just looked up at Hayden. "It hurts don't it Ben," Hayden remarked, and his evil grin emerged, taking full form. Toying with them both he counted the money saying, "I guess that's enough to buy you a little more time. Time can be a precious thing, trust me."

Ben told Hayden to let Ashley go. He was willing to use himself as a bargaining chip if necessary, but Hayden informed Ben he didn't take orders. Ben clarified he was now asking. "You're starting to grow on me Ben. We might not be friends but even you can't deny we are partners in crime," Hayden jested. He added, "I think I'll keep both of you around awhile." That brought no relief to Ben's face, but Ashley knew more time in Hayden's world was a rare thing indeed. It also meant more time to escape from his clutches which is all she so desperately wanted to do.

Hayden lowered his window, then he pulled out Roy's lighter. He lit it staring at the flame a moment, then he held the lighter out the window next to the gas pump. Hayden asked, "do you know the most effective way to try something Ben?" Ben looked at him as he sat there clutching his injured shoulder. Hayden's hideous face had a smug look on it as he said, "I thought not. It's fire Ben. That's how you test something for all its strength. That's when you discover what something is really made of."

"Why are you telling me this," Ben asked.

Hayden responded saying, "it's what you must go through. We all have to go through the fire at some point. The question in my mind is will you parish or endure. You see

Ben, I am a betting man and I say you don't have what it takes to walk through it. I think you are just like all the other weak bastards out in the world. You cling to what you have in fear of what happens when you let go."

Ben didn't care what Hayden thought of him. He was betting he and Ashley would somehow make it out of this situation alive. Hayden stared at him saying, "I hope you're ready Ben cause I'm going to put you through the fire, and you will beg me to end your sorry life before it's over. I assure you." Hayden found more humor in a thought he kept to himself, *at that point - I may actually be the best friend you got.*

"Why don't you just let us go," Ben asked.
Hayden looked back at the road they drove in on saying, "now what would be the fun in that?" Hayden looked into Ben's eyes making sure he could see the crazed look within his, and that's when he said, "we can end it all right here." It came across as a threat more than an option. He moved his hand holding the lighter just feet away from the old gas pump. He then looked up in the rear view mirror at Ashley asking, "what do you say Ashley, should we all go out together in a blaze of glory?"

She slowly shook her head no, and Hayden flipped the lighter closed snuffing out the flame as he peeled out of the gas station. He knew the road to hell was paved with good intentions, and Ben was in no short supply of those. Maybe Hayden was right about Ben. Perhaps there really was nothing he wouldn't do to save the girl from dying a horrible death. Hayden figured time would tell if he was right about him. In the meantime, he would find out exactly what Ben and Ashley were made of by torturing them until one of them begged to be killed.

Hayden drove back up the highway toward Ben's car pointing out the obvious, "I reckon that's the first time you've been shot Ben. Move your hand and let me see it." Against his better judgment Ben slid his hand down revealing his gunshot wound to Hayden. "Hell that's just a flesh wound," Hayden said. A heavy rush of air left Hayden's nostrils as he said, "I've had plenty of those. You'll live as long as I let you." Then he laughed saying, "the real funny part is the old man back there had his sites on you Ben when he probably should have been a little more concerned about me. What do you think Ashley?"

She didn't answer Hayden's question. She wasn't playing his game. She lashed out at him screaming, "what do you want from us?"

Hayden replied, "everything, nothing, does it really matter?"

Hayden addressed Ben warning him, "you better watch it Ben. Your girlfriend there seems to have quite the temper." As he drove out of town Hayden told Ben there was no justice in this world for either of them. Just at that moment, Hayden's headlights shone directly in the eyes of the drunken man he almost hit before pulling into the gas station. Hayden added, "and there ain't no justice for this bastard either," as he floored it. This time Ben couldn't stop Hayden from running him over as he plowed right into the man.

When the grill guard of the SUV struck the intoxicated chap, his body was thrown onto the hood of the Tahoe. It rolled across the hood before bouncing right into the windshield directly in front of Ben. It looked as though he was actually coming through it, and Ben turned his head in a knee jerk reaction to avoid being struck by the hit and run victim.

Hayden turned the vehicle sharply flinging the man's body off the hood of the Tahoe. As the drunkard hit the ground, Hayden jerked the wheel toward Ben making sure the rear tire of the SUV ran over the body. There was no question as to whether or not the man was dead. It didn't faze Hayden in the least. The back of the SUV jostled up and down as the rear tire rolled over the poor guy. Hayden thought nothing more of it than rolling over a speed bump. All he said was, "see Ben, it's dangerous walking on the road at night."

Chapter 28

The Hunt For Hayden Keller

It was late and Sheriff Baker was still sitting at his desk inside his office. He looked over the photographs taken out at the Ferris farm laying them out on his desk. He finished reading over the coroner's report and he placed it back inside the folder. He got up from his chair and walked over to the map which was hanging on the wall right next to his door. The sheriff studied it for a moment before placing a pushpin in it right near the county line. That marked the place where the Ferris' were found. There were other pins positioned on the map marking points where Hayden had previously struck. The trail of dead bodies were leading right through Chanceville, and Sheriff Baker knew another body would probably turn up in his county within the next day or two. He only hoped it wasn't the body of Ashley Pennington as he tried to get inside the mind of the animal responsible for the carnage in Jefferson County.

People throughout the town were now afraid to leave their homes in a community that once never bothered to lock its' doors. The sheriff ran his finger over the map as he heard a noise at the door. It was Ratley, and he had his hands full of food. The sheriff walked to the door unlocking it to let him in. "What the hell are you doing," the sheriff asked.

Ratley replied, "I saw your light on and figured you might be hungry. So, I got you something to eat. Oh by the way, Stella said for me to tell you hi."

Ratley held up the food, and the sheriff pointed to the table sitting outside his office. As Ratley sat the food down the sheriff told him, "you should be at home getting some rest."

Ratley looked around at the sheriff questioning, "what about you?"

The sheriff admitted he couldn't rest until the son of a bitch responsible for this was dead or behind bars. Ratley could certainly identify with that, but he felt the need to remind him of something, "even you gotta eat sheriff."

The sheriff responded to that explaining, "I just keep thinking about that girl. She's out there somewhere, and I'm hoping we don't find her ripped to pieces on the side of the road."

Ratley sat down in the chair next to Singer's desk asking, "you don't think anything will come of what Sister Lee said do you?"

The sheriff opened up the box of food and began shoveling some of it into his mouth. He chewed on that question and paused thinking about how he should answer that. "I can tell you he will strike again, and this stays between us," he said. "From what I have seen on the map he has killed numerous times in the same general vicinity."

Ratley was all ears. He downed another gulp of tea listening to the sheriff. "This bastard has a quota to fill and he won't move on permanently until he has bagged his limit here," said the sheriff.

Sheriff Baker may have understood Hayden better than anyone. He simply couldn't determine where he would actually strike next. Part of him wished Sister Lee was gifted enough to pinpoint where the next body would turn up, but he didn't hold out that hope. The sheriff explained how Hayden's travel patterns were damn near impossible to predict especially to the degree Sister Lee had gone to, but he stopped himself confessing to the young deputy, "I wish she really could tell us though."

Ratley was still a little freaked out by the ride he took with her earlier that day. All he said to the sheriff at that point was, "I don't know sheriff. That was sure weird out there. Hell, I hadn't ever seen or heard of any shit like that before. You can ask Singer. It was like she was somewhere else, and the damn sky turned dark in almost no time."

The sheriff listened to the sound of Ratley's voice but his mind was elsewhere. He looked up at Ratley raising his fork telling him he better get on home and get some rest because he had a big day ahead of him tomorrow. Ratley said, "I know. It'll be here before we know it. You going home too?"

Sheriff Baker answered him saying, "yeah, I reckon I will." Thanking Ratley for the food, he led him to the door saying, "come on, let's get out of here."

The sheriff couldn't go straight home without patrolling Chanceville one last time. He felt as though he had let the people of the town down by allowing a predator such as Hayden Keller to enter into their peaceful little community. He cruised down the streets looking for anything that seemed unusual. If there was something he could do to prevent another Jefferson County resident from suffering the fate of the Ferris' the sheriff was intent on doing it.

It was quiet for the most part and the streets were deserted. There was no sign of Hayden Keller anywhere inside town. Sheriff Baker hoped it would remain that way overnight, but he knew nothing good would happen under the cover of darkness. He made a trip all the way out to Sister Lee's before he crossed over the main highway. He noticed her lights were still on, but he didn't dare approach her place at that hour. Pulling into the diner parking lot Ben had visited that morning, he questioned whether or not he should take

Highway 80 back home. He figured old Blue would be waiting on him when he pulled into the drive, and if he had waited this long another thirty minutes wouldn't amount to much in Blue's world. He was the best damn hunting dog in Jefferson County, and the sheriff was dead set on using old Blue's nose to help him find Hayden Keller.

Taking one last look at Sister Lee's little white house, the sheriff pulled back onto the road following the path Ben had made earlier that day. Sister Lee walked over to her window where she had watched as Ben sped into town. This time she saw the taillights of the sheriff's car as he headed back toward Chanceville. She slowly turned letting go of the curtain, and she took a seat in the chair Ben had turned over that afternoon. It was fast approaching the eleven o'clock hour, and in Sister Lee's world that was the hour of darkness where all things were concealed from her sight. Still, she sat there in the chair placing her hands on the table in front of her, and she meditated in an effort to see through the eyes of the man with two lives.

Sheriff Baker wasn't the only soul hunting for Hayden Keller. Sister Lee had now made it her mission to bring balance to the world, and that entailed stopping Hayden Keller before he took another life. She knew nothing of justice, nor did she believe in it, but she did understand that the world is filled with good and evil. Hayden was obviously the latter of the two, but one could not exist without the other.

In a spiritual realm where all things are possible and nothing is as it seems on the surface, Sister Lee could prove to be the most dangerous human being God ever put on this earth. She barely weighed a hundred and twenty pounds, but she held secrets to the universe others simply couldn't understand. She used the stars to predict destinies, and sometimes she used them to change fate. This came easy to her since she wasn't bound by the typical constraints of time and space. She now set her sights on hunting down the scarred lion using Ben as her arrow, and Hayden had no idea of her existence, but she knew more about him than even she revealed to Ratley.

Chapter 29

Startling Revelation

Attempting to tap into her clairvoyant abilities she softly chanted, "revelet ut mihi faciem malum," which in the language of old meant reveal to me the face of evil. As Sister Lee searched the mystical world to find it, Ben stared right into it.

Hayden removed his jacket revealing his many battle scars, and to Ben's horror he pointed to his right shoulder. He too had been grazed with a bullet, and that was just one of the numerous gunshot wounds he wore on his body. Hayden said, "looks like we have something in common Ben."

Ben's eyes opened with astonishment. It wasn't the scar on Hayden's shoulder that had his complete attention, it was the lion tattoo which covered it. Suddenly, the words of Sister Lee made sense, and Ben now knew he was destined to die. Hayden said, "you look as though you've seen a ghost Ben. Don't tell me I scared you again."
Ben blurted out, "the mark on your arm." He stopped himself from saying anything further.
Hayden glanced down at his shoulder admiring the handiwork placed there by a now deceased tattoo artist. He said, "you like it I see. Who knows, you play your cards right and maybe we'll get you one before you leave this shitty old world."

Ashley saw it as the mark of the beast, and she referred to it as such. Hayden smiled as he confessed, "I am that now."

Just to add some enjoyment to the road trip, Hayden said, "I'll tell you what Ben, you recall my name and I'll let you go, but you only have until sunup."

Ben had no idea what his real name was and even if he did Hayden wasn't about to let him go regardless of what he said. Sarcastically, Ben muttered, "you sure as hell aren't Rumpelstiltskin."

Hayden let go of a laugh as he commended Ben on his sense of humor. Hayden said, "you're one funny bastard Ben. I always liked that about you."

Ben was more perplexed by something else Sister Lee had said as he made his way out her door. He thought about it as Hayden continued to drive, but the answer never came to him. Hayden could tell he was in deep thought about something. "I see I've got you thinking Ben. You'll figure it out soon enough." That was all Hayden said. He drove back toward Chanceville to dispose of the severed body he was still carrying in the back of the SUV. He figured the trunk of Ben's car was a good place to stow it. He just neglected to make Ben aware of what his plans were. Hayden liked delivering surprises, especially gruesome ones that had his name written all over it.

Ben grew tired, and he was having trouble maintaining his focus. Ashley pointed out he was losing a lot of blood as Ben's hand slid lower down his arm and his eyes closed.

Hayden shouted, "wake the fuck up Ben. This ain't no time to fall asleep on me." Hayden swerved pulling the SUV off the road for a moment. He reached under the edge of his seat telling Ben he had something that might help stop the bleeding. When Ben opened his eyes to look down at his shoulder, Hayden grabbed hold of the large flathead screwdriver he used to disable Ben's car. Grasping it by the handle he quickly retrieved it jabbing it into Ben's arm. He pushed it in as deep as it would go striking the bone, and Ben let out a hellacious yell just before passing out from the pain.

Ashley pulled her hand to her mouth in horror as she screamed. Hayden left the screwdriver blade sticking in Ben's arm. He looked back at Ashley saying, "how's that for a quick fix?"

Ashley sat back in her seat afraid to utter a sound. She was trembling with fear as Hayden pulled back onto the road in search of Ben's car. Within less than two miles he rolled up next to it, and he shut off the engine. Ben's eyes remained closed, and Hayden pulled up next to his BMW. He rummaged through Ben's pockets pulling out his keys and then he slipped on his coat. One cold dark stare was given to Ashley. All Hayden said was, "take care of him for me until I get back," then he climbed out of the vehicle.

He reached down unlocking the doors so he could get the body out of the back, and Ashley shook Ben as Hayden walked over to unlock Ben's trunk. She said, "come on, wake up please. He's going to come back. We gotta go now."

Ben cracked his eyelids. He watched Hayden out of the corner of his eye. He was walking back to the SUV as Ben said, "you run when I tell you, not until then."

Hayden opened up the rear door, and he pulled out the bloody bedspread filled with severed remains. Ben carefully pulled the screwdriver out of his shoulder trying not to make a sound. Hayden carried what was left of Jamal over to Ben's vehicle and he forced it into Ben's compact trunk. In fact, he struggled to get it inside. Jamal's left leg wasn't cooperating. Hayden thought to himself, *it's a good thing I diced this one up.* He didn't see how it would fit otherwise.

Ben leaned over telling Ashley to run like hell, and don't look back as soon as he opens the door. Ashley asked, what about you? Aren't you coming?" Ben responded saying, "I'm in no shape to run but I can hold him up long enough for you to get away. Now you do what I say." Ashley knew this was her only chance and she could tell Ben was serious. In fact, he was right. If she could get away maybe she could get help before Hayden killed him. That was all just wishful thinking on the part of a young girl, but she was determined to do just what Ben said regardless of how afraid she was of failing to escape.

Hayden couldn't see what was taking place inside the SUV. He was preoccupied with stuffing Jamal's torso and the pesky left leg into the trunk. He forced the trunk shut and wiped his hands of the bloody mess. It was a job well done in his mind. He then turned to walk back to the SUV and Ashley whispered, "here he comes." She knew this was her only chance of getting away, and she had better not fail because there wouldn't be a next time. That's what she kept telling herself.

Hayden approached the driver's side door of the SUV, and Ben clinched the handle of the screwdriver firmly in his right hand. He could feel the adrenaline rush through his veins, and at that moment the pain he felt in his shoulder didn't matter much at all.

Ashley could hear the sound of the door unlatch as Hayden pulled the handle to open it, and she breathed heavily as her heart raced. The pounding it made beating inside her chest could almost be heard while she prepared to make her escape. Her chest suddenly tightened and her breathing became shallow right before Hayden climbed back inside the vehicle. That's when Ben yelled for her to run as he forcefully stabbed Hayden with the screwdriver, ramming it through his right thigh with every ounce of strength he had left in him. He held on tight to the handle pinning Hayden's leg to the seat of the SUV and Ashley exited the vehicle leaving the rear door hanging wide open. She fled straight for the trees searching franticly for an opening in the woods where she could enter. She knew without question the wolf would soon be behind her, tracking her down like helpless prey.

Hayden drew his breath holding it in his lungs sensing the pain which shot through his leg. Looking toward the backseat he could see her getting away through the open door of the Tahoe as she scrambled through the brush before disappearing into the trees. His face became contorted in utter anger. He refrained from making any sound other than a pained grunting noise which escaped his throat as he exhaled. Filled with rage Hayden gasped, "damn it Ben!" He reached for his gun taking the butt of it to Ben's head, and he repeatedly struck him with it.

Ben released his grip on the screwdriver handle as Hayden pummeled him without mercy pounding the butt of the pistol against his brain. Knocking him unconscious, he earnestly admitted, "you're learning Ben. I think I may have underestimated you."

There was blood spatter all over the front seat. He could even taste Ben's blood on his teeth as he spoke, and Hayden wanted to finish what he started, but there wasn't time. Looking over at Ben's bludgeoned face, Hayden realized he had to retrieve Ashley before she gained too much of a head start. The fact that he was now injured made it much more challenging, but Hayden lived for that.

Placing his gun inside his jacket, Hayden lifted his right leg slightly before dragging it across the seat and stepping out of the SUV. He was forced to put all of his weight on his left leg as he hobbled to the rear of the Tahoe. With his teeth firmly clinched, he opened the back door to retrieve the roll of duct tape he had stashed there for just such an occasion. Quickly removing the screwdriver from his leg, he wrapped the wound securely with tape. Hayden drew his knife slicing through the tape as if it were butter, and he then looked up to see if he could tell where Ashley had run off to.

Limping across the road, his eyes scanned for any sign of her. Hearing the rustling sound of leaves deep in the woods, he knew he would find his prey soon enough. All he had to do was follow the sound knowing it would lead him right to her. Hayden's mouth began to salivate as he entered the woods after her. Carrying the knife in his left hand, he wasted no time. The hunt was underway, and he stalked the girl once more.

Chapter 30

No Safe Haven

Hayden relentlessly pursued her through the trees. He chased after her as she struggled to make her way through the darkness. Hearing something behind her Ashley paused. She looked over her shoulder. She knew Hayden was in the woods with her. She just didn't know how close he was to finding her. Ashley could see the headlights of the SUV in the distance through the trees, but no sign of Hayden. In fact, she couldn't see anything else at all. She took several more steps holding her hands out in front of her. Blindly trying to feel for obstacles blocking her path she started to run deeper into the woods, but she fell to her knees. She had tripped over something, probably a root or a branch of some sort. Ashley attempted to get up. She turned looking all around her trying to recover her bearings. Her mind flashed back to the last time she attempted to hide from Hayden in the woods. Ashley stood regaining her balance as a shadow blocked out what little light she could see coming from the SUV.

Her face was filled with anguish as she turned seeing Hayden's silhouette against the headlights, and he was coming after her. His shadow was rapidly moving toward her. Ashley let out a panicked cry and she began running once again. This time she didn't stop to look back over her shoulder. She sobbed, franticly searching for an opening to make her way out of the woods. She became confused not knowing which way to turn. Unsure of where she was going she ventured deeper into the woods. Continuing to run full speed until she neared a clearing, Hayden followed losing ground, but he was determined to catch her no matter what the cost.

Reaching the edge of the clearing, she peered at what looked to be a light way off in the distance. Ashley could tell it was coming from the porch of a house that sat several hundred feet away. She hyperventilated making a mad dash for the little house hoping someone would be there. Her tears had temporarily stopped. She was focused only on reaching the door of the small house.

Hayden watched her as she crossed the clearing in a useless attempt to find a safe place to hide from him. Standing there at the edge of the woods, Hayden's face carried a stone cold look about it as she raced toward the little house. The emotionless scowl he directed toward Ashley was as serious as death itself. Hayden's eyebrows pulled in close to the bridge of his nose as he continued pursuit, struggling to catch up to her. He was determined to make her pay for causing him so much trouble.

Ashley ran up on the front porch and began pounding on the front door. Mrs. Harris awoke from her not so peaceful slumber to the sound of Ashley beating on her door. Now startled by the sound of Ashley's panicked voice, and the ruckus she was making on the front door, Mrs. Harris remained completely motionless. Still in her bed, she pulled her hand to her chest trying to catch her breath. She slowly turned her head looking over at her window. Seeing a ominous shadow pass by it she exclaimed, "oh, dear God!" The elderly woman's hand shook as she reached over toward her nightstand. She pulled open the drawer and reached inside retrieving a .44 caliber revolver. Holding the gun in both hands she sat on the edge of the bed tormented by the sounds she heard outside her isolated country home.

Fearing for her own life, she stood as she made her way into the hallway just outside her bedroom door. She recited the Lord's Prayer as she walked down the hallway while pointing the gun at the door.

Ashley continued beating on the door incessantly. She pleaded for someone to open it. Tormented by the thought of Hayden placing his hands on her again she screamed, "please! Open the door. Can anyone hear me? Help me, please! I'm begging you. Please open the door!" She was in utter tears begging for help as Mrs. Harris prayed, "deliver us from evil."

Hayden turned the corner without making a sound. He stood at the foot of the steps right behind Ashley. She had yet to see him, but she made one last attempt to get someone to the door. Desperately, with a fear filled shrill present in her voice she cried out, "he's coming for me!"

Mrs. Harris moved closer to the door. She saw the shadow which passed by her window casting itself on the window closest to Ashley. Trembling, she raised the gun a little pointing the barrel of it at the horrifying shadow that took her breath away. She knew whatever loomed outside her door was unholy in every sense of the word. She deliberately squeezed the trigger as she finished the prayer, firing a shot right through the window next to the door.

Ashley screamed as the bullet pierced the window right beside her head. Hayden moved slightly to avoid being struck by the bullet. He then stepped onto the porch, and Ashley heard his footsteps hitting the old wooden planks. She didn't even have time to turn much less flee.

Hayden came up behind her, and she could see his shadow overtake hers against the house. She screamed, "No! He's here! Somebody please." For her there was no sanctuary.

Mrs. Harris sat on the floor with her back against a chair. She stared open-eyed at the window and the front door. Her mouth was partially agape adding a look of confusion to the shocked expression which covered her face. All she could hear were Ashley's petrified screams.

Hayden was enraged. Grabbing her by the hair he pulled her to the ground before dragging her off the porch. Mrs. Harris could hear Hayden's heavy footsteps leaving the front porch, and she heard Ashley's heels kick the boards as she struggled to free herself.

Hayden drug her away from the house and her screams soon faded. Knowing she was about to die, Ashley began to cry uncontrollably. The last thing Mrs. Harris heard in the distance was Ashley pleading with evil itself. "Don't kill me. Please don't, I'll do anything. I'm begging you."

Hayden scoffed at her saying, "that's all you seem to be able to do. Begging is very unbecoming Ashley, especially for a young lady such as yourself. Didn't your parents ever teach you that?"

Ashley cried out, "why are you doing this to me?"

Hayden responded with, "it's not all about you Ashley. It's about us." He ruthlessly dragged her through the woods reminding her of their previous agreement. "I thought we were working on our relationship. You know, trusting one another." He then purposely jerked her hair just to inflict more pain on her as he announced, "you disappointed me Ashley. Someone is going to have to pay for this you know."

Hayden was still livid that Ben had gotten a leg up on him by jamming that fucking screwdriver into him. He was determined to kill one of them, but now wasn't the time. The pain Hayden felt in his leg was now excruciating, but Hayden loved pain, even his own. It's what made him feel alive. He steadily made his way back to the SUV pulling Ashley through the woods over rocks and fallen branches which scraped against her body and legs. He informed her she could never escape from him, no matter what she prayed for. Then he added, "that cross you carry around your neck, it won't do you any good out here. Out here, I'm the one in control of things. You and Ben will soon come to understand that. I'll see to it."

Hayden found it amusing that either of them thought it possible to escape. Still, he appreciated the effort and he told Ashley that right as they neared the edge of the woods next to the highway. Hayden pulled her toward the SUV expecting to find Ben right where he left him. Shoving Ashley into the back seat he said, "well, here we are - you, me and Ben together again." Noticing his other passenger was missing, Hayden voiced his immediate thought out loud. "Where the fuck is Ben?"

Chapter 31

Power Of The Third Eye

The hour of darkness drew to an end. Sister Lee brought her hands together touching the tips of her thumbs and forefingers together. Forming a triangle using her hands, her eyes were closed as she focused all of her energy on the man with two lives. His name, she knew not. She only knew Ben by what was written in the palm of his hand. That, however, didn't prevent her from seeing the events that were unfolding through his eyes. She was sitting right where Ben had sat, and she was connected to him in a mental state of consciousness that Ben had never experienced before. Sister Lee saw the ground moving in front of Ben's feet. He was putting distance between himself and the black SUV.

Hayden took the duct tape, and he used it to restrain Ashley in the back seat of the Tahoe once more. This time he hastily wrapped the tape around Ashley's arms and legs and he shoved her into the rear floorboard. Locking her inside the SUV, he followed the blood trail Ben had left him knowing he couldn't have made it too far. Hayden hollered, "ready or not, here I come!"

Ben paused hearing Hayden's voice. Sister Lee could see the dark outline of Hayden moving toward Ben. He was beating the brush away with something as he hobbled closer. Suddenly, she saw nothing but tall grass in her vision, and she knew Ben's face had to be against the ground. Unable to tell if the scarred lion had found him, she opened her eyes losing sight of what was happening. The last thing she saw was total darkness and that could mean one of two things. Either Ben shut his eyes or he had been devoured by the beast which stalked him like prey, and still she knew nothing of the girl.

Hayden came upon Ben clinging to the ground. He laid there motionless on his stomach in the tall grass trying desperately not to be found. Hearing Hayden approach, he tried to crawl away without being seen. The tall grass moved directing Hayden to his exact location. Hayden informed him, "you're giving away your position Ben. Now, I'm going to have to kill you."

Ben immediately rose to his feet and ran for cover toward a stand of trees less than fifty feet away. Hayden pulled his gun firing two shots, one of them hitting Ben right in the leg. He watched Ben fall to the ground, and he could hear the impact of his body hitting the dirt. Hayden took that moment to remind him that he was in control, and told him point blank, "I'm going to pick you apart until you beg for it to end." He stood over Ben adding, "I don't guess either one of us will be running anymore. Now get your sorry ass back in the Tahoe. Ashley's waiting for you and she's probably worried sick about now."

Ben covered his wounded leg with his left hand, his right hand held firmly to his left shoulder. Hayden stood putting full weight on his injured leg and he kicked Ben which ironically delivered pain to both of them. Hayden told him in no uncertain terms, "you're going to pay for this Ben." Ben needed help and Hayden was going to give it to him just to keep him alive a little while longer. He forced him back inside the SUV, and he inspected Ben's recent collection of wounds. Hayden couldn't refrain from saying, "damn Ben you're starting to look like Swiss cheese. I guess this night just went from bad to worse."

Ben was too exhausted to muster much of a response, all he mumbled was, "it's a bad moon."

Hayden retrieved the roll of duct tape from the back seat and he administered his special brand of first aid. Tearing off a piece of tape he instructed Ben to place it over his shoulder. Hayden tightly wrapped Ben's leg to stop the bleeding using up the last of the tape. Ben couldn't figure out why Hayden even bothered.

Sister Lee attempted once more to gain a glimpse of the scarred lion as she sat at the table inside her parlor. Leaning forward slightly, she closed her eyes again. She concentrated placing the palms of her hands on the tapestry which rested on the table in front of her. Forming the same mystic symbol she made before using her hands, she raised it to her brow holding it in the place of her third eye. The words she spoke this time were, "succurro ostendo sum volo," which in her tongue meant help reveal to me. She softly whispered the words using her mind's eye to connect with Ben. Within seconds she was staring through his eyes once again.

A strange feeling came over Ben as if he suddenly gained an awareness he had not felt ever before. It was almost as though Sister Lee was right there with him. Ben never consciously made that connection though, he simply felt different. Ben looked over his shoulder at Ashley as Hayden walked around to the driver's side of the Tahoe. Hayden moved a little slower climbing back in the SUV. He grabbed hold of the wheel, and Ben glanced over at his injured leg.

Sister Lee had seen the girl's face but not Hayden's. For some reason Ben avoided looking at him, and it frustrated

Sister Lee that she still had no face to put on the evil one.

Ben was exhausted. He had lost a fair amount of blood. He closed his eyes thinking about what Sister Lee had said to him. That's when her vision went black once more. Still, she focused on her connection with Ben hoping he would open his eyes to allow her to see the evil one.

Hayden scolded them saying, "you two are something else, you know that. The fact that either of you think you can escape from me is downright laughable." He began to ramble at that point as he said, "I guess you don't get my sense of humor though. Do you? Maybe I'm the only one that sees the humor in that. Never mind I get it. That's all that matters, but now one of you is going to have to die. Question is, which one will it be."

Ashley was terrified, but Ben didn't flinch. He just sat there with his eyes still closed. Hayden drew his gun to get their attention, and he extended his arm pointing it directly at Ben's temple. He growled, "any last words?"

Ben's eyes opened feeling the cold metal barrel of the gun touch the side of his head. Still, it didn't make sense. Why bother patching him up just to shoot him minutes later? That being logical, Ben had to realize Hayden was insane, and logic simply didn't apply to him. Could he pull that trigger and end Ben's life? The answer was absolutely, but Ben didn't feel as though it was his time to die just yet. He knew not his purpose for enduring Hayden's wrath, but he figured there was reason behind it and it would reveal itself in time. He also believed Hayden would kill him at some point because Sister Lee had warned him not to touch the scarred lion with cancer. That was the part Ben struggled with as he tried to figure it out. His mind flashed back to when he first bumped into Hayden, and that's when the gun moved away from Ben's head.

Hayden now pointed it at the back seat where Ashley sat with her hands and feet bound together. Hayden questioned her saying, "how about you?" Looking straight down the barrel of the gun she remained speechless as well.

Ben spoke up, drawing Hayden's attention to him asking, "why does anyone have to die?"

Hayden replied, "you only have one life Ben and that's borrowed time. Everyone has to give it back sooner or later."

Ben posed another important question to him, "why does it have to be now?"

Hayden took the gun pointing it back at Ben holding it right in front of his face so he couldn't help but see it as he replied, "balance, fate, my will take your pick. You ask a lot of questions Ben. Don't worry, I like that about you. It shows you wish to get to know me better. I think I'll miss that about you most of all. You still don't know who I am, do you?"

Ben begrudgingly said, "I know you're nothing but pure evil."

Hayden said, "you're getting closer Ben, but there's nothing pure about evil, and I aim to prove it to you."

With Ben's eyes now open looking at Hayden's hand holding the gun on him, Sister Lee could see all. Shadows covered Hayden's face to the point she couldn't describe it in detail. Still, she viewed everything through Ben, and she had a hard time separating herself from him. Their chakras were linked and Ben now understood another piece of Sister Lee's vision. They were tied together in such a way that it was difficult for Sister Lee not to feel as though the gun was being pointed directly at her. All she could do at that moment was offer him her wisdom and strength.

Suddenly, Ben became aware that he was sent to save Ashley from Hayden. Maybe that's the only real purpose his life served in the end, but Ben knew he had to stay alive long enough to see Ashley free from Hayden's control. How that would come about he didn't know, but it certainly entailed both of them living a little while longer.

Now mentally drained, Sister Lee struggled to maintain her supernatural connection to Ben, but the power of her third eye weakened to the point where all she saw was darkness. Only time could now reveal what would happen as Sister Lee hung her head with little hope.

Chapter 32

Dire Consequences

Ben was Sister Lee's only link to Hayden even though she had not yet discovered his name. Still Hayden's captive, he stared at Hayden's trigger finger as it repeatedly tapped the trigger of the gun. Hayden enjoyed making Ben sweat. He toyed with pulling the trigger. Unexpectedly, Hayden offered up a proposal saying, "I think we should let Ashley decide who lives and who dies Ben. Ladies choice if you will."

Hayden turned the pistol around and he handed it to Ashley. Her hands were taped together resting in her lap and Hayden pushed the handle of the gun toward her telling her to take it. She had never touched a gun before in her life, much less fired one. Hayden encouraged her to make good on her promise, "here's your chance to prove to me you'll do anything to stay alive Ashley. All you have to do is shoot old Ben here, and put him out of his misery, but make it count cause you only have one bullet."

Ben tried to reason with her, "listen to me. No one has to die Ashley. Not you and not me. I promise."

Hayden cut him off saying, "that's real touching Ben, but you're not holding the gun, are you." He then looked at Ashley as he said, "I don't think he'd feel the same way if he were in your shoes Ashley, but like I said someone has to die."

Ashley looked back at Ben listening to Hayden's words, "this is pretty exciting, huh Ben." Her palms became moist as she held the gun with both hands. She didn't know what to do. She sure as hell didn't want to shoot Ben.

Hayden felt the need to educate her saying, "let me give you a pointer or two. First you need to point it at him in order to accomplish the task, and the second thing you have to do involves squeezing the trigger." Casually shrugging his shoulders Hayden added, "that's all there really is to it. Isn't that right Ben? You've seen me do it."

Against her will she raised the gun pointing it at Ben. She didn't want to die. Hayden had made it clear one of them was going to have to lose their life as a result of their failed escape attempt. Hayden yelled, "it's time for someone to die Ashley," pressuring her to pull the trigger.

Ben looked into her eyes. She was scared as hell. She ever so slightly moved her head from side to side hoping Hayden wouldn't notice. Ben cut his eyes toward Hayden encouraging Ashley to shoot him instead.

Hayden continued taking in the show. He directed his comments toward Ben as he said, "she seems to have a strong desire to keep breathing, although I don't know why. If she were smart she would use that bullet on herself and avoid having me kill her Ben. I guarantee you if I do it, it won't be near as quick and painless." Hayden started to lose what little patience he had and that's when he shouted, "come on Ashley, do us all a favor. Hell he's already half dead, now shoot him."

Ben looked into Ashley's eyes saying, "don't do it Ashley. He's trying to play you. Put the gun down." Hayden took his eyes off of Ashley, and he scornfully stared at Ben. Just as Hayden started to speak, Ashley quickly moved the gun pointing it directly at Hayden's head, and she squeezed the trigger. Hearing the clicking sound the gun made as she attempted to fire it, Hayden grinned. He looked directly at her, a scowl took the place of the wretched smile he had on his vile face. Thoroughly disgusted by the sight of him still breathing, she pulled the trigger again and again. Still no shot was fired. There was no round in the chamber to fire. Hayden had set her up, and she fell for it.

Now faced with the reality that there were no bullets in the gun, Ashley started crying. This nightmare seemed as if it was never going to end. Fearing the worst, her hands shook as Hayden reached over snatching the gun out of her hands. His gruff voice sent chills through Ashley's spine as he said, "that was a grave mistake you made there Ashley. I think you'll live to regret it." Turning his attention to Ben he cranked up the SUV saying, "you didn't think I'd hand a loaded weapon to a girl did you? No, that would just be plain crazy, now wouldn't it?"

Hayden pointed out that he was in total control as he drove down the dark stretch of road headed toward Chanceville. He reminded Ashley that God had deserted her, and the necklace she wore around her neck offered her no protection. He mocked her faith, and he told her to take it off promising he would allow her to live to see another day.

Ben shook his head as he silently mouthed the word "don't."
Hayden glanced over at him and he confronted Ben saying, "you got something to say Ben?" Hayden slammed on brakes throwing the Tahoe in park as he plunged the pistol into Ben's shoulder. Ben's eyes opened wide feeling the pain of the blow to his injured arm. Hayden hit him several more times as he shouted, "I'm the one running this show Ben, not you." He then ran his fingers through his hair

trying to regain his composure by stifling his temper. In a more reserved tone he spoke directly to Ashley without looking at her. He pointed out that Ben would now pay the price for her silly attachment to the cross hanging from her neck. He made it clear that Ben would suffer greatly until she did as he said, and he added, "but that's okay. God made men to suffer Ben. He made me to see to it. Who am I now?"

Ben said nothing, but Ashley spouted, "you're the devil." Hayden delivered a wicked laugh saying, "oh now you try to flatter me, I see. That's alright. You're not the first person to mistake me for him Ashley, and my guess is you won't be the last."

"If you're not Satan then who are you," Ashley questioned. "Oh, now that you see is for Ben to figure out," Hayden replied. Hayden lied saying, "I hope for his sake he comes up with the right answer." In another attempt to get Ashley to remove the cross from around her neck Hayden told her, "I will kill him. You know that, but if you don't do as I say I'll put him through hell before I take him out of this world." A devilish look appeared in Hayden's eye as he said, "don't be afraid Ashley. Trust me, he doesn't care about you." Looking in the rear view mirror at the cross Hayden attested, "even Peter denied him thrice in one day, and he was his favorite you know. Surely, he wouldn't hold it against you. I asked you once before what has he done for you, and still you have no answer. So, why hang onto him when he has cast you aside to the wolf?"

Ashley looked down at the crucifix her grandmother had given her, and she remembered the words her grandmother spoke when she placed the chain around her neck. They were words of courage, sacrifice, love, and hope. Ashley believed in that even after all she had been through, but Hayden had placed a question in her mind about God's concern for her. Perhaps all mankind was enough to move him to action, but the prayers of a seventeen year old girl were not so important. It was a dangerous line of thinking she had entered into, and Hayden knew he was on the verge of shaking her faith to the point where she would question if God cared at all.

Hayden told her to think about it as he drove off down the highway in search of a place to lie low. He knew she would give into his demands when the time came. All he had to do was threaten her with Ben's life. Hayden also figured the state police would surmise that he had continued west after shooting the old man back at the gas station in Justice. The last place they would expect him to be was Chanceville.

Sheriff Baker, however, had figured out Hayden's unusual nature. He knew he would kill again in Jefferson County unless he was stopped. On the surface, it would seem illogical, but in retrospect it bordered on genius. It was simply unfortunate that the gift be bestowed upon one so, evil as Hayden Keller.

Hayden had been at this game a long time, and the choice was easy enough for him. Hell, he liked Chanceville, the name of the town mostly. Truth was Hayden couldn't think of a better place to hang out with Ben and Ashley. What better place on earth could there be to determine which one lived and which one died? It was just fitting that it should all end there. Besides, that was the place where he and Ben first met. Hayden appreciated the irony in that.

Chapter 33

Final Hour Of Darkness

It was a cold dark night which led into early morning. Plenty of evil filled it, both out on the roads, and in the minds of those that feared it. The sun had yet to rise, and the people of Chanceville were still asleep in their beds. Many of them were unable to sleep as a result of the recent killings which had taken place near their little town.

Ratley found himself among those that couldn't get a peaceful night's rest to save their life. He had been awake for well over an hour, all due to a nightmare he had which wouldn't allow him to fall back asleep. The dream he had was so real and vivid, he questioned whether or not it was actually happening. It was probably a collection of things that had gotten to him.

What he saw out at the Ferris farm, which Singer had accurately called a slaughterhouse, gave Ratley some idea of what kind of evil lurked outside. He knew the night provided the perfect cover to conceal it. He wasn't the only one that feared what existed in the shadows. Even his conversation with some of the townspeople had made an impression on him he couldn't shake. The ride he took with Singer and Sister Lee added another frightening element to the uneasy feeling he carried around inside. All that combined was enough to give anyone a nightmare, but never had he experienced one like this.

Looking over at the alarm clock next to the bed he noted the time. Recounting parts of his nightmare it all seemed real. He woke up in a cold sweat short of breath. He sat there in his bed looking around the room trying to process what he saw in his dark vivid dream, telling himself it wasn't reality. That didn't change the fact that it alarmed the hell out of him. He thought of Mrs. Harris and then about Sister Lee, and what she would have to say regarding his God awful nightmare.

As Ratley fought to put himself at ease, Ben fought to stay alive still trapped inside the SUV right along with Ashley. Hayden flipped on the light inside the Tahoe. He sat in the driver's seat administering his unique blend of philosophy and torture. Blowing a steady stream of smoke through his nose, he looked over at Ben. His detest for Ben lessened some, mostly because he presented a challenge, one which Hayden hadn't encountered in some time. Ashley had also endeared herself to him, simply out of her stubbornness to continue to live, and her will to pull the trigger.

Ben's eyes were closed. Even under the stress of being held captive, he rested. He was biding his time, waiting to make his next move. Prudently, he tried not to expend any more energy than he had to.

Hayden grew bored waiting for the sun to appear, and he snuffed out his cigarette on the back of Ben's hand just to cause him more pain. Determined to rattle his cage further, Hayden bellowed, "you still alive Ben?" Ben jerked his hand away. He opened and closed it trying to suppress the pain he felt from the cigarette burn, but he didn't utter a sound. His eyes were now wide open though, and Hayden had his complete attention. Hayden then said, "that's good. No fair dying on me in your sleep. The sun will be up in a little while, and we have business to tend to." Pulling out his revolver, he loaded a bullet into the cylinder. Then he closed it rolling it over his forearm. He made sure Ben knew there was a live round inside it. Pointing it at Ben's head, he said, "I don't think I can wait until sunup Ben. Are you a sporting man? I know I am."

Ben was tired of Hayden's twisted games. He wanted it to end, but his only thought was for Ashley. Maybe that was what allowed him to endure all that Hayden had put him through. Regardless of how Hayden attempted to torture him Ben remained silent. He deprived Hayden of his satisfaction simply by keeping his pain to himself. He knew it wouldn't stop Hayden from causing him further discomfort, but he realized as long as Hayden's vengeance was directed at him, Ashley remained alive. Ben tried not to show his fear to Hayden, but his greatest fear was that Hayden would use Ashley once again as a means of working on him psychologically. Ben told himself as long as the girl lives nothing else matters, and that's how he dealt with Hayden's malevolent personality.

Hayden taunted him by saying, "let's give this a shot shall we." Then he pulled the trigger as he listened to the hammer click without firing the round he placed inside the gun. Ben's eyes quickly blinked when Hayden pulled the trigger, and they opened stunned to still be alive.

Time passed slow after that. Ben's heart no longer raced regardless of what Hayden did or said. He had reached that pinnacle point where one accepts their demise. What Ben wouldn't have given to have the upper-hand. He would have done things much differently if only given the chance, but time was on Hayden's side and with the exception of the wounded leg all was going to plan.

He and Hayden continued waiting for the morning sun. With it came another life which Hayden could take and that made a total of two. He informed Ben it was the final hour of darkness they were in, and although it wasn't his time to die at that moment, eventually it would come. Hayden continued saying, "I bet you got a real nice life back home, don't you Ben. You probably got a nice house, even a little family, maybe a few friends that put up with you." Is that what has you hanging on Ben? Something does, I know. Why don't you tell me what it is you live for? I'm curious Ben."

Ben looked into Hayden's hollow eyes and he said, "seeing you burn in hell."

Hayden casually looked away breaking eye contact with Ben for a moment before looking back at him. That's when Hayden said, "now come on Ben, I think you're taking this way too personal. That's a terrible thing to say. Have you ever seen hell up close? I'm telling you it's no place you want to spend any time in." Hayden then pointed out that in order for that to happen Ben would have to actually be there himself to see it. That brought out a detestable laugh. Hayden made certain to tell him, "see you in hell Ben."

He revealed his true face, the one only seen by his victims, right before death. His eyes were now filled with fire and rage as he stared back into Ben's eyes.

Ben was scared stiff to the point he could not look away. He was forced to face his demons just as his horoscope predicted. Hayden was a demon in his own right and the words Sister Lee spoke had come true. Hayden Keller would see to it that Ben burned in hell right along with him, but there was one life which Hayden knew nothing of, and it was dedicated to destroying him. Only time could prove whether or not it would come to be more powerful than him.

Hayden said, "to tell you the truth, I don't know why you keep hanging on. Most guys in your shoes would have begged me to end it long before now. You must just love my company Ben." Hayden banged the butt of the gun against Ben's shoulder. He wanted to see his painful look once again, and Ashley asked him to stop. That's when Hayden looked over his shoulder at her telling her to shut up.

Placing the gun back inside his coat, Hayden pulled out his knife threatening to cut out Ashley's tongue if she said another word. Hayden talked down to her as if she were nothing. He assaulted her verbally using words like cancer and garbage. He began to blame her for all the problems in the world, but Ben became incensed and he interrupted Hayden's chide remarks. Instantly, Hayden became silent as Ben shouted, "it's not her fault you're fucked up!"

Hayden placed the tip of the blade under Ben's right eye and applied pressure. "Maybe if I cut it out, we can see eye to eye on this Ben." That was all Hayden said before he pulled the knife away from Ben's face leaving a sizable gash on his left cheek. Not another sound was made inside the vehicle. Evil had shown its face, and they all had much to think about as Hayden, Ben and Ashley all planned their escape. Hayden, of course, sought to stay free from capture while Ben welcomed death when the time came, and Ashley longed to be free from Hayden Keller. The last hour of darkness was dismal indeed.

Chapter 34

Guts And Bloodhounds

Sheriff Baker was up at the crack of dawn as usual. He normally fixed himself a bite of breakfast while he savored the first few sips of his morning coffee. This particular morning was no different except he hadn't slept well knowing a killer was still on the loose in his jurisdiction. He questioned what the day would hold as he threw on his shirt before walking to the front door.

Blue was waiting for him on the porch like every other morning they had shared together since he was a pup. Sometimes there was a table scrap in it for him, but there was always a soothing scratch on the head followed by a nice pat on the back. It was the same old routine for both of them. However, this morning Sheriff Baker carried Blue's leash in his hand when he walked out to his car and Blue happened to notice. He sat there on the porch his eyes following the sheriff's every move.

The sheriff said nothing walking toward the car, and old Blue adjusted his head trying to figure things out. He started to lay down on the porch, but his head was facing in the direction of the sheriff's car, and his eyes remained trained on it never looking away for an instant. That's when the sheriff hollered, "well come on, get your ass in here if you're going. I don't have all day." Blue's ears moved slightly. He raised his head as the sheriff spoke.

When Sheriff Baker opened the car door, old Blue bolted for the vehicle, and he wasted no time jumping right in the passenger seat. He was ready to track down something or somebody. Whether or not it was a serial killer they were after made no difference to Blue. To him, he was just another man to hunt, another scent to track, but to the sheriff, he was the fugitive from hell.

Singer pulled up just about the time Sheriff Baker got to the office. He knew what the sheriff had in mind as soon as he saw old Blue riding shotgun. He wanted to catch that cold blooded bastard just as much as the sheriff did, but he figured the man they were after had put many miles between himself and Chanceville by now.

Getting out of his car, Singer shook off the cold morning chill saying, "well from what I hear around town this morning it seems like it was a quiet night."

Sheriff Baker nodded his head as he led Blue up the steps to his office. All he said in response was, "let's just hope it stays that way."

The sheriff's tone sounded worrisome, and Singer asked if he was concerned about what Sister Lee had said. The sheriff responded, "until this guy is caught, hell yeah I'm concerned, but I don't put much stock in a vision. When I see it with my own eyes then we've got a problem, but right now I want us to focus on the evidence."

Singer offered, "well, maybe we'll get a match on those prints and identify our suspect."

The sheriff told him he was counting on that, and he caught Singer up on his latest findings.

Singer grumbled about not having any coffee while he checked the voicemail, and Sheriff Baker looked over some information which was faxed overnight. It was a quarter after eight and there still was no sign of Ratley. They soon began to question if he was going to make it into the office at all. He was normally there before the sheriff to open the door and put the coffee on.

Singer complained about not knowing where the coffee filters were just about the time Ratley walked through the front door nearly twenty minutes late. Predictably, the senior deputy started to give him a hard time saying, "I was wondering if you forgot how to get here. We're trying to track down a killer, you know."

Ratley removed his hat, and he shook his head a little taking off his coat. He seemed somewhat out of sorts. That's when he told Singer he had a terrible dream that woke him up in the middle of the night and he walked over to his desk. Ratley still looked deeply disturbed by it as he said, "it was about Mrs. Harris. I hope she's alright."

Singer scoffed at his unwarranted fear saying, "look anybody that road in the car with that woman yesterday is probably bound to have a nightmare or two as a result. Hell, I know I was up half the night myself."

Ratley replied, "that's different you hardly ever get a decent night's sleep."

Singer boasted saying, "four and half hours. That's all you need, anything more is just a waste."

Ratley questioned Singer about what he did with all the extra time, and Singer told him he could tell him every line there was in every Andy Griffith episode. He then added, "and I'm not going to lie to you, I watch a lot of *Matlock* when I can't find a good *In The Heat Of The Night* on." Ratley shook his head. He even snickered a little forgetting all about Mrs. Harris and his dream.

The sheriff stuck his head out of his office hearing that, and he put them both on notice, "good maybe you can figure out who killed Mr. and Mrs. Ferris." That, of course, got their attention. Then the sheriff said, "I can't believe between the two of you my coffee mug is still empty. Do you think one of you could manage to figure out how that machine works?"

The sheriff was in a foul mood, and for good reason, two more dead bodies found in the next county. He closed the door to his office as he walked back to his desk, and his deputies scrambled to fix him a cup of coffee. They could see him through the window into his office and the sheriff appeared highly agitated, picking up the phone.

"Damn he's on edge, ain't he," Singer gasped. Ratley confessed that the sheriff didn't leave the office until a little after ten the night before and Singer said, "it's the girl."

Ratley knew the sheriff was highly concerned with finding the missing girl, and he wanted her recovered unharmed. It was a lot to ask for obviously. He also wanted the bastard that took her dead. Still, Ratley had a puzzled look on his face when Singer walked over to his desk to pick up a folder. He flipped through some of the pages within it and Ratley started the coffee brewing.

Singer eventually said, "I just saw this yesterday after we got back from our drive through the twilight zone." Ratley nodded his head toward the folder, and Singer pulled out a photograph which he showed to him. The young deputy paused looking at the picture of Ashley. Singer asked, "does this look like anyone we know?"

Ratley looked up at him with a serious look plastered on his face admitting the obvious, "looks a lot like Rebecca."

Singer nodded his head in agreement adding, "and don't you think he has noticed it too?"

Rebecca was the sheriff's only daughter. She was older

than Ashley with a family all her own, but the sheriff still had a picture of her on his desk that was taken of the two of them when she was younger. The resemblance to Ashley was remarkable. There was simply no way for him not to think of his daughter when he looked at the photograph of Ashley Pennington. This case had become very personal indeed. The sheriff realized her immediate family had been killed by this psychopath they were in search of, but she still had a grandmother that prayed for her safe return. The sheriff was committed to doing everything in his power to find her. Despite the odds of surviving after missing over forty-eight hours in the hands of a twisted killer, the sheriff believed she still had a chance. He only hoped he could get to her in time.

Singer took the photograph from Ratley and placed it back inside the folder. Ratley now watched the sheriff through the glass window next to the door of his office. The sheriff was placing another thumbtack on the map next to his door. That could only mean one thing, more bodies were found. Singer looked over to see what had Ratley's attention. Leaning his head slightly to get a better look, he said, "damn, that don't look good." Ratley remained speechless wondering if Sister Lee was right. He didn't dare raise that question though. He knew both Singer and Sheriff Baker didn't believe in that mumbo jumbo.

Sheriff Baker picked the phone back up, and he leaned up against his desk staring at the map on his wall. It was peppered with pushpins, and the look on Sheriff Baker's face was one of deep thought. His deputies watched him through the window only looking away when he glanced up at them. Ratley began to fumble through some papers on his desk, and Singer poured himself a cup of coffee just about the time the sheriff ended his call. They couldn't really hear anything through the glass, but they knew another body had been discovered. They could tell by the sheriff's demeanor it wasn't the girl's.

Sheriff Baker grimly opened the door to his office and he clued his deputies into what was going on. The sheriff said, "well, I was right. He struck again they believe, but this time it wasn't in our backyard."

Singer pressed him for the exact location asking, "where?"

The sheriff's reply was, "they got two dead bodies in Justice and they believe he's headed west.

Ratley asked, "is there any sign of the girl?"

Sheriff Baker replied, "no not yet, but I'm not so sure he's moving on that quickly." He paused a minute before speaking as he looked down at Blue. Then the sheriff said, "I'm taking Blue out there, and we're going to determine for sure what direction he's headed in." He confidently added, "and I'll bet you dollars to donuts he's coming back here."

The deputies looked at one another trying to gain a gut feeling for what the sheriff was saying. When you got right down to it that gut feeling the sheriff had was similar to Sister Lee's prediction in a sense. The sheriff would never refer to his gut as a sixth sense, but he trusted it wholeheartedly. It had yet to let him down. He had preached to his deputies over the years to never doubt it by saying, "you always follow your gut, no matter what." That was the sheriff's first rule and he never broke it.

Ironically, the only concrete difference between what the sheriff felt deep within him, and Sister Lee's extra sensory perception was the sheriff could point to his pushpin dotted map, and rest his assumptions on years of investigative work. It was easy enough to discount the lifetime Sister Lee had spent predicting that which was yet to come. She didn't have a badge or a certificate of achievement for years served in law enforcement hanging on the wall.

Seconds passed while the deputies stood there pondering what the sheriff said and it finally hit Singer. He looked right at the sheriff saying, "the quickest way to get to Justice is out Highway 80." They all knew that was where Sister Lee had predicted the next body would turn up. Suddenly, no one said anything. Ratley was glad Singer brought it up and not him. That didn't change the fact that it still felt strange that Sister Lee was able to name that highway even if she was off concerning the exact location of the body. Coincidence maybe, but they all had to tell themselves it was just a shot in the dark taken by a crazy woman that could no more predict what would happen than they could.

The sheriff pointed out, there were only three main roads which ran all the way through Jefferson County. It would stand to reason that the killer would most likely take one of them, and in this case it just happened to be the one Sister Lee mentioned. Sheriff Baker's attempt to reason away the unexplainable seemed to settle Ratley's nerves to a degree.

The sheriff changed the subject of conversation as he poured himself a cup of coffee. He looked over at Blue telling him they had a good little ride ahead of them, and he walked back into his office to grab his jacket. After taking a sip of coffee, he placed the mug on the corner of his desk figuring he'd best use the bathroom before he and Blue set out for Justice. He felt certain the killer, they had yet to name, was throwing the state police off his trail by doubling back one more time. Only an insane person would attempt such a thing with a hostage, but Blue would tell the sheriff for certain if he was right about the killer's whereabouts.

Chapter 35

A Growing Body Count

Nearly two hours after sunup a highway patrolman by the name of Whatley ventured down Highway 80 after hearing reports of bodies found thirty miles away from his location. He didn't expect to find the killer or anything really on that stretch of road. He had cruised it more times than he could count and early in the morning there was hardly ever any traffic on it whatsoever. Still, the state police had issued a manhunt in an effort to capture the person responsible for the recent rash of murders, and Trooper Whatley was doing his part.

He had been instructed to pull over any vehicle he saw on the road that morning, and to be on the lookout for anything unusual. That covered a lot of categories. Whatley had seen his share of off the wall shit in his time, most of it bordering on asinine in nature. However, this morning held something else in store for him. Was it unusual? Hell yes! How many brand new BMWs did Whatley run across stranded on the side of the road along Highway 80? This was a first. That was reason enough for him to proceed with caution.

Rolling up on the vehicle, he slowed down surveying the area. *What the hell it was doing there God only knows*, he thought. Pulling over to the shoulder, he switched on his lights. It wasn't until he got out of the car that he could tell it had been abandoned. He looked around noticing something that took him by surprise as he approached the vehicle. That's when he reached for his radio calling in his location.

Crime scene tape was already present close in proximity to the silver BMW. His eyes were fixed on the crime scene tape tied to the tree on the other side of the road. Suddenly, Whatley had a bad feeling about this one. He looked in both directions, and he stepped around to the side of the vehicle. He looked inside the car through the windows after he checked to see if the vehicle was locked. Nothing appeared unusual, but there was an unpleasant odor coming from inside beamer that made Whatley jokingly remark, "hell, I see why they left it."

He walked to the rear of the car to look at the tag, and that's when he saw blood on the trunk. Immediately, his blood pressure shot up several points. He radioed dispatch telling them, "this is Whatley, I have a plate I need you to run, and I need you to put me in touch with Sheriff Baker right now."

Sheriff Baker had just stepped out of the bathroom right when the phone rang. He walked back into his office to get Blue leaving Singer to answer the phone. Sheriff Baker fastened the leash to Blue's collar while Singer stood motionless listening to what Whatley had to say. His face became ghostly white as his said, "hold on a moment. I'll get the sheriff." Singer lowered the phone from his ear and he placed Whatley on hold. He got up from his desk and walked to the door of the sheriff's office. Sticking his head in slightly he said, "you got a call, and you're going to want to take this one."

Sheriff Baker's face looked somewhat perplexed, but he could hear the serious tone in Singer's voice. The sheriff looked over at his phone scratching old Blue on top of the head saying, "don't worry we'll get there. Believe me, I want to find him a whole lot more than you boy." The sheriff gestured to Singer to close the door as he picked up the phone. He answered propping his feet up on his desk saying, "hello."

Whatley confirmed he was speaking to the sheriff and he forewarned him he probably wanted to sit down if he wasn't already. The sheriff just asked, "what can I do for you?"

That's when Trooper Whatley proceeded to explain he was with the highway patrol, and he came up on what was left of a body alongside Highway 80. He then added, "which still appears to be inside your jurisdiction."

The sheriff questioned him, "did you say Highway 80?"

Singer and Ratley's eyes were glued to the sheriff. This time they didn't care if he saw them staring at him or not. The sheriff moved kicking his cup of coffee onto the floor as his feet came flying off the desk. He saw Singer and Ratley outside his window, but he didn't even bother to walk over and close the blinds this time. Instead, he just tossed what was left of yesterday's paper on the floor to help soak up the spilled coffee, and he listened while Whatley painted a grizzly picture of the decedent.

Whatley started by saying, "this guy is in pieces sheriff, and it's not pretty. He's been dead a while. I was calling you to let you know about it, but the odd thing is there's already crime scene tape on the scene. Do you know anything about it?"

Sheriff Baker answered him by saying, "that scene was marked as a potential dump site. I'll explain as soon as I get out there. Don't move that body until the coroner arrives."

Glancing back at the severed remains of what once was Jamal Morris, Whatley tried to hold down his breakfast saying, "well, he's not going anywhere, that's for sure. We'll see you when you get here."

The sheriff slung open the door to his office and yelled, "I want you to ride out and pick up that palm reader, and I want her in my office by the time I get back. You understand?"

Singer immediately sounded off, "yeah sheriff."

That's when the sheriff lowered his voice some telling Singer he better take Ratley with him. He added, "don't tell her a thing about this. People in this town are already spooked enough. Just tell her I have some more questions for her."

Singer grabbed his coat saying, "shit sheriff, I'm about freaked the hell out myself."

Ratley chimed in with, "that makes two of us."

Suddenly, Sister Lee's predictions had come full circle. The body was found just where she said it would be, and they were returning to the little white house on the hill where she lived much sooner than either of them anticipated. She was also right about their faith in her abilities. Yesterday they doubted her, but today they were forced to believe.

The sheriff assured them they were going to get this son of bitch and today was the day. He then instructed them to keep their eyes open out there. Seconds later, the sheriff picked up his hat and grabbed his partner. Moving in unison, Ratley and Singer followed him and Blue out the door.

No one was left there to answer the phones, but they would soon begin ringing off the hook, and all that was a result of Hayden Keller returning to Chanceville. The nightmare never ended.

Chapter 36

Smells Like Road Kill

Hayden sat behind the wheel of the SUV without saying a word long after the sun had crested. He was faced with a choice of who to kill, and when to do it. He knew he needed another vehicle, and as soon as he got it that would be time to part company with Ben. A question still left unanswered was whether or not Ashley would be accompanying him on his next hunt. For Hayden, it was of the utmost importance that she voluntarily take that cross from her neck, and toss it aside. Only then could he kill her, and harvest her soul for Satan. In order to get her to do that, he would have to bring her to the point of loathing all she ever believed in. That was no easy task even for Hayden, but if he accomplished it that would probably be the closest they would ever come to seeing eye to eye on anything.

Hayden looked over at Ben. He was the man with two lives as Sister Lee knew him, but at that point he was half dead, half alive with little life left in him. Hayden knew he had one foot in the grave, but he saw Ben as his tool to convince Ashley to set aside her faith. It would prove to be a long morning for everyone in Jefferson County, Hayden included.

With Ashley bound securely in the back seat, and Ben unable to put up much of a fight Hayden stepped out of the vehicle. He told them he wouldn't be long, and if he saw anyone stick their head out he would blow it right off their shoulders. Then he added, "this time the gun is loaded." Leaving them no options, he slammed the door locking them inside the Tahoe.

Ashley watched Hayden as he walked away from the vehicle. She searched for something in the back seat that she could use to cut the tape he had wrapped around her wrists, but nothing seemed to work. Scared out of her wits, she hysterically asked Ben, "what are we going to do?" Can you start this car somehow?"

Ben knew nothing about how to hotwire a vehicle. Hell he had trouble operating one with keys, but for Ashley's sake he attempted. Ben knew Hayden would kill him soon enough, but he also knew deep down inside, without question, he was sent to protect Ashley from suffering the same fate.

Hayden pissed against a tree while keeping an eye on the SUV. He craved a smoke as Ashley and Ben made a last ditch effort to flee from him in the stolen Tahoe. Ashley started to cry while Ben fumbled with the wires in the floorboard of the Tahoe. Stuck in an awkward position, he was becoming dizzy from the blood loss. That's when Ben assured her that regardless of what happened she was going to live.

Ashley said, "just start the damn car." She was losing it, and Ben knew he had to calm her down.
He calmly told her, "listen whatever happens you don't take that cross from around your neck. You hear me?" Ben was serious, and Ashley listened to every word he spoke before asking him why. Ben responded saying, "because he wants you to for some reason." He said nothing else on that subject. He just focused on crossing two wires together. He was good at making sparks, apparently.

Hayden looked up from his smoke break seeing the hazard lights flash several times on the vehicle. He shook his head and he took another drag from his cigarette before he started walking back toward the Tahoe.

Filled with fear, Ashley's voice cracked telling Ben what she had seen take place. "You don't know what you're talking about this sick-o killed my entire family, and he's coming back here to kill us. Now hurry up."

Ben pointed out she was still alive for a reason, and then he confidently said, "I know more than you think. You're a cancer aren't you?" Ashley looked a little puzzled asking, "what?"

Ben clarified things for her. "Your sign, its cancer right."

Ashley admitted he was correct. Then she had to ask, "how did you know that?"

Ben just confessed, "it's a long story. I'll tell you when we have more time. Right now, I have to face my demons, but I have a feeling you're going to survive."

Ashley couldn't make sense of it. "I don't understand." The panic was present in her voice as she spoke.

Hayden was coming. They could both feel it. Ben informed Ashley, "he's the scarred lion, you're cancer and I'm the man with two lives." He touched two more wires together and the horn started going off. He quickly separated them, and Ashley looked out the window at Hayden. He was steadily approaching, hindered some by his wounded leg, but still able move faster than Ashley would have liked.

Ben might have known her sign, but he sure as hell didn't know how to start the vehicle without keys. "Try something else quick," she urgently ordered. Ashley could see their only chance to get away vanish with each step Hayden took.

Ben acknowledged, "he's almost here, isn't he."
Ashley sadly faced that reality as she said, "yeah."

Ben grabbed a hand full of wires in his fist, and he started snatching them out from underneath the console, ripping away at them in a final effort to disable the vehicle. Ben figured if he couldn't start it, neither would Hayden Keller.

Ashley turned seeing what he was doing and she freaked out. Ben said, "trust me," as he sat back up in the front seat.
Ashley bluntly asked, "do you know what you just did?" Ben took a breath as Hayden tried to unlock the door. Unable to do so, he yelled, "I'm going to enjoy killing you Ben. Now let me in."

Ben wasn't about to make Hayden's job any easier. A subtle smile came to his face for a moment as he overcame the pain he felt in both his arm and leg. Ben knew Hayden wasn't going anywhere inside that vehicle. He also took comfort in knowing, if only for the moment, he and Ashley were shielded from him at least for now. He realized the next move was Hayden's, but he had done something to buy them a little more time. That was a precious thing to have in their situation, and Ben could hold out hope that they would soon be found.

Hayden finished off the cigarette pissed to no end that he was now locked out of the SUV. He needed a different set of wheels now more than ever. Out in the middle of nowhere, he knew of only one way to get them, and that was to wait. He withheld the overwhelming urge he had to bust out the window and strangle Ben right there on the spot. He had other plans for Ben, and it entailed a great deal more pain and suffering. There was no price Hayden wouldn't pay at Ben's expense to see Ashley burn in hell.

Hayden could smell death and it was getting near. All it took was a passing car, and the bloodshed would soon commence.

Sheriff Baker rolled out Highway 80 to the crime scene which had been marked with tape the day before. Seeing the flashing blue lights atop Whatley's car, he applied the brakes pulling off to the side of the road. He left Blue inside the vehicle when he got out to speak with Trooper Whatley. He could smell the stench coming from the trunk long before he laid eyes on the body.

Whatley warned him, "it's awful sheriff. There really isn't any other way to describe it." The sheriff figured it couldn't be any worse than what he found out at the Ferris farm as he opened up the trunk, but even he was at a loss for words seeing the sawed up body parts. He looked over at the crime scene tape Ratley had tied to the tree, and he knew Sister Lee held the key to finding the killer. He figured he could count on Blue to give him a direction to follow and he would pursue it to the bitter end if that's what it took to find the girl.

The sheriff asked the state trooper about the car, and who it belonged to. The name he was given was that of Ben Goodman. Seeing the tire tracks from another vehicle pulling off the road within thirty feet or so of the beamer, the sheriff snapped a picture.

Trooper Whatley asked, "is that your partner?" He pointed to Blue sitting in the passenger seat of the sheriff's car. The sheriff nodded as he looked back at the old hound claiming, "he'll find this guy. I promise you that."

Whatley couldn't see how that dog could smell anything other than that rotting corpse. Confirming several more facts with the state trooper about what he found at the scene when he first arrived, the sheriff said, "I'll take it from here I guess."

Whatley offered to remain with the vehicle until the medical examiner arrived, and Sheriff Baker took him up on it. Using a flat metal rod, Sheriff Baker popped the lock to open up the vehicle. He took several prints from the door and steering wheel. He then held his breath as he dusted for some on the trunk. Walking back to his vehicle he told Whatley, "when the coroner gets here you can go ahead and call for the tow truck."

Whatley said, "10-4," and he climbed back inside his vehicle closing the door.

He watched Sheriff Baker lead Blue toward the vehicle, allowing him to sniff inside a moment in order to gain the scent of the killer they were searching for. Then, Sheriff Baker allowed Blue to lead him in both directions, and he realized he'd have to follow the trail all the way to Justice to see whether or not it went cold. Within minutes he and Blue were back in the car headed to the town where two dead bodies were discovered hours before about sunup.

Whatley was left with a broken down BMW, numerous body parts and little faith that bloodhound could track down the nearest McDonalds. *That was a sobering way to start off the day*, he thought as he looked at his watch.

Sheriff Baker thought he was closer than ever to finding the girl, and stopping a serial killer from taking another life. Blue had a scent and they were hot on the trail.

Chapter 37

More Questions For Sister Lee

Singer pulled into the drive in front of Sister Lee's house. She was standing at the window watching them as they drove up. Ratley looked over at Singer asking, "do you think she knew we were coming?" This time Singer didn't say anything. His eyes expressed his concern. Ratley then asked, "you want me to do the talking?"

Singer replied, "she won't talk to anybody but you and that's alright by me."

Singer got out of the car and walked to the door with Ratley leading the way. Sister Lee opened it for them as she invited them in saying, "I knew you would be back. Have a seat."

Ratley declined her offer telling her, "the sheriff would like to meet with you down at his office, and he sent us out to give you a ride there."

Sister Lee knew everything Ratley had said was true, and she also knew there was more to it than that. She asked, "were there bodies found?"

Ratley simply responded by saying, "I'm not quite sure what the sheriff has found, but he definitely wishes to meet with you.

Sister Lee said nothing as they walked to the car, and Singer remained closed lipped as well. When they started to pull out of the driveway Ratley broke the awkward silence by asking, "is there anything else you can tell us about the scarred lion you haven't already shared with us?"

Singer felt like he was now riding in the car with two

weirdos, but still he said absolutely nothing. If Ratley spoke her language that meant he didn't have to, and that suited him just fine.

Sister Lee confessed she had discovered more about him since they last spoke, and she had seen him again through her third eye. She expected some remark from Singer, but he kept his thoughts to himself. He just continued to drive.

Ratley was as much interested in what she referred to as the third eye as he was about hearing what she saw in her vision. "This third eye thing, how does that work exactly," he asked.

Singer couldn't believe his ears, but all that could be heard coming from him was a forceful rush of air exiting his widened nostrils. That's when he looked over at Ratley.

Sister Lee answered Ratley saying, "you wish to know, but all things reveal themselves in time. Time is something you do not have much of at the moment. You should ask the other question."

Ratley had a confused look on his face. "What question," he asked.

Sister Lee smiled a little. She looked out the window. Honestly, she liked Ratley. She even found him amusing at times, but this was time to tend to more important matters than reading one's mind. Sister Lee said, "you ask the question when I give you this answer." Then she said, "I saw a field of tall grass and the lion was lame as he hunted his prey. His leg is injured, and when you find him you will know it is him by the tape which marks his wound. Blood will cover his body and he will hardly be able to walk." Ratley listened to every word she spoke. It sounded as though she was predicting they would find this killer and soon. Sister Lee added, "I then saw the girl through the eyes of the man with two lives, and both of them are still alive but not for long." She finished speaking saying, "that is the answer. Now ask the question that entered your mind."

Ratley paused before asking, "how did you see this?"

Singer's eyes widened and he stepped on the gas. He even flipped on the lights. He wanted the sheriff to hear what she had said, and he wanted him to hear it directly from her. He was now a believer of sorts, and Ratley was long before they set out to pick her up that morning.

The young deputy had to ask more questions about where they would find the killer, and Sister Lee closed her eyes saying, "he is close. He waits on the side of the road for something. A black vehicle, parked next to a field and down from it is a rusted barn. There is a road of dirt in front of it. That's where you will find him but you must hurry."

Sheriff Baker reached the near nonexistent town of Justice about the time Singer and Ratley pulled up to his office with Sister Lee in the back of the squad car. They led her inside while several townspeople watched with great interest. Singer overheard parts of the conversation taking place between some of the folks passing by, and he tried his best to ignore it.

When Hal Thornton asked, "is everything alright," Singer lied convincingly.

Trotting up the steps he replied, "yeah Hal, there's not much going on you don't already know about." Hal started to share the news he had heard on the radio, but Singer didn't give him a chance to speak his thoughts. He just quickly unlocked the door to the office so Ratley and Sister

Lee could enter. Following them inside, he then closed the door and he closed the blind to limit the visibility of onlookers.

The discussion that took place among those that saw Sister Lee exit the car centered on whether or not she knew anything about those murders. Inside, Ratley removed his jacket as he said, "you got to love small towns don't you." His remark was directed at Singer, but Sister Lee responded saying, "now you see, I am not the only one here that knows about other peoples' lives." It was an amusing remark under the circumstances even though she had no intention for it to be. While everyone in that town knew everything about everyone else, Sister Lee was the only one that could know of what was to come through her powers of perception.

Singer pointed out that the whole town would soon know they brought Sister Lee in for questioning, and that made both he and Ratley a little uneasy. Ratley looked over at the chair next to his desk and he led Sister Lee toward it confessing, "yeah. The grapevine around here is something else."

Sister Lee looked around the office, now confused by the words Ratley had used to describe the town's rumor mill. She looked at Ratley's desk. "This is where you work I see," she said.

Ratley replied, "yes. This is where I was sitting when we first spoke."

Papers cluttered his desk, and Sister Lee felt uncomfortable sitting next to the mess. She found it difficult to collect her thoughts, much less concentrate. She blurted out, "you need a bigger desk, more drawers maybe." She looked through the window of the sheriff's office and she said, "like that one perhaps."

Singer damn near spit his coffee back into his cup suppressing the urge to laugh a little. Ratley informed her that was the sheriff's office, and she responded by saying, "and you think I do not know this."

Ratley's serious look faded to a quirky smile as he admitted to himself he was speaking to Sister Lee of all people. Of course she knew which office belonged to the sheriff, and she could probably tell you who would be sitting behind that desk ten years from now. All the young deputy said was, "no, that was rather silly of me, I suppose."

Sister Lee always had the last word even if it was terse, and she said the first thing that came to mind, "at least you are honest."

Singer walked back to lock the door, and Sister Lee said, "him, I'm not so sure about."

Ratley just looked at her motioning with his head, pointing it in Singer's direction. That's when he said, "he's alright, you just have to get to know him. That's all."

Looking at Singer over her shoulder she said, "he will not show me his palm. Therefore, he has something to hide. Let me see your hand."

Ratley hesitantly extended it not knowing what would happen or what she would say. She looked at his hand studying it for a moment. Still, she said nothing. Ratley asked," do you see anything?"

Sister Lee replied, "yes, a hand." Then she admitted, "you can tell a lot by an man's hands." Ratley listened closely becoming captivated by the words which she spoke. That's when Sister Lee said, "you need to use moisturizer. You should take better care of your skin you know."

Singer found humor in that as Ratley asked, "is that all you are going to tell me?"

Sister Lee said, "that depends. You have twenty dollars?" Ratley looked at her shaking his head, and he dug into his front pocket pulling out thirteen dollars and seven cents. He laid it on his paper plastered desk, and Sister Lee looked down at it saying, "you need a raise. I can tell you that without looking at your hand."

Unafraid, Ratley asked, "what do you see when you do look at it?"

Sister Lee tried to focus, but the environment she was in didn't help. She stood, and she led Ratley into the sheriff's office telling him to sit down at the desk. Much like a small child he did as she instructed without questioning it one bit. She stared into his palm and she focused all of her attention on it. Singer watched, curious as to what she was doing. Even he wanted to hear what she had to say.

Placing her finger in Ratley's palm, she ran it over the lines in his hand. Her finger stopped and she spoke these words aloud, "soon you will be faced with a life or death decision, and it is up to you to make the right one. It is not your life which hangs in the balance though, and that is all I can tell you." Those weren't comforting words, but it was what Sister Lee saw in his future according to his palm. Even she wished she had never read it. Letting go of Ratley's hand she changed the subject by saying, "this sheriff of yours, he is busy doing something."

Ratley assured her he was on his way, and he tried not to reveal anything to her she hadn't spoken of already. He and Sister Lee engaged in limited conversation inside the sheriff's office. Wondering what was taking the sheriff so long, Singer picked up the phone to call him just to let him know they had Sister Lee in custody. As he spoke with the sheriff he could hear Blue baying in the background.

The sheriff explained he had to drive all the way to Justice to see if the trail ran cold or not. He then informed Singer he was right about the killer doubling back, and he was headed directly for Chanceville. He admitted, "he could be anywhere inside Jefferson County by now. Maybe even out of it all together, but one thing's for certain, he didn't keep going west."

Singer became tense at the sound of that, and the sheriff told him he wanted to know what Sister Lee had to say. The deputy recalled fragments of the conversation he heard take place in the car between her and Ratley that morning. He started by saying, "she said he's close sheriff, something about a black vehicle he was driving, and right now he's on the side of the road somewhere. Hell that's all I could really understand. You need to talk to her yourself. Oh yeah and she said, he's injured, something about he couldn't walk good."

The sheriff instructed him, "you keep her there until I get back, and you keep this between us. I don't want the whole town up in arms trying to gun down anybody driving by in a dark colored vehicle. We've got enough to deal with."

Singer agreed asking him how long he expected it would be before he got back there. The sheriff looked at the time and he estimated he would be there in less than thirty minutes. Singer hung up the phone while Sister Lee stared out the window, and Ratley said nothing. He just sat there in deep thought in the comfort of the sheriff's cushy chair.

When Singer walked into the office Sister Lee said, "he is coming. I know. He is hunting the hunter and there will be more bloodshed to come before it is over." Those words which she spoke took whatever Singer had to say, and made it not so important. He just looked over at Ratley and back at the front door.

Several faces peered inside the glass to catch a glimpse of what was going on. Seeing Singer look toward them drove them away though. Their voices could be heard as they scurried down the steps of the courthouse. They continued chattering away about the most recent murders as they walked down the sidewalk toward a nearby store. Thirty more minutes stuck there under those conditions made for a long God-awful wait. Reflecting on the sheriff's words, Singer felt he should be out there trying to find the killer.

Chapter 38

Help Us Please

Hayden was anything but a patient man. Sometimes he questioned if Satan himself didn't take great delight in his most miserable moments. Still, he had a master to serve as most of us do, and part of that entailed a trial in one's willingness to sit and do absolutely nothing while time passed slowly. Honestly, he had his fill of Ben and the hour in which to kill him was fast approaching, but even Hayden didn't know when he would take his last breath.

His plan was to flag down a passing motorist and borrow his vehicle. In Hayden's world that, of course, consisted of killing him first though. He never like leaving whiney witnesses behind to provide law enforcement with a fuzzy sketch of what he looked like. He preferred to take their life and then their vehicle. It was a system that had worked pretty well for him over the years, and he never deviated from it, not without good reason. He had his work cut out for him though. With a killer on the loose, people were much less apt to stop and lend a hand to a total stranger on the side of the road, especially one that looked as intimidating as Hayden.

Just about the time Sheriff Baker arrived in front of the courthouse, Hayden heard a car coming. He knew exactly how to play this moment, injured leg and all. He removed his leather jacket using it to cover the duct tape he had wrapped around his leg. It hurt like a son of a bitch, but he knelt down by the rear tire of the SUV. Hunched over it, he pretended to be hard at work trying to fix the tire. He had already let the air out of the tire after Ben rendered it inoperable.

The approaching vehicle slowed as Hayden raised his hand in the air in an effort to wave down the motorist. He never stood. He just moved his hand back and forth figuring he had a fifty-fifty shot of him stopping to see what was wrong. That percentage paid-off. Clarence Passmore pulled over to the side of the road not knowing what he just got himself into. He was by himself, a middle-aged man somewhere in his forties.

Ashley saw him get out of his vehicle and she franticly shouted at Ben, "honk the horn." Ben looked over his shoulder and he laid on the horn, but no sound was made at all. He had gutted most of the wires under the dash and the wire going to the horn happened to be one of them. To make matters worse, Ashley couldn't get out of the vehicle without busting out the glass in the window, and neither she nor Ben were in a position to do that. Ashley saw this as her last hope. If she didn't warn this man of the extreme danger he was in before he came any closer, they would all end up dead.

Clarence asked, "what seems to be the problem?"
Hayden replied, "I've been having problems with this tire. You wouldn't happen to have a tire iron on you, would you? I think this thing has about had it."
Clarence stopped where he stood, and turned around walking back to his vehicle as he said, "I've got one but I don't know that it'll work. That's a pretty big vehicle you got there."

Hayden stood while his back was turned. He held his jacket in front of his injured leg as he hobbled toward

Clarence closing ground rapidly. Ashley started beating on the window with bound hands as she shouted, "help us! Please help us!"

Clarence looked inside his trunk unable to hear her from where he stood. Moving some stuff aside, he searched for a lug wrench or anything that would help Hayden out of the spot he found himself in at the moment. Hearing a faint sound coming from the Tahoe, he stopped shifting stuff around as he asked, "what's that I hear?"

Hayden moved closer telling him that was just his kids begging for him to help, but he told them they would have to stay inside the car. Clarence nodded his head as he placed his hand on the tire iron. Looking at it, he gripped it firmly saying, "I don't know that it'll get the job done. You might have to call for a tow truck."

Hayden walked up next to his vehicle just as Clarence raised his head closing the trunk. He was standing just three feet away from him, and Clarence was taken by surprise seeing Hayden's unsettling appearance close up. Before looking up at Hayden, he had started to say, "you can give this a shot," but he stopped before uttering another word.

Hayden took the tire iron out of his hand saying, "oh, I think this will work just fine."

Just at that moment the sound of a busted window caught Clarence's attention. Ben had managed to kick out the driver's side window. Glass covered the pavement next to the Tahoe, and Clarence knew Hayden was not the person he pretended to be. Unfortunately, for him it was too late. Hayden began bludgeoning him with the tire iron striking him repeatedly in the face until his identity was impossible to see. As Clarence fell to the ground, Hayden stood over him pounding on him relentlessly. Blood spattered onto his face while he brutally beat the man to a pulp, and Hayden took his wrist wiping away the man's blood from his lips and cheek.

Ashley screamed in horror at what was unfolding, and Ben told her not to look. Instead, he told her to use the glass to cut the tape. It didn't work of course even though she leaned forward into the front seat desperately trying to free herself, and all she could say is, "we're going to die. I know it." Ben tried to calm her down by saying, "I'm going to die. He's injured Ashley. You're going to live to get away."

The thought of being left alone again with Hayden didn't seem comforting in the least. Living another day, still his captive, was not a pleasing thought, and she wanted Ben to stay alive at all costs. Without Ben, Ashley feared she would not make it. After what they had been through together, watching him die the way Hayden was tearing that man apart was more than she felt she could take.

At that moment, Sheriff Baker walked into his office telling Sister Lee he needed her help. His voice was earnest and much less contemptuous than the day before. "Can you help us find the girl," he asked. She closed her eyes almost as if she were meditating, and she opened them saying, "yes I believe I can, but you don't have much time."

The sheriff pressed her for landmarks, road signs and anything that would give them a clue as to which direction to take. Sister Lee didn't work at her best under pressure, but the sheriff's focus was on ending the killing spree.
Sister Lee was unable to tap into Ben's mind, even small peeks into what he had seen were blurred to where she could barely make them out, and she knew he was dying. She only saw a rusted building which had the faded word

FIRE painted on it. That was the only real landmark she could give them but it was enough.

Singer questioned, "she's not talking about the old volunteer fire station is she?"

The sheriff asked her to describe it in detail. Sister Lee did her best saying, "it's small, overgrown with vines and the top is not good at all."

Ratley said, "the top. You mean the roof is caved in on it." Sister Lee looked lost to a degree and Ratley said, "it's dented isn't it." He pointed to his hat and drawing the parallel Sister Lee nodded yes.

The sheriff knew what Ratley was referring to, but he asked Sister Lee if it looked as though it had burned many years ago, just to make sure Ratley had identified the right landmark. Sister Lee thought for a moment somewhat unsure of how to answer, but again she nodded yes. Ratley looked over at the sheriff and Singer asked, "you think she's referring to Smitty's old fireworks stand?"

Ratley pointed out, "that's only fifteen miles from here, twelve if you cut across Johnson Mill."

Sheriff Baker wanted to know if that's where they would find the girl, and Sister Lee replied, "I don't think so, but it's close to where she is now." That was all she could tell them. There wasn't much around it for sure. There were a half dozen roads within a three mile radius of the old burned out building Sister Lee had described. Which road to take was anyone's guess.

The sheriff instructed his deputies to focus on searching the lesser traveled roads just north of town. He planned on taking Sister Lee with him, figuring they would cover the lower part of Fortune Hole Road together in search of the missing girl. Ratley and Singer wasted no time. Grabbing their hats, they scrambled to their car.

Picking up Blue's leash the sheriff said, "come on," as he took Sister Lee by the arm leading her out the door right behind his deputies. He locked the door to the office as Singer and Ratley laid tracks for the old abandoned building Sister Lee spoke of. With blue lights flashing they hastily made their way through town as Sheriff Baker loaded his traveling companions in the cruiser.

Chapter 39

The Reckoning

Hayden dug inside Clarence's pockets relieving him of his wallet and keys. Placing them inside his coat pocket, he kneeled over Clarence's dead body looking back around at the SUV. Taking in one last view at the bloody mess that was Clarence Passmore, he turned gripping the tire iron in his left hand as he moved toward the Tahoe. Hayden was now hell bent on killing Ben, but not before he put him through hell just as he had promised.

Now covered in blood and injured, Hayden needed to end his reign of terror in Jefferson County. There was no better way to do it than to rid himself of both Ashley and Ben. All Hayden had to decide was how to go about doing it. After killing Clarence he could only take one more life before the Sabbath, and Hayden could never break that rule. If he did, he would suffer the fate which eventually awaited him in the end. Severe consequences hinged on his ability to work within the confines given to him by the prince of darkness himself. His bargain with Satan had bought him time to kill and to bring about mayhem, but one day it would all end.

Even in an unjust world such as the one we live in, good will triumph over evil in the end. Hayden knew it to be true. That's why he hunted all good men and Ben was one of them. Hayden yelled out for him saying, "I'm coming for you Ben!"

Looking over his shoulder at Ashley, Ben told her to stay inside the vehicle, no matter what. Her hands and feet were still bound, and Hayden was thirsty for blood. Killing Clarence just fueled his lust for it. He walked up to the SUV tapping the tire iron against the rear window. Hayden tormented them a little further dragging the end of the tire iron along the side of the SUV, scrapping it against the metal as he circled it. He took his sweet time as he rounded the rear corner of the Tahoe, and he slowly made his way down the passenger side toward the front of the vehicle. Stopping at Ben's window he rapped on it with the tire iron as he said, "I'm here." Ready to unleash his pent up aggression and show true terror on his victims, Hayden drew his left hand back and forcefully struck the tinted window of the Tahoe shattering it into little pieces.

Ben moved trying to avoid the glass, but it pelted his face and showered him with fragments filling his lap. Hayden quickly shoved the steel bar under his chin, and he gripped each side of it with both hands as he pulled Ben's head toward him. Ashley screamed loud enough to wake the dead when Hayden tore Ben away from the SUV pulling him through the busted window.

Showing no mercy, Hayden choked him as he drug his body over the broken glass. Ben struggled using his one good arm, but there was little he could grab onto. He was just trying to keep breathing at that point. Hayden applied more pressure to his throat using the metal bar. Ben only hoped he could put up enough of a fight to possibly injure Hayden some more. He had no idea what his plans really were.

Hayden warned Ben saying, "I'm not going to lie to you Ben. This is going to hurt you a hell of a lot more than it's going to hurt me." Ben let go of the vehicle. Keeping one hand on the tire iron in an effort to keep breathing. He formed a fist using his other hand and he pounded it against Hayden's wounded leg as they both fell to the ground outside the Tahoe. Trying to strike him again with his fist he failed to inflict any real damage. Hayden was definitely experiencing real pain though.

He released his grip around Ben's neck, but that's when he struck him in the chest with the tire iron. Ben wailed out in pain. On his knees, Hayden assured him this was only the start, and there would be lots more pain to come. He then said, "this is the end of the line for you Ben. I think this is where you and I part company. I don't think this town is big enough for the two of us."

Another vicious blow to the head left Ben incapacitated. Hayden stood looking back over his shoulder, and he started back toward the SUV as Ashley cowered in the back seat afraid he was coming after her. Ben reached with his wounded arm trying to grab Hayden's leg as he limped away toward the rear door of the vehicle. He was unable to reach him though. Ben shouted, "no!"

Hayden sadistically announced he wanted Ashley to see this up close for herself. Taking the tire iron he busted out the rear window. He wasted no time. Reaching inside snatching Ashley's hair once again he pulled her out just as he had Ben except he didn't choke her with the tire iron this time. She struggled to get away from him, but she was no match for his strength, especially with her hands and feet still bound. She landed hard on the ground and the wind was knocked out of her. The crucifix remained around her slender neck though, and Hayden played his last card in an effort to get her to part with it.

Holding the tire iron over her face, Hayden stared down at her. Ashley was petrified, but Hayden said, "it doesn't have to end this way. You can save Ben you know." Hayden turned limping away from her. He moved toward Ben telling her, "all you have to do is take off that stupid cross, and I promise I won't kill him." He turned looking directly at her as he struck Ben in the head with the tire tool. He reminded her if she didn't do as he said, he was going to pick Ben apart.

Ben knew he wasn't going to make it, and even if he survived the damage inflicted at that point, Hayden's promise held no value. All he could physically do at that point to protect Ashley was remind her of what he said earlier in the SUV. He looked into her eyes, and he slowly shook his head no. In a final breath he begged her, "don't do it."

Tears began to stream down Ashley's cheeks when Hayden yelled, "what kind of God allows this to happen? Don't you realize? There is no God." Powerful words spoken by the deceitful serpent himself, Hayden Keller added, "no one can save him but you, and no God will save you from me."

Hearing those words caused Ashley to lose hope. It shook her faith. It even brought her to the point of clinching the religious symbol which represented the sacrifice made which paved the way to eternal salvation in her hands. She didn't want Ben to die. Tugging at it sharply, Ashley broke the chain which carried the cross and she dropped it on the ground in front of her. She looked down at it and back up at Hayden. She watched him let go of Ben, believing he had ceased his attack.

Hayden kicked Ben in the head causing him to black-out. Ashley felt nothing but pure terror as a despicable look came over Hayden's disgusting face. He still gripped the tire tool in his hand and he turned his attention to Ashley. His eyes were filled with hatred and bloodlust. He growled, "welcome to the reckoning, Ashley. Looks like I'm going to have to kill you instead." Hayden moved toward her and she tried to shield herself from him by rolling over.

With her face against the ground, she tried to squirm underneath the SUV in search of protection. Hayden grabbed her bound legs pulling her behind the Tahoe and she screamed at the top of her lungs. He unleashed his wrath upon her, stabbing her repeatedly with the sharp end of the tire iron until her cries of agony and pain were silenced for good. A pool of blood formed around her as Hayden drove the tire tool through her stomach.

Hayden left it there for Ben to discover whenever he came to. By then, Hayden would be miles away and he knew what to do to cover his tracks, wiping off his gun. Placing him closer to Ashley, Hayden rolled Ben over onto his stomach. Hayden derisively said, "I hope you will remember me next time we meet Ben. By the way, my name is Hayden Keller, just so you know." Hayden added, "I sure as hell won't forget you." He then tucked his gun inside Ben's pants. He even wiped his prints from the tire iron before he hobbled away toward Clarence's car.

Hayden climbed in the car taking one last look at the carnage, and he knew he had to get back on the road. As he pulled away passing the black SUV he picked up speed, headed for parts unknown. Hayden had watched the light go out in the eyes of his victims many times while watching their spirits crossover to the other side. Never had it been such a rewarding experience than when he killed Ashley. Knowing that Ben would agonize over what he could have done to prevent it made her blood taste that much sweeter. Hayden only wished he could be there to see Ben's face when he discovered her dead body lying next to him. He was certain Ben would die at the hands of someone other than him, and fairly soon. He was counting on the sheriff and his deputies to do his bidding. He figured he would read all about how the killing spree was brought to an end in the paper the next day.

Chapter 40

A Not So Happy Ending

Singer and Ratley were headed north, neither of them sure which way to go. That's when Ratley suggested they take Lynch Road. It was seldom used by anyone, but the dilapidated building in Sister Lee's vision was less than two miles in that direction.

Ben laid there on the ground next to Ashley. His eyes remained closed, but he had heard Hayden's final words to him. Feeling something wet touch his hand, he opened his eyes. It was Ashley's blood, and she was lying right beside him. Nearly dead himself he called out to her as he raised his head, but she didn't move. He reached over touching her shoulder and he saw the blood which covered his hand. That's when he looked down seeing the tire iron which Hayden had stabbed her with, and it was still sticking out of her abdomen. A small stream of blood escaped from the corner of her mouth and tears still filled her eyes. Ben wiped them from her face.

"It wasn't supposed to happen like this," he said out loud. *It should have been him*, at least that's what he thought. Ben looked down at her noticing Ashley's necklace was gone. In unrestrained anger he yelled out Hayden's name. He was distraught as he knelt down beside her. He never planned on finding her that way. Ben reached over grabbing the tire iron and he withdrew it from her abdomen. He could see her blood drip from the end of it, and he promptly threw it away. It landed in the grass a few feet from Clarence Passmore's bloody corpse just as Singer and Ratley rolled up on the black SUV. Ben's back was turned toward the deputy's vehicle.

Singer looked over at his partner confirming, "do you see what I see?" They got closer and it was easy to make out the bodies of both Ben and Ashley at the rear of the Tahoe. Singer said, "I hope you're ready for this," and he quickly jerked the wheel pulling the car over. That's when Ratley pointed out Ben had a gun. Singer said, "I see it. You just watch my back." He brought the car to a stop and Ratley flung open the passenger door drawing his weapon. Crouching behind the door for cover he pointed his gun right at Ben.

Singer opened the driver's side door reaching for his gun as well. He drew it in an instant and he had a bead on Ben's head. He was aiming the kill shot. Knelling next to her, Ben hovered over Ashley's dead body. He pushed her hair back out of her face gaining a final look at her. He was in shock. None of this seemed real. He was injured and covered in blood. He had played right into Hayden's hand.

Singer and Ratley both saw the tape which was wrapped around Ben's leg marking his wound. It was just as Sister Lee had said in her vision regarding the evil one. That's when Singer yelled, "get away from the girl, now!"
Ratley shouted at Ben to keep his hands where he could see them, but Ben could hardly stand up. When he turned they couldn't believe what they saw. His shirt and hands were covered in blood.

He looked up saying, "I didn't do it. It's not me." He stood and Singer yelled at him to drop the gun. Ben informed him, "I'm not armed."
Ratley shouted, "what's that behind your back?"

Ben had no idea what he was referring to as he reached around behind his back feeling for the pistol Hayden had placed on him before driving away. Using his right hand, he grabbed the handle of the gun, and he pulled it out of his pants.

Singer yelled at him again, this time telling him not to do it. Bringing the gun around his waist, he was stunned to see it. Ben looked down at the weapon Hayden had shot him with thinking *this can't be happening*.

The gun was now in full view of the deputies and they had him firmly in their sites. Ben's eyes opened wide as he looked up at the guns that were drawn on him. Ratley didn't have time to think about the words Sister Lee spoke earlier at the station. He had a split decision to make as he yelled to Singer, "he's going for it!"

Singer fired a shot hitting Ben right in the heart. The impact of the gunshot spun Ben to the left, bringing his right arm forward toward the deputies. With the gun still in his hand Ratley fired a shot hitting Ben in the head. The impact of that shot was deadly too. Ben fell backward. His right arm rose in the air slightly before he finally dropped the gun. Singer and Ratley had already fired another shot each as he fell to the ground in a puddle of blood.

Seconds after the sound of the shots cleared, Singer ordered Ratley to call it in as he rushed over to Ashley to see if she was still alive. Seeing her up close, Singer looked back at Ratley. A sorrowful expression covered Singer's face as he shook his head no. At that very moment Sister Lee became ill just before hearing Ratley's voice come over the radio. The sheriff looked concerned, and he knew something was wrong. That's when Ratley picked up the radio saying, "sheriff this is Ratley. We had shots fired out off of Old Lynch Road. Singer and I are on the scene. We got him sheriff, but the girl - well she didn't make it. I'm sorry sheriff."

The sheriff hung his head as he stopped the car. He picked up the radio and asked, "did you take him down or is he still breathing?"

Ratley responded by saying, "that son of a bitch is dead sheriff."

Sheriff Baker was almost at a loss for words once again. He simply told Ratley that he was going to contact the state police to inform them and then he said, "I want you to wait to bag the evidence until I get there." The sheriff paused a moment realizing he had failed in saving the girl. Then he said, "I guess it's finally over."

Ratley assured him it was right before he got off the radio. That's when he noticed the body of Clarence Passmore lying in the grass a ways off the road. Ratley pointed toward it as he walked over to investigate. The last thing Ben saw was Singer standing over him. He stared down at Ben with a condemning look in his eyes, convinced he was the killer they had been searching for.

Chapter 41

The Awakening

Ben's body twitched and then it became motionless. He laid there on the mattress from hell without moving a muscle. The rays of the morning sun pierced the blinds hanging in the dingy window of his motel room. Light began to fill the room, and suddenly he woke from the nightmare of a lifetime. It was so real he actually questioned if he was alive or just having an out of body experience. The pain he felt in his back as he sat up answered his question though. Whatever he was experiencing it wasn't out of body. He was alive and he realized it was all a horrid dream as he placed his hand on his left shoulder rubbing it a little. He certainly wasn't injured other than the backache he sustained from the worn out mattress.

He sat there propped up on his elbow thinking about parts of his nightmare, and found them to be too disturbing to recount. He wiped the sleep from his eyes pinching his fingers together at the bridge of his nose as he winced. Whatever the day held in store for him had to be better than what the night before delivered without question. For Ben the day started off as planned, but the outstanding day the weatherman mentioned didn't turn out so grand for everyone.

As Ben rolled out of bed he began to get dressed. He envisioned a leisurely drive on the open road which would undoubtedly help him clear his head of everything, including the terrible life ending nightmare he just had. The

SUV which was parked near the back of the motel was no longer there when Ben climbed into his car that morning. The door to one of the rooms was left standing wide open, but Ben paid no attention to it as he drove out of the parking lot. No one really noticed it since it was toward the back of the motel.

It was almost noon when the maid screamed into her walkie-talkie for the manager to come quick. She immediately backed away from the door trembling as she waited for her boss. The walls inside the room were spattered with blood, and the bedspread was missing. The gray sedan parked in back of the motel was still there. It belonged to Edward and Sandra Pennington, the couple found dead the night before on Highway 30 along with their son.

When the manager reached the room, the maid was standing several doors away holding onto her radio. Her cart was just outside the open door. He could see the petrified look on the maid's face. She couldn't even speak at that point. He looked inside the room not sure what he would find, and his mouth slowly opened when he saw the walls for the first time. He couldn't believe what he was seeing. It had been over a week since he rented that room to anyone. Whatever happened there wasn't good.

He didn't want to go inside, but he called out asking, "is anyone in here?" Obviously, no response was heard. He turned to the maid saying, "no one goes in here. You understand?" She nodded her head with a look of fear firmly planted on her face. She looked over her shoulder as the manager passed her on his way back to the office. Her attention was focused in the direction of the door which he pushed to.

As soon as he got back to the front desk he dialed 911 telling the dispatcher he needed an officer at the Greenbriar Motel. The woman on the other end of the phone questioned him asking, "what seems to be the emergency sir?"

The manager just responded saying, "I've got what looks like blood on the walls in one of my rooms, and I don't know where it came from." Hearing that, the dispatcher assured him an officer would be there shortly. The manager hung up the phone, and he looked through his guest register.

Ben had left the motel that morning around 8:30 a.m. There were less than a dozen vehicles in the parking lot when he exited his room to load his stuff in his car. The black SUV parked near the rear of the motel was not one of them. It belonged to Robert Watson, the only problem was it was no longer in his possession. It had been reported stolen ever since Jamal Morris had taken it three days earlier. Unfortunately for him someone else decided they wanted it as well, and that was of course Hayden Keller.

When Officer Kirkland arrived on the scene, the manager showed him the vacant room with the bloodstained walls. He carefully entered the room in search of a body, but he found nothing more than blood on the doors, walls and floor. There were signs of a struggle, but they were minimal. No one loses that much blood without some sign of a struggle though. Forced entry was evident. That's when Officer Kirkland asked the manager for the names of everyone that stayed there that night as he searched the rest of the premises.

He couldn't help but notice the unattended car parked in back of the motel. It fit the description of the one they had been looking for. Kirkland drew the manager's attention to the gray sedan and asked, "whose car is that?"

The manager responded saying, "I don't know. I've never seen it before."

When the officer ran the plates on the vehicle it was determined to belong to none other than Edward Pennington. It had been listed as missing, but it had never been reported stolen. Mr. Pennington never had the chance to make that call. He, his wife and son were now dead, and his daughter was missing according to reports. The question immediately became is this her blood they were looking at on the walls. The manager stood there in shock as he listened to the voice coming back over the officer's radio.

Officer Kirkland looked at the motel manager asking, "do you have any cameras on the property?" The manager just shook his head no still in disbelief any of this was actually happening. The officer said, "you might want to think about getting some," as he continued making notes for his report.

It was Jamal's blood found on the walls of the vacant motel room even though police hadn't determined whose blood it was. It didn't take them long to determine it was the work of a cold blooded killer though instead of some kind of prank committed by a bunch of teenagers. The car belonging to the Pennington's which was left in the parking lot would lead them to that conclusion.

Where the killer was now, and what vehicle he was in were questions left unanswered for the moment. Ben would soon uncover those answers though. He was headed to meet his fate that afternoon while Officer Kirkland concluded his business at the Greenbriar Motel.

Crime scene tape was placed on the door marking it for forensics personnel to investigate. When his police cruiser drove out of sight, the maid turned in her resignation. The manager tried to convince her to stay on, but her mind was made up as soon as she saw those blood covered walls. She wasn't listening to a word he was saying at that point. All she knew was she needed to find a new line of work preferably far away from there. The thought that went through her mind as she left the office on her way to her car was the blood found on those walls could have been hers. That sobering thought made it easy to quit without giving the standard two week notice.

She had heard some of the news reports that morning about the family which was found killed the day before, and this was closer than she ever intended to get to the person responsible for their demise.

Ben's name was listed on the registry, and it was given to Officer Kirkland along with a dozen others that had stayed there that night. Ben, unfortunately, had no idea what he was in for.

Chapter 42

A Revelation

Once again, Ben found himself out on the open road. This time it really was just as the weatherman predicted. The weather was perfect. Every mile he covered seemed very familiar to him as if he had traveled down that road once before. Even though that was the case, he never drew the parallel to the landmarks he passed on his way toward the next town which he had envisioned in his dream the night before.

Driving past the wheat fields, he paid little attention to anything he saw until he looked out the window at a rundown shack in the distance. It was standing in the midst of an open pasture, and he couldn't help but wonder where he had seen it before. The stone chimney which was still standing caught his eye for some reason. He questioned if he had seen a picture of it somewhere. Still, it wasn't clear to him that he had seen it in his dream, but then he saw the windmill which was no longer in operation. He soon became aware of what it stood for. It stood there to remind him of what was ahead and the terrible dream he had before driving down that stretch of road.

Ben's imagination stirred as he ventured further, opening his mind to possibilities he once never considered at all. It was a deserted stretch of lonesome highway in the middle of nowhere just like he pictured in his nightmare. The images he saw were consistent with the ones he saw in his dream. That was extremely difficult to overlook staring out at the landmarks which stood off to the side of the road.

Those things did pave the way to the future, Ben's future. It was drawing nearer with each passing fence post.

Ben flew down the road in his silver beamer, and for once California was no longer the focus of his thoughts. He tried to block out images of Hayden Keller and the girl which police were now searching for. Suddenly, the Pacific Ocean seemed further away than ever. Ben tried to shake the uneasy feeling he had, telling himself that kind of stuff just happens. He labeled it merely a coincidence. That's when he noticed the old rusted silo near a stand of trees off to his left. Immediately, he became nervous not quite sure what to expect next.

Ben felt his life was about to change, and he didn't believe it would be for the best. This trip suddenly offered more adventure than he ever anticipated at the onset, and it was far from over. Ben no longer felt secure as he drove past the fence posts which lined the side of the road. Knowing what was around the next curve was what scared the hell out of him as he stared at the silo. He continued down the deserted stretch of two lane road reaching into his pocket pulling out his cell phone. Just as he suspected, he still had no signal. He tossed the phone in the empty passenger seat next to him.

Ben turned his attention to his gas gauge. It was nearly on 'E' just like in his dream. That's when he looked up seeing the sign which read, *Chanceville 20 Miles*. Suddenly, it hit him. That was no bad dream he had. It was a premonition. Ben had never bought into such things, but now he didn't question it. It was far too on target to be anything other than a look into the future. For Ben it was the immediate future, and he knew he had to play his cards differently this time because he wouldn't get a second chance.

He wasn't sure if Ashley even existed or what Chanceville would look like when he got there. He was just on edge, telling himself if Chanceville looked anything like what he envisioned in his sleep, he would have to hunt down Hayden Keller before he hunted him. His concerns were elevated as he crossed the Jefferson County line. The café was there just as he had pictured, along with Sister Lee's sign. He pulled into the parking lot of the café, and he stared over at Sister Lee's palm reader sign.

The white house was there just as he envisioned, and Ben didn't grin when he saw it this time. He turned seeing a familiar face. It was the man he had seen coming out of the café in his horrifying dream. He had a toothpick in his mouth as well as a folded paper, and without fail he waived to a passing car.

From where Ben sat, it appeared to be a real life nightmare unfolding before his very eyes. He only had one question which centered on Ashley as he got out of his car.

He didn't bother to lock the door, he just quickly walked inside the diner. Sidestepping the man leaving the cash register, he looked toward the end of the counter. There was a man seated at a table with a newspaper, and he was talking to the waitress. Overhearing the tail end of their conversation, Ben heard the waitress say, "I know. That's so awful, isn't it?"

Ben walked straight over snatching the newspaper off the chair next to the man's table just to read the headline. It, of course, read, *Family Killed Girl Still Missing*, and Ben knew what purpose his life served. Without saying a word Ben threw the paper back down. He turned seeing the black SUV pass by, and he froze for a second as he watched it head into town. He felt the same chill he experienced the night before.

The man seated at the table behind him looked up at Ben, and the waitress paused before asking if everything was alright. Ben said absolutely nothing. He immediately headed for the door. As he exited the diner the waitress looked back at her customer trying to figure Ben out. The man seated at the table looked at her saying, "well, I don't know what to tell you. There are some crazy damn people in this world, that's for sure."

Ben looked at the little white house across the street as he made his way to his car. He stared at it only a second, then he quickly slung open the door and jumped inside his BMW. Looking in his rear view mirror he cranked the car. He quickly backed out of the parking space and shifted the car in drive laying rubber pulling out of the parking lot.

The waitress inside the café walked over to the window hearing the squealing tires hitting the pavement. She knew something was wrong and she even wondered if she should call the sheriff. Sister Lee walked over to her window pulling back the curtain as she watched the man with two lives peel out of the parking lot across the street from her house. She watched him drive away as she said, "today is a new beginning. You have much to live for. Prepare for the road ahead. For you will face a demon in this life. Her life depends on it."

Ben could hear those words in his mind as he drove into town. He could remember much of what Sister Lee had said to him in his dream, and he was frightened at what awaited him. He knew the name of the demon he would face, and he knew where to find him. Still, he never thought twice about coming to Ashley's aid. For him it was destiny.

Sister Lee now knew Ben's name and she knew he was in fact a good man. That is why she chose him to put an end to evil. She looked down at the phone next to her window and she turned walking over to the table which sat in the center of the room. She carefully placed her hands squarely on the tapestry which covered it. She positioned her hands so they rested on each side of the yin and yang symbol. Staring down at it intently, she closed her eyes as she concentrated using the power of her third eye, and she directed Ben using her thoughts.

Chapter 43

Prepare To Face A Demon

Ben drove into town looking all around at the shops which lined the street on both sides of him. He turned into a parking lot next to a drugstore which sat directly across from a small pawnshop. The lettering on the glass window out front read, *Guns, Jewelry, Electronics and more.* Ben stared at it for a minute, debating what to do. Arming himself seemed like the most prudent thing given the circumstances, but Ben had never fired a gun before.

He would have no problem shooting Hayden if given the chance after what he had experienced in his dream. Saving Ashley was all that mattered at that point. He looked down the street in each direction, then he got out of his car and hastily made his way into the second-hand store. The bell which rang above the door when he walked inside the shop made it clear someone had entered.

Ben could hear the voice of the pawnbroker coming from the backroom of the store. Sounding somewhat agitated, he yelled out, "I'll be with you in just a minute!" Apparently, he seemed to be in the middle of something. Whatever he was doing didn't matter much to Ben. He just looked around the store for something that could even the odds between he and Hayden Keller. All he saw were shelves filled with stereo equipment, TVs, and a couple of outdated laptop computers. He even saw several guitars near the window next to the door, but that wasn't what he came there for.

Not finding what he wanted, a look of disappointment and serious concern swept over Ben's face. He continued to look the place over as he started to head back toward the door. That's when the old fellow that owned the place walked out of the back room. He groaned wiping off his glasses as he stood behind a glass case which contained watches, rings and several gold chains. Observing Ben for a moment he asked, "what can I do you for?"

Ben looked up at him saying, "I need a gun. You have any of those?"

That caught the old fellow by surprise. He hadn't figured Ben to be looking for a firearm. The old man said, "I got a few. What kind are you looking for?"

Ben told him he needed a handgun, something powerful. That's when the old guy behind the counter suppressed a laugh asking, "have you ever shot a gun before?"

Ben confessed that he hadn't had that much experience with guns as he said, "I don't know much about guns, but it's high time I learned."

The pawnbroker twisted his head accepting Ben's assessment, and he motioned with his hand saying, "step over here." Unlocking a covered showcase, he revealed well over a dozen guns to Ben while telling him, "I got more back there." Ben pointed to the biggest cannon out of the bunch, and the pawnbroker said, "now that's quite a hog leg son. What are you planning on hunting, bear?"

Ben looked up at him with a serious look on his face as he asked, "how much?"

The pawnbroker told him, "that one is six hundred and eighty dollars, but I'll let you have it for six."

Ben pulled out his wallet, and he handed the store owner his driver's license along with his credit card. The old man made a questionable sound and his lips twisted a little. He informed Ben he didn't take plastic. He said, "you can pay cash down, and I'll gladly hold it for you."

Ben didn't have time for that. He took the cash he had out of his wallet and he laid it on the counter. He said, "I need a gun now and I need bullets for it. What will this buy me?"

The pawnbroker looked down and he counted about two hundred and eighty five bucks. He admitted, "that won't get you much son." He paused a minute looking down at the money, then he looked back up at Ben asking, "are you in some kind of trouble?"

Ben didn't want to answer him. If he told anyone what he was thinking they would swear he was crazy, and the last thing they would do is sell him a gun. Ben just looked at him asking, "can you help me mister? All I want to do is buy a gun."

The pawnbroker nodded his head feeling it was none of his business at that point as long as the background check panned out. He motioned with his finger directing Ben's attention to a slightly rusted .38 special he had sitting in that case which had been collecting dust. Ben looked at it hardly impressed, but he asked if he had bullets for it. The pawnbroker reached around pulling a box of bullets off the lower shelf behind him and he laid them on the counter as he asked, "is that enough?"

The old man locked up the case after he picked up the cash. That's when he told Ben, "I'll get you a receipt as soon as I do the background check. Have a seat this shouldn't take but a minute." He then took the money along with Ben's driver's license and he walked toward the back room where he was when Ben first entered the store.

Ben was nervous. The pawnbroker watched him pacing the floor through the mirrored glass window in the back of the store. He knew something was wrong. That's what compelled him to pick up the phone and dial the sheriff's office, but all he got was a busy tone. Ben leaned his head over in the direction of the door leading to the back room and he asked what was taking so long. About that time the fax machine started printing. The background check came back showing Ben was clean as a whistle and the pawnbroker handed him his receipt along with the gun. Ben held the rusty weapon in his hand familiarizing himself with it a little.

Seeing a lighter sitting on the counter that resembled the one Hayden used in his dream, Ben was reminded of the words Hayden spoke. The old man could tell he was in deep thought about something. He asked Ben if he had any questions regarding the gun but all Ben heard was Hayden's voice saying, "it's fire Ben. I'm going to put you through it. That's when you discover what something is really made of Ben. We all have to go through the fire at some point. Will you perish or endure? I'm going to put you through the fire. See you in hell Ben."

The old man asked, "did you hear me?"
Ben looked over at him as he moved his head in the direction of the lighter which had caught his eye, and he asked, "how about the lighter."
The old guy knew he was out of cash. Looking down at Ben's watch he said, "I can always use a good timepiece." He looked back up at Ben never expecting him to make that trade.

Ben said nothing, he just placed the gun back in the bag with the ammunition. To the old man's amazement, Ben took off his watch and he laid it on the counter. He exchanged it for the lighter placing it in his pocket, and the pawnbroker turned his head slightly jerking it sharply thinking Ben was a little off his rocker. That's when the old guy picked up the watch admiring its quality. He walked back to place it in the case with the rest of the watches offering some words of advice to Ben, "you be careful with that now son." He then told Ben he needed a permit in order to carry it. Ben walked out of the store assuring the old man he would get one. He thought he might do it right after he killed Hayden Keller.

Ben's mind raced as he walked toward his car. His hands shook when he went to unlock his door. Once inside he opened up the box of bullets, spilling them in his passenger seat, he loaded the gun. He knew where he had to be, and when he had to be there as he cranked his BMW.

One scenario after another ran through his mind as he thought about how things would go down between him and Hayden. He was now hunting him, and he questioned if he could successfully do it. Ben was concerned about ensuring Ashley's safety, not about firing the gun. When he pulled into the gas station he saw no sign of the black SUV. He first questioned if he had missed him or if he was early. Time seemed to pass in slow motion while he waited, and part of him wished it was all just a figment of his imagination.

As Ben sat there, he out right asked himself if he was going crazy. Maybe he was already being hunted by Hayden and he didn't even know it. That started him thinking the way Hayden would. He immediately started the engine and drove away. Concerned he may have been followed after leaving the pawnshop, he looked for any sign of the black SUV. Positioning his car where he could see the gas station from a distance, Ben parked waiting for his prey.

Chapter 44

Burn In Hell

Ben watched the convenience store which sat at the edge of town. There was no doubt it was the one he had seen in his nightmare. He anxiously waited for the black SUV to appear. He sat there fighting the urge he had to use the bathroom. That made time move even slower for Ben, as if it were possible, until he finally lost the desire to go.

Thirty minutes passed, and there was still no sign of Hayden or the girl. Ben continued waiting, but he was losing his patience. He wasn't a stalker by nature, not like Hayden. This part of the hunting process was nothing he enjoyed. In fact, it damn near drove him crazy. He hated the wait, but there was nothing he could do about it. Within minutes he started to question if he had made a mistake. Maybe Hayden wasn't coming or he had already been there. The whole timeline may have been changed simply by Ben stopping off at the pawnshop to pick up that gun.

Ben's frustration grew along with his temper. He questioned what he should do. He looked at the road which led toward Justice, and then he realized he needed gas to get there. He knew that's where Hayden was headed. Ben figured if he couldn't find him in Chanceville he would surely find him there, but he also risked the chance of breaking down too. Ben reached feeling for his wallet. He was out of cash but he still had plastic. He started to think about parts of his dream, the part where he first met Hayden. He couldn't be sure, but he soon became convinced Hayden had something to do with what happened to his car. Either way, he figured if Hayden didn't show within ten minutes he would gas up and hunt for him on the road to Justice.

Ben picked up the gun he had purchased, and his compulsive nature got the best of him. He was paranoid to the point that he opened the cylinder to verify it was fully loaded, wanting to make sure it would fire when he pulled the trigger. He closed it as he looked down the barrel, pointing it as if he were going to shoot something. That's when it happened. The black SUV which he had been waiting for pulled into the gas station. Ben saw it out of the corner of his eye. He quickly turned his head as he gasped, "oh shit." This was really fucking happening, and he damn near dropped the gun in the seat beside him. Attempting to grip it, his fingers fidgeted a little. Trying his best to overcome his nerves, he quickly stuffed the gun into his jacket pocket.

He sat there clinching the handle of the small firearm as a fearful look on his face subsided. In his mind Ben actually asked himself, *now what do I do*? The answer which followed was, *kill that son of a bitch* of course, but to do that Ben had to come face to face with Hayden. That meant getting a hell of a lot closer than where he sat inside his BMW. He watched Hayden get out of the Tahoe. Then he watched him walk toward the convenience store.

Hayden stopped before entering, and he turned looking over his shoulder. It was like he knew he was being watched. Ben looked at the SUV knowing Ashley was in there. He looked back at Hayden as he continued to stare in his direction. It was eerie how he scanned over the surrounding landscape, and almost pinpointed Ben's exact location. The nervous feeling Ben had in his stomach increased ten times over as Hayden stared straight at him for what seemed like a minute or so.

Ben sat there in his car almost frozen trying not to breathe or make a sound. Being the hunter he was, Hayden's instincts were extremely acute. He could feel Ben's eyes watching him from a distance. Even Ben knew it. He felt as though he was staring right into Hayden's sinister eyes even from a distance. That feeling soon became intense. Not sure of what to do, Ben closed his eyes just to break the connection between them. He hoped it would dispel the feeling Hayden was sensing. That's when he made a very grave mistake.

A hunter should never take his eye off the target, but Ben was new at this game. He was learning, unfortunately for him it was the hard way. Ben kept his eyes closed much like a small child who's afraid of something. He simply prayed Hayden would turn around and enter the store. He figured that would be the best chance he had of rescuing Ashley. That was his number one concern.

When he opened his eyes, Hayden was gone just as he hoped. The black Tahoe sat right where it was when Ben first closed his eyes, but obviously Hayden was now in the store. Ben cranked up his car and he drove up next to the gas pump adjacent to the Tahoe. He paused a moment before getting out. Ben had that uncomfortable feeling come over him. It was the same one he experienced in his dream, almost as though he was being watched. Still, he didn't have much time if he was going to save Ashley. He knew he had to act fast. That's what compelled him to brush aside that feeling as he climbed out of his car.

He looked over at the SUV as he started to put gas in his car. He casually looked to see if he saw any sign of Hayden inside the store. That's when he made his move toward the Tahoe, but Hayden stepped out of the driver's side door of the SUV. Taken totally by surprise, Ben stood there dead in his tracks. Hayden stared at him as he slammed the door. Ben reached inside his jacket pocket feeling for the gun. Placing his hand on it he brandished it, pointing it directly at Hayden. Ben was frightened, but he held the gun on him. His hand hardly trembled as he said, "you're going to pay for what you've done."

Hayden looked at him as if he was trying to place Ben's face. Not recognizing him, Hayden asked, "have we met somewhere before?" That was his best effort to play dumb as he sized Ben up. Hayden's hand inched closer to his gun as Ben stared at the scar on his face.
Ben coldly replied, "oh, I never forget a face."

Hayden moved toward Ben telling him to never point a gun at someone unless you plan to use it, and there was no fear showing whatsoever on Hayden's face. Ben took several steps back toward his car as he yelled out Ashley's name. He hollered for her to get out of the car. He even tried to assure her it was okay. Ben wanted to pull the trigger and end the nightmare, but he had to see Ashley's face. Hayden moved a step closer telling Ben to go ahead and fire the thing. Hayden warned him saying, "killing me might cost you your soul. Are you okay with that?"

Ben wasn't worried in the least. He wanted to see Hayden burn long before he reached hell. He couldn't forget the images he had of Hayden threatening to burn Ashley alive using gasoline. The best thing he could do for Ashley and the rest of the world would be to kill Hayden Keller. Ben knew it, and he spoke Hayden's name out loud as he squeezed the trigger telling him, "see you in hell."

Hayden was outright stunned Ben knew his name. The first bullet struck Hayden's shoulder and the second bullet jammed locking the trigger in place. Ben was now left to his own defenses. He became paralyzed not knowing what to do. He now held a worthless piece of metal in his hand that had no chance of stopping Hayden Keller.

Taking another deliberate step, Hayden moved closer and Ben threw the gun right at his face. Hayden dodged it, locking eyes with Ben. He wanted to know how Ben knew his name and where to find him. Ben's left hand was now near the gas hose as he scurried to find the lighter he had placed in his pocket. Touching the lighter with his fingers Ben picked up the hose. Hayden snarled at him asking, "what are you going to do with that?"

Staring at the hose, Hayden pulled his gun. He looked right into Ben's eyes a second time. That's when Hayden said, "I think I'll strangle you with it." Ben planned to set him aflame as he pulled the lighter out of his pocket. He squeezed the handle pointing the hose directly at Hayden. Ben dowsed him with gas from head to toe just as Hayden fired his pistol. The flash from the gun ignited the accelerant which now covered Hayden's body. Instantly, he was covered in flames. Burning full blaze, he continued firing.

Ben scrambled to avoid being consumed by the flames which now engulfed Hayden's face and upper body. The clerk inside the store heard the shots outside. Holding a carton of cigarettes in his hand he ran over to look out the window. With his mouth wide open he dropped the carton of cigarettes he held and he picked up the phone to call 911. He could see Hayden fully consumed by the flames, and he was staggering close to the gas pumps. All the clerk could say at that point was, "oh fuck, oh fuck, oh fuck."

As the convenience store clerk tried to explain there was a burning man outside his building, Ben raced to save Ashley before they were all blown up. Opening the door to the Tahoe he could see Ashley was bound, both hands and feet. Her head was covered where she couldn't see, and her mouth was taped. Ben took the pillowcase off her head as he said, "we got to get you out of here." Pulling her out of the vehicle, Ben could hear Ashley say, "umm huh," loud and clear even through the duct tape.

Meanwhile, inside the convenience store the clerk was giving directions to Hayden through the glass as if he could actually hear him. He even swatted his hands in a particular direction as he said, "no dude, go the other way."

Ben ran carrying Ashley away from the gas pumps. She looked over Ben's shoulder at Hayden. The demonic killer was totally ablaze. He violently jerked and twisted trying to rid himself of the raging flames. It was no use though, he was covered in flames.

Ben couldn't rest until he knew she was safe. He didn't look back until they were a fair distance away. Placing her on the ground, they both watched as Hayden Keller burned. Neither of them had to wish he burned in hell. For him there was no other place. They both knew he was already there.

Chapter 45

Saving Grace

Ratley hung up the phone yelling to the sheriff, "we got a man on fire at the gas station near the edge of town." Sheriff Baker looked up from his desk with a stunned look on his face. Grabbing his hat he hollered, "radio Singer and tell him to meet us there."

Ben removed the tape from Ashley's mouth and assured her it was all over. He worked to free her hands as he informed her, "you're safe now, I got you." She could hardly believe what she was hearing as she looked at him somewhat in shock that she was still alive. How did he find her and who was he? Those were now the questions she had in her mind. She had prayed someone would find her, but she never expected it to be Ben. She didn't even know his name but somehow he knew hers. Tears started to flow from her emerald green eyes as she said, "it's you. You saved me."

Ben knew what had saved her, and he knew something divine was at work to allow him to come to her aid in her desperate hour of need. He couldn't explain about the premonition he had, and what role Sister Lee played in leading him to her. He reached over placing his hand on her necklace. Ashley looked down at the crucifix which seemed to have Ben's complete attention. His fingers gently lifted it from her neck. Ben carefully slid his fingers behind it as he examined it. This wasn't the first time he had seen it, but only he knew that. It rested in the palm of his hand, the same palm that had helped determine his recent course of fate. Ben looked up at her as he held the necklace where she could see it and he said, "it's true I came for you." He glanced back down at the crucifix adding, "I believe he sent me for you, but this, your faith, that is what saved you."

Ashley was left almost speechless by his confession of faith. He let go of the necklace not knowing what to say at that point. Ashley placed her unbound arms around his neck hugging him tightly. She thanked him again as she cried both tears of joy and pain. She was thankful to still be alive herself and mournful concerning the loss of her entire family. She felt she had no one other than Ben at that moment, but he wasn't going anywhere. Ashley said, "I don't know why you did what you did but I can't thank you enough."

Ben cut her off saying, "you would have done the same for me."

Ashley wasn't so sure about that, but she wasn't privy to what had taken place in Ben's nightmare. He would eventually share how he came to find her, but now was not the time. She had already been through more than anyone should ever have to endure. Leaving it as divine intervention was good enough for the time being.

About that time the clerk from the convenience store exited the building carrying a fire extinguisher. He dashed across the parking lot with it as he tried to put out the flames. Hayden was already dead of course, at least that's what Ben and Ashley thought.

It was true his burned body showed no sign of life, but his evil spirit now resided in another place. He had visited that place many times before, never wishing to stay. This would not be the last time he saw it, and it would not be the end of

Hayden Keller by a long shot, not as long as he did the devil's bidding. There would soon again come a day when evil takes on another face in a place far away. Ben knew nothing of that though, in his mind he and Ashley were safe.

The clerk wrestled with the fire extinguisher trying to pull out the cotter pin in order to operate it but the damn thing was jammed. He cursed a little as he struggled with it, then he finally managed to remove it only to find it didn't work anyway. The clerk stared down at the charred remains of what was left of Hayden Keller. His face was burned beyond recognition. Parts of his body were still on fire, but most of it was now smoldering. Using his forearm, he covered his mouth and nose as he got closer. He looked at the gas pumps. Then he looked over at Ben and Ashley. In shock all he could say is, "damn this dude is fucked up." Ben's thoughts escaped his lips as he said, "you have no idea."

Ashley looked at Ben as the sheriff and his deputies pulled up. The sheriff jumped out of his car and he immediately asked Bruce, the store clerk, "what the hell happened?" Right at that second, the fire truck and ambulance arrived on the scene. Bruce had a lost look on his face as he explained he was stocking cigarettes and the next thing he heard were shots being fired. "When I went to the window all I could see was the guy covered in flames," he said. He looked in Ben's direction saying, "ask him. I think he saw the whole thing."

Sheriff Baker looked over at Ben and Ashley. He recognized her from a photo he received just several hours earlier. He was studying that picture when Ratley received the distress call which sent them out to the scene. There were quite a few similarities she had in common with the sheriff's daughter.

Ratley continued taking Bruce's statement as the sheriff made his way over to check on Ashley. Singer walked over to the SUV, and he looked around the gas pump next to Ben's BMW. The sheriff confirmed Ashley's identity. He turned his head as he heard Singer say, "I've got a gun over here." Ben admitted that one was his and the other one they would find belonged to Hayden Keller.

The sheriff had plenty of questions at that point. Ben just told him to look in the back of the SUV. He forewarned the sheriff, "you won't like what you find, but I guarantee you, he's your killer."

The sheriff told Ratley to give Singer a hand as he opened up the rear door of the Tahoe. A severed limb fell out of the blood soaked bedspread and Singer looked down at it saying, "you've got to be kidding me."
Ratley's face became pale and his stomach started to churn a little. He turned away holding his breath then he said, "I think I'm going to be sick sheriff."

Singer reached in the toolbox which was sitting next to the bloody bedspread. What he found were several wallets which belonged to Hayden's victims. Reading one of the names, he had to inform Ratley he was looking at part of Jamal Morris.

The sheriff turned back toward Ben telling him not to go anywhere. It wasn't like he could go too far without his car. Sheriff Baker then escorted Ashley over to the ambulance, but she kept looking back over her shoulder at Ben. She didn't even know his name, but she felt a strong attachment to him. He nodded his head trying to reassure her it was alright, but she wasn't going anywhere without him. That's when the sheriff mentioned her grandmother. He told Ashley he was going to have her meet her at the hospital.

She didn't say a great deal to the sheriff even though she had been Hayden's captive for quite some time, she had spent most of it with her head covered or locked in the trunk. All she could tell Sheriff Baker was the man on fire killed her family and Ben saved her life. The sheriff certainly believed every word she said as he placed her in the hands of the paramedics. He still had more questions he needed answers to, and he figured Ben could provide him with some.

The sheriff looked over at the black SUV knowing they had just solved the biggest killing spree case the state had ever seen and recovered the kidnapped girl in the process. It was the best outcome he could've hoped for given the circumstances. He ordered his deputies to bag the evidence as he made his way back over to speak with Ben. Looking directly at him the sheriff said, "well, I guess it's finally over."

Sister Lee looked up opening her eyes as she sat at her round wooden table. She drew her hands together clasping them over the yin and yang symbol. The stars were aligned in perfect order and balance had been restored to the universe once more.

As Sheriff Baker approached Ben the first question he had for him concerned how he knew Hayden Keller. That one was a little tricky to answer. Ben just said, "I had a bad feeling about him. I can't explain it. He pulled his gun and I did the same. The next thing I knew he was on fire."

The sheriff said, "well you followed your gut. That's good.

It's probably why you're still alive son. You don't know how lucky you are." The sheriff looked over at Hayden's torched body adding, "that was one evil man you came into contact with, someone must have been watching out for you."

Luck, fate, call it what you will. Ben knew how evil Hayden truly was. He never saw the carnage the sheriff viewed out at the Ferris farm, but he saw Hayden's wrath in his nightmare close up. Was someone watching over him? Yes. Someone is always watching, always waiting and they are vigilant in their pursuit. Wherever there are good men, they will be there guiding them to protect that which is worth saving.

Chapter 46

The Spirit Knows No End

It had been almost a year, months had come and gone since Hayden Keller's demise. Even though that was the case, the sheriff and his deputies would never forget that day. It wasn't everyday they found a serial killer burned alive, especially one that had wreaked such havoc across the entire state.

Sheriff Baker closed the file drawer in his office. He walked out telling Ratley to mind the place until he got back. The calls had subsided in the office for the most part. People were once again comfortable walking down the streets of Chanceville, even late in the evening.

Singer drove past the sheriff's office as he was leaving. He waived to the sheriff but he patrolled the town in an effort to keep it safe. Sheriff Baker climbed in his cruiser and he headed out to get a bite to eat.

Sister Lee sat at her table in deep meditation as she did this time every year. For her, this day would be a long one indeed. It would be nearly fourteen hours before she stopped channeling her thoughts and got some sleep. Only during the hour of darkness would she cease her efforts and take a break.

As for Ben, he found himself out on the west coast. He had made it, a change of scenery and a new job to boot. It looked like things were finally going his way. Occasionally, he would think about the past and how Ashley was doing.

Sometimes she'd pick up the phone just to call and say hey. He always enjoyed hearing her voice. She had started college, but she was two thousand miles away. She often joked about coming to visit Ben in California instead of spending her vacation with her grandmother, but she was serious about doing it someday. Life continued even though it had changed.

Hours passed as Sister Lee meditated focusing all of her energies on the constellations above her. They served as her gateway to mystical realms. In another small town in the southern part of the country, someone else was experiencing a transformation of epic proportion all their own which held great importance for Sister Lee.

It was now four o'clock in the morning eastern standard time when the buzzer on the alarm clock sounded. It was incessant the way it kept blaring. The man lying next to it just continued to lay there. He didn't make a move, he just stared straight up at the ceiling. "It's time to get up Vincent," his wife murmured in her sleep. Turning her back to him, she rolled over covering her ears with her pillow. Agitated by the sound of the alarm, she kicked him with her heel hoping he would shut the damn thing off so she could go back to sleep. Still, he laid there as he looked over at the clock and then at his wife. He could hear her complain even through the pillow as she said, "what's wrong with you? Turn that damn thing off."

He reached over snatching the cord out of the wall which immediately put an end to the loud buzzer blaring into his ear. He could hear his wife say, "it's about time you got your ass up." That's when he reached over grabbing the pillow she had placed over her head, and he forcefully shoved it into her face. Cutting off any airflow she had, he held it in place. She struggled as she tried to pull away. He aggressively applied more pressure as he suffocated her with her own pillow. She squirmed and wiggled to no avail as he kept the pillow over her mouth and nose. Finally, she stopped moving altogether and then he took the pillow away. The only thing he said as he got out of bed making his way to the bathroom is, "this is going to be a hell of a day."

Suddenly, Sister Lee's eyes popped open wide. She was no longer in deep meditation. She now had a foreboding look on her face. Blood drizzled from her nose. She didn't bother to wipe it away knowing of the bloodshed yet to come. This was just the beginning. Terrible deeds would be done at the hands of the merciless.

The moon was full and the wheel of years was positioned at a very dangerous place. The watchtowers were out of sync, and Sister Lee knew what it meant. The portholes in time were in alignment with one another forming an open door allowing Hayden Keller to escape. Sister Lee knew evil had once again taken on a human shape. The dark days were at hand and they would have no end, not until she put an end to him. Nearly breathless, she gasped, "he's back!"